C000170608

the lonely hearts beach club

BOOKS BY AMY MILLER

They Call Me the Cat Lady
The Day My Husband Left

WARTIME BAKERY SERIES
Heartaches and Christmas Cakes
Wartime Brides and Wedding Cakes
Telegrams and Teacakes

AS AMY BRATLEY
The Girls' Guide to Homemaking
The Saturday Supper Club
The Antenatal Group

AMY MILLER

the
lonely
hearts
beach club

bookouture

Published by Bookouture in 2023

An imprint of Storyfire Ltd.
Carmelite House
50 Victoria Embankment
London EC4Y 0DZ

www.bookouture.com

Copyright © Amy Miller, 2023

Amy Miller has asserted her right to be identified
as the author of this work.

All rights reserved. No part of this publication may be reproduced, stored in
any retrieval system, or transmitted, in any form or by any means, electronic,
mechanical, photocopying, recording or otherwise, without the prior written
permission of the publishers.

ISBN: 978-1-83790-401-3
eBook ISBN: 978-1-80314-701-7

This book is a work of fiction. Names, characters, businesses, organizations,
places and events other than those clearly in the public domain, are either the
product of the author's imagination or are used fictitiously. Any resemblance
to actual persons, living or dead, events or locales is entirely coincidental.

For Jimmy, Sonny and Audrey

PROLOGUE

It was the last day of Olivia Fryer's old life.

The wind, that late July morning, was unseasonably wild. Hairstyles were wrecked. Sunflowers bowed to invisible audiences. Clean laundry blew off washing lines and dogs' ears blew inside out. Seagulls hovered, their beady eyes searching for chips. And, as she walked along Milton-on-Sea's promenade, past the beach shop stuffed with buckets and spades, sticks of neon-pink rock and postcards curling at the edges, Olivia felt a stab of nostalgia for the south-coast seaside resort she was leaving.

'You're so brave,' friends had said in astonishment when she'd told them she was moving away. They hadn't been able to imagine leaving their settled lives, 'forever' homes and jobs for life. But Olivia secretly knew that courage wasn't a factor. It was more of a necessity. Of outrunning the past, before it caught up with her.

Packing up her two-up, two-down Victorian terraced house, ready to rent to friends of friends, had been easier than she'd anticipated. Boxing up her past and storing it in the attic had felt quite cleansing. There were things about the house she wouldn't miss: the floorboards that creaked and squeaked, the back door she had to slam her shoulder against to make it shut properly. And things she would: the bountiful plum tree in the garden, the whistling of the kettle in the small, sunny kitchen.

In her mind's eye, she held on tightly to the image of the modern flat she'd rented for herself and her fourteen-year-old daughter, Beau, in Dublin. The owners of the haberdashery Olivia worked for as an assistant manager had offered her a relocation package and promotion she couldn't refuse. They were moving their business to Dublin and wanted Olivia to manage their new shop. They'd also dangled another carrot: an offer to help develop Olivia's textile designs and potentially sell her hand screen-printed fabrics in the shop – a long-held ambition.

She'd just about made her mind up to take the plunge when news of her ex, Oscar Gregory, moving back to the area for business, after years of living in New Zealand, had made the offer irresistible. The memory of the lie she'd told him all those years ago made her breathless with worry. There was no way she wanted him to find her in the same place he'd left her. A sitting duck.

Dublin was the chance of a fresh start, of fulfilling a dream. It was also, she could only admit to herself, the chance to get away from what she couldn't face. Yes, Oscar could still track her down if he wanted to – she supposed he always could have – but at least she wouldn't be on his doorstep.

And today they were leaving! Flights were booked, bags packed, travel documents checked and rechecked. While Beau said goodbye to her best friend, Olivia was at the beach to say a final farewell to her mum, Hattie, and stepfather, Jesse.

'We'll still be here when you get back,' said Jesse warmly. 'Touch wood and whistle.'

Hattie and Jesse were in their usual positions, comfortably seated in their green-and-white-striped deckchairs in front of their pale-blue beach hut, chairs pulled close together. If not there, they'd often drag the deckchairs across the sand to the water's edge, to cool their blue-veined feet in the seawater, always side by side.

'What do you mean "when you get back"? She's not coming back!' said Hattie, shielding her eyes from the sun as she looked up at Olivia. 'It's not a holiday. They're moving four hundred miles away, as far away as possible it would seem.'

'Not quite,' said Olivia gently. 'Anyway, it's economics. They're offering me a great salary.'

I also need to get away. Far away, she thought.

'I know, but it's such a long way...' said Hattie, wearing a wounded expression.

Olivia sighed.

'I would walk four hundred miles and—' Jesse burst into an edited version of the Proclaimers' song until Hattie silenced him with a whack on the arm.

Jesse grinned. His jacket was draped over the back of his deckchair and his arms, in rolled-up shirtsleeves, rested on the money bag slung around his middle. He wore a bucket hat with a wide brim, which shaded his smiling face. His skin was deeply tanned and creased like the skin of a dried chilli, and his pale-blue eyes contrasted handsomely.

'You and Beau will visit us regularly, won't you?' he said, looking at her questioningly.

'Of course we'll visit,' said Olivia. 'And you can visit us.'

'How can you leave me with only Jesse for company?' Hattie said with an affectionate laugh, turning to her husband, taking his face in her hands and giving him a big kiss.

Compared to Jesse, Hattie was tiny. Only five feet tall and incredibly slim, she seemed drowned by her blouse and pale trousers that flapped like flags in the wind. Hattie had very pale blonde, almost white, hair, an almond-milk complexion and dark, darting eyes. She too wore a hat – hers was straw and seemed close to being snatched by the wind.

Hattie and Jesse made an incongruous pair to look at, but their personalities were enviably well suited: jelly and ice cream; cheese and pineapple. They made each other laugh and shared the same sense of fun. When they were younger and stronger, they would suddenly get up from their deckchairs and leapfrog one another on the beach in a gymnastic display, collapsing into laughter afterwards to a round of applause from passers-by. Certainly, Olivia had never found a lasting love like theirs, even though she'd once foolishly hoped she had.

An image of Oscar loomed in her mind and her palms started to sweat. The prospect of him turning up on her doorstep made her stomach turn inside out.

'She loves me really,' said Jesse.

'I do,' Hattie said. 'I'd have to, after all we've been through.'

They shared a glance and said something to each other without words. Jesse took Hattie's hand in his and gave it a gentle kiss.

Olivia smiled. Her mum and stepdad seemed to belong to the past somehow, like the Victorian theatre on the pier that had been bulldozed, or the children's donkey rides that had been replaced with a surf school. The whole town was going through a period of modernisation; people were moving out of London to the coast, polishing and painting the faded buildings and weathered wood. Out with the old, in with the new. Though the area did need renovating, Olivia hoped that the old-timers would stay – that the cobbler and the bingo hall would stand their ground among the trendy coffee shops and gin parlours.

'Remember to lock up the beach hut when I'm not here to remind you,' Olivia said. 'I can't believe you don't lock it – it's not the 1970s! Are you going to be okay left to your own devices?' A wave of panic shot through her. Most people her age were moving closer to their parents, even inviting them to live in their homes, not moving hundreds of miles away.

'Jesse and I can look after each other,' Hattie said. 'Don't you worry.'

Olivia almost laughed. She'd spent most of her life worrying. If there was something she had a PhD in, it was worrying.

'Honestly, stop fretting,' Hattie said. She grabbed Olivia's hand and gave it a squeeze and a shake in that way older people did.

A lump formed in Olivia's throat. 'I'm going to miss you,' she said.

Jesse laughed. 'Like a nail in your head.'

Olivia *would* miss them. And worry about them. Sometimes Hattie could be forgetful: names and places would often leave her blinking blankly. And Jesse was prone to overworking.

Throughout their retirement, Hattie and Jesse had run a small business during the summer season hiring out deckchairs on the beach, as Jesse's father had done before him. They had dozens of old-fashioned deckchairs, striped and colourful, which they kept in storage close to their beach hut. Hattie and Jesse relished meeting the holidaymakers who rented the deckchairs; day trippers who poured out of coaches, their legs stiff as posts after long journeys; hen parties; newlyweds; families. There were drifters too, homeless souls who came to the coast to sleep out in warmer climes – Hattie always gave them a free deckchair to snooze on.

And then, on quieter days, Hattie and Jesse would sit side by side on their own green-and-white-striped deckchairs, faces tilted to the sun. Sometimes they'd hold hands as they snoozed. Other times they'd people-watch and steal knowing glances at one another, observing the sunburned tourists and their giant inflatable unicorns. They'd sat together like that every summer season for years, a portrait of a bygone era: a kind of animate iconic British seaside postcard.

'Let me take a picture of you both in your natural habitat,' Olivia said, locating her phone in her pocket and snapping their image. 'All you need is a knotted hanky on your head, Jesse, and you could be a 1960s throwback.'

'Don't give him ideas!' Hattie said. 'And I think he's more 1940s.'

'Hey!' said Jesse. 'I'm young at heart, despite my wrinkles.'

Turning towards the sea, Olivia frowned. The waves were high and breaking messily, but she'd wanted to have a swim before leaving. The red flag was flying outside the lifeguard hut, several beaches down, indicating the sea wasn't safe for swimmers, so she decided to settle for a paddle in the shallows.

Inside the beach hut, she slipped out of her clogs and grey linen pinafore dress and changed into her swimsuit. She patted her bloated stomach and sucked in her breath. She tended to overeat when she was stressed – dark chocolate in fresh baguette, or roast pork with crispy crackling depending on whether her mood was sweet or savoury. But when they got to Dublin, she would be a better version of herself; it would be kiwis and kale all the way.

The familiar smell of the beach hut squeezed her heart: coconut sun cream, gasoline, salt.

Catching sight of her reflection in a porthole-shaped mirror, she stared at her forty-six-year-old self. Her hair, tight narrow ringlets, like the catkins of a weeping willow, hung around her face. In the July sunshine, her skin had turned an oaky bark brown and was lined in a wise rather than wizened way. Her eyes were a rusty hazel colour – as if someone had squeezed in a pipette of orange dye – and were framed with thick dark eyelashes. She tried to see herself through a new person's eyes – how would they view her in Dublin? Would they see her? Or was she in the bracket of middle-aged women who seemed invisible to everyone else but charity fundraisers.

She pushed her shoulders back – she was prone to slouching. She had a strong upper body, short torso and giraffe-long legs – inherited from her father, Hattie's first husband, Michael, who had been six foot four.

'Your dad's legs were so long, his feet dangled off the end of the mattress,' Hattie had told her as a child. 'I had to put the washing line up really high to hang his trousers out to dry and they took an age to iron.'

Olivia had relished those stories. It linked her to the father she'd only known for six years; the father who'd gone out on his bicycle one day, his long trousers in ankle clips, and never come home, no matter how fervently she'd wished he would, her little nose pressed up to the window, waiting.

Nobody can ever live up to your dad!

From nowhere, Oscar's sharp voice suddenly burst in her head. Even now, after years of being apart, he made himself heard. She took a sharp intake of breath and forced herself not to think about him but instead focus on imaginings of her new life.

The plans for the haberdashery in Dublin were impressive. The shop would be packed with rolls of vibrant coloured fabrics, cottons, buttons and shelves of beautiful trimmings. And perhaps one day her fabric would be on the shelves too. Tomorrow she would be a long way away from Oscar, waking up in a new city and starting a new life with Beau.

Throwing a towel over her shoulders, Olivia stepped outside the beach hut, a gust of wind whipping sand into her eyes. Hattie and Jesse were standing shoulder to shoulder, looking out to sea. Their striped windbreak was wobbling precariously beside them.

'Olivia,' said Hattie. 'Can you see that boy out there on the surfboard? Do you think he's in trouble?'

Olivia followed Hattie's gaze. The glare of the sun combined with the strong wind made it difficult to see clearly, but in between sets of roughly breaking waves, she caught sight of a boy – a teenager around Beau's age with hair tied back in a ponytail – very far out. He'd come off his surfboard and every time he tried to get back on it, a wave appeared to move the board just out of reach.

'I think he's just trying to grab his board,' Olivia said. 'He's probably getting tired.'

'What if he's in trouble?' said Hattie. 'The water's like a washing machine – there'll be an undertow. If there's one thing about me that's razor sharp, it's my sight. Jesse, I'm worried. I think he needs help. You should have a closer look...'

The lifeguards were a good ten-minute walk away. Olivia scanned the beach and couldn't see anyone obviously looking out for the boy – perhaps he'd come alone. There were a couple of other surfers who'd disregarded the red flag, but they were closer in and didn't seem to have noticed him.

'Let's go down to the shore,' said Jesse, tugging at Olivia's wrist, then handing his money belt to Hattie. 'You stay here and, if I indicate, call for help.'

Hattie gave a nod, while Jesse and Olivia jogged down to the water's edge.

The waves were several feet high, breaking quite far out, and there was barely any time between each wave, so the boy intermittently disappeared from sight. He didn't seem to be making any progress in the water one way or another. His hair was covering his eyes, but he wasn't moving it out of the way. He seemed strangely still, occasionally tilting his head back. The board was now some distance away from him – the surf-board leash must have come undone. Olivia felt a tightness in her throat.

'What shall we do?' she asked. 'Shall I run to get the life-guards? Call the coastguard?'

Jesse took off his shirt, sandals and socks and waded into the water. 'Not enough time.'

'Jesse, you can't go in. It's really rough – he's too far out.'

'He's just a boy. I can't leave him!'

'I know, but it's too...' Olivia's words trailed to nothing as she watched Jesse dive through the middle of a wave, not reappearing for what seemed like forever. When he did surface, the next wave crashed over his head.

'Jesse!' Olivia shouted. 'Jesse, come back! For God's sake – it's too rough for an old man!'

'Who are you calling an old man?' he shouted back, breaking into front crawl.

Olivia stood in the shallows, not knowing what to do. The water tugged at her calves like hands trying to pull her over. She felt helpless, and though she tried to call Jesse back again, he couldn't hear her shouting. She wasn't a strong enough swimmer to reach him, or even get beyond the breaking waves. What could she do?

She waded in a bit further, waving her arms at the other surfers and pointing towards Jesse and the boy, but they didn't seem to register her distress.

'Damn it,' she said. There was no way of communicating. She felt useless.

A powerful wave knocked her over, and she plunged into and under the cold water. She raised her head and gasped for breath, swallowing a mouthful of seawater. Coughing, she tried to get up, the undertow pulling at her legs. She panicked; the sea was wild and powerful.

Staggering out onto the sand surrounded by frothy white breakwater, she saw that a few people had gathered, concern written on their faces.

Someone called out to her, shouting that they should form a chain, to try to reach Jesse and the boy. A moment later she was holding hands with a middle-aged man on one side, a woman in her early twenties on the other, water swirling around her ankles, digging her toes into the sand to stand firm.

Others joined, men and women, young and old, holding hands to reach Jesse. Olivia scanned the sea, but Jesse was far out and kept disappearing from view. She searched the beach for Hattie, who was running to the shore, her hat lost to the wind and wheeling down the beach.

The chain of people grew longer and stronger until the person at the front, a young man in a wetsuit, was at the furthest point you could be and still stand. Olivia could hear his muffled shouts to Jesse: 'Over here! This way!' and feel the grim, tight grip of the strangers' hands she held. In the distance, she saw Jesse reach the boy and reunite him with his surfboard. The boy struggled onto the board and lay flat, his head to one side. Was he exhausted? Had he swallowed a lot of water? At least he was safe.

Suddenly, a powerful wave crashed over Jesse and the boy, flipping over the surfboard, which whacked Jesse on the head and tossed the boy into the sea. The crack was audible from the beach. Another surfer, who'd got close to them, managed to pluck the boy from the water and pull him onto his own board and paddle back to the shore.

'Oh my God, Jesse, please be okay,' muttered Olivia, her eyes flitting to the lifeguards now on the scene, one checking out the boy, another heading for Jesse on a rescue board. But there was no sign of her stepfather.

Hattie, now knee-deep and unsteady in the water, shouted his name at the top of her lungs, her voice brittle, shrill, horrible. There was more shouting all around now, urgent voices. The wind blew harder. The clouds grew darker.

'Come on, come on, please...' Olivia urged under her breath, but there was still no sign of Jesse.

'There!' someone shouted as Jesse became visible a few metres out. He'd been dragged in by the current, but he was face down in the water.

The lifeguard paddled determinedly towards him and the chain of people moved abruptly as the first in line tried and failed to reach Jesse. The lifeguard, not much more than a boy himself, reached Jesse and managed to haul him onto the rescue board.

The man and woman on either side of Olivia suddenly let go of her hands, and she stumbled towards Jesse and the lifeguard, now on the sand, her teeth chattering in shock and cold.

'Oh my God,' she said, her heart pounding in her chest.

Where the board had hit Jesse's head, blood was leaking down his neck, soaking into the sand. His body was limp, his eyes closed. Hattie dropped to her knees beside him, her hands reaching out towards him as the lifeguard tried to revive him.

Olivia held her breath as a loud, high-pitched note rang out in her ears. She crouched down next to Hattie, who was saying, 'I told him to go, I told him to go, it was me, I told him to go,' under her breath.

Moments later, paramedics arrived, and Hattie and Olivia were ushered into an ambulance with Jesse.

The journey was bumpy, blurry and silent. At the hospital, a nurse gave Olivia a hospital robe to wear over her damp swimsuit, but she continued to tremble.

When they were told that Jesse wasn't going to make it, Hattie's eyes were perfectly round circles, her skin drained of colour. She didn't say a word; she just blinked. Jesse was dead. Life had changed in an instant – the bat of an eyelid, the snap of a twig.

When Olivia put her arms around Hattie, she stood still and rigid as a post.

'I can't understand...' Hattie muttered. 'I don't know what... We were just on the beach, chatting, laughing, when...'

Her broken sentences went unfinished. There were no words.

That night, Olivia and Hattie stumbled to the beach hut to collect Hattie's bag, which had her purse, house keys and phone inside. The sea, calmer now, was a pool of black oil in the darkness. There were no stars. Hattie and Jesse's deckchairs were where they'd been left, a supermarket carrier bag spilling open with their uneaten sandwiches nearby.

Hattie perched on her deckchair for a moment, her fingers gripping the edges of the wooden frame, shaking her head in disbelief.

'What will I do without him?' she asked. 'I don't want to be on my own. I don't want to be without him.'

'I'm here,' Olivia said, shivering. 'I'm not going anywhere.'

The flight to Dublin was forgotten, the ticket to a new life of no consequence now. The striped fabric seat of Jesse's empty deckchair flapped hopelessly in the breeze. The lovely old seaside postcard had been ripped into pieces and carried away by the wind.

ONE

ONE YEAR LATER

Hattie sat in the passenger seat of Olivia's old yellow VW camper van, wearing sunglasses, with some of Jesse's ashes in a box resting on her knee.

'Before you ask, I don't want to think about which bit of him I have in this box,' Hattie said grimly as they drove towards the beach. 'I haven't slept a wink, wondering if it's right to divide his ashes, but I think he wouldn't mind.'

Olivia, driving, and Beau, in the back seat, were unfazed by the comment. In the twelve months since Jesse's death, Hattie had been profoundly sad and felt wholly bleak; her grief an enormous, unwieldy rucksack she couldn't put down.

But despite her paralysing misery, the year had galloped by like a happy little pony. Spring had been and gone, pink blossoms had faded and, now, the schools had broken up for the summer and peak tourist season had begun. Billboards advertised the beach, even though the beach could advertise itself perfectly well.

'I wasn't going to ask,' said Olivia. 'Of course Jesse wouldn't mind. You must do what you think is right.'

Olivia glanced through the windscreen at the sky. Dark

clouds loomed angrily overhead, threatening rain, plunging the usual vivid colours of Milton-on-Sea into shade. An ice-cream van rattled out its eerie tune regardless.

As they neared the beach car park, Hattie started to recount a phone call she'd had that morning. Every now and then she pushed up her sunglasses and dabbed her eyes with a tissue.

'The man on the phone said I'd been a victim of fraud. He asked my name, date of birth, address,' she said. 'He was investigating the fraud and said that he'd send a courier around to my bungalow to collect my credit card so they could make some security checks. He said I should put the card in an envelope and hand it to the courier as soon as he arrived.'

Olivia tightened her grip around the steering wheel until her knuckles were white. She glanced over at Hattie.

'And did you do that?' Olivia asked. 'Because you do realise it's a sca—'

'No!' interrupted Hattie. 'I couldn't find my bank card! I didn't answer the door because I was too embarrassed to tell the courier I'd lost my card, after all the effort he'd made to get there from London. My memory isn't what it was and, anyway, I was thinking about Jesse's ashes.'

'He wouldn't have come all the way from Lond—' began Olivia, but Hattie interrupted again.

'He rang the doorbell nine times!' she said. 'I hid in the bedroom cupboard and waited there for fifteen minutes to make sure he'd gone. I expect he'll call back soon, but what will I say?'

Olivia let out an exasperated sigh. 'Mum, don't answer the door or the phone. You need to block the number. It was a scam. They're conmen, rogue traders. You should report it to the police.'

'What?' said Hattie, her expression wounded. 'But he said he was *from* the police!'

'He wasn't,' said Olivia. 'You need to be less trusting.'

'There are loads of warnings about it, Granny,' said Beau.

'Check with your bank that they haven't stolen your identity. They prey on old people and might be committing major crimes. You'll have to spend years trying to clear your name or paying off debt they rack up with your personal details. I heard this awful story of a man who lost his house in a scam like that.'

'Beau,' said Olivia, trying to catch her daughter's eye in the rear-view mirror to give a slight shake of her head to deter her from continuing her story, but she was plugging in headphones and staring at her phone as if it held all the answers to life in its tiny screen. Her hair, dyed a shade of silvery blue, obscured her face. With every passing day, Beau was becoming more distant, less likely to meet Olivia's eye. It was one of many entries on Olivia's 'Things to Worry About' list.

'Why would anyone want to steal an old lady's identity?' Hattie asked, throwing her hands up in the air. 'I don't understand the world today, I really don't. People stealing identities, for heaven's sake. What a thing. Why can't people be satisfied with stealing a banana?'

'I've stolen a banana,' said Beau.

'Beau!' said Olivia. 'I hope you haven't.'

'Of course she hasn't,' said Hattie. 'My gosh, I could fill the pages of a Bible with what's wrong with the world today.'

'Remind me to buy a copy,' muttered Olivia.

Hattie gave her a sideways glare. 'Do you know what?' she said, shaking her head. 'I wish it was me in that grave, not Jesse.'

He's not in a grave; he was cremated, Olivia thought meanly, indicating left at the last second and pulling sharply into a parking space close to the beach. The driver in the car behind sounded their horn, to which Beau stuck up her middle finger and pressed it against the rear window.

'Beau!' said Olivia again with a deep sigh. 'Don't be so rude!'

Hattie had wished herself in the grave countless times since

Jesse's death – there wasn't much raging against the dying of the light going on.

Yanking on the handbrake to almost ninety degrees, Olivia switched off the engine. The weight of Hattie's grief – and hers – sometimes felt oppressive and made her abrasive and snappy, for which she felt constant gnawing guilt.

She rearranged her lips into a smile. 'Don't worry about it now. The important thing is you didn't give him your card. Let's get down to the beach hut with Jesse's ashes,' she said, leaning across Hattie to open the glove compartment to locate the beach-hut key.

A heap of leaflets she'd collected over the months skidded out over Hattie's lap. Ballet for seniors, walking for widows, cold-water swimming lessons, craft clubs for over seventies – all had been angrily dismissed by Hattie.

'I'm not interested in any of that,' she said, scowling. 'Put them in the recycling bin!'

'Not now, but you might be,' Olivia said gently.

But Hattie shook her head, her eyes suddenly moist. 'I will not,' she said before changing the subject. 'Did you manage to pick up that prescription for me?'

'The antidepressants, blood-pressure tablets and psoriasis cream?' Olivia said, winding up the van window, which jammed on every other turn. 'Yes, I gave them to you. They're in a paper bag by the bread bin. We had a conversation about it.'

Since Jesse's death, Hattie's health had deteriorated – small things, but it was as if her immune system couldn't fight the sadness. Olivia was seriously worried about her and had accompanied her to appointments with the GP, trying to communicate to the doctor that grief was making her mother ill. The best he could do was offer antidepressants and suggest a hobby, hence the leaflets.

Hattie had scoffed at the GP. 'Do I look like I play golf?'

she'd said, before Olivia had apologised and steered her mother out of the consulting room.

'We did not have a conversation about it,' said Hattie.

'We did!' said Olivia, massaging her temples in small circles.

Beau sighed an enormous sigh.

A woman walking past the van, holding her young son's hand, gave them a sympathetic smile through the windscreen. Olivia felt a pang of longing for when a five-year-old Beau would seek out her hand to hold, gripping her fingers as if they were lifelines. She remembered a time in a clothes shop years ago, when Olivia had leaned over to pick something up and was momentarily out of Beau's view, and she'd immediately burst into tears and screamed 'Mummy' in a voice that could be heard above the shop's loud music. She was lucky now if her lovely daughter even looked in her direction.

'I remember telling you the psoriasis cream is a spray nozzle so you can reach the patches on your back,' said Olivia.

'You don't need to share my medical history with the world!' said Hattie, her eyes misting over. 'That woman might be able to lip-read! Are you sure you told me?'

'Yes,' said Olivia, the knots in her neck crunching as she shoved the leaflets back in the glove compartment.

Hattie's yo-yo moods left Olivia feeling utterly exhausted. Since Jesse's death, she felt Hattie had been unravelling, stitch by stitch, at the seams. One moment she was abrasive and rest-less, the next rendered immobile by the weight of grief, fright-ened to do anything alone.

'I just feel like all the meaning in my life has gone,' Hattie said, stroking the box on her lap. 'There's no point to it anymore. Even getting out of bed in the morning is a struggle.'

Olivia sighed internally. The plans for her life – and Beau's – had been cancelled. The new opportunities in Dublin, the new flat, the new start, the chance to run away, gone. She swallowed hard. Although she would never leave Hattie alone now that Jesse was gone, she sometimes found herself dreaming of the new life she never got to start.

For the time being, she'd managed to get a part-time job in the costume department at the university, but it didn't pay well, and she'd promised herself to look for a new job during the summer break. Beau had reluctantly returned to school. The friends who'd thought Olivia brave for moving away told her that the grass wasn't always greener, relief audible in their voices.

Thankfully, the tenants due to move into her house had been understanding when she'd retracted the agreement, but all the 'new people, new start, new experiences' promises she'd made to Beau had evaporated. And the secret reason she'd wanted to go, the prospect of Oscar Gregory coming back to the area, still loomed over her neck like the glinting blade of a guillotine. Since she'd bumped into one of Oscar's old colleagues and he'd told her Oscar was planning to return, she hadn't heard anything more. So she didn't know if he was definitely in the UK – he'd thankfully not made his presence known to her – but whenever she heard a car pull up outside the house, or the doorbell rang unexpectedly, she'd find herself trembling, only to discover it was the postman with a bundle of letters.

'Maybe the keys are in my bag,' Olivia said, turning round and reaching into the back seat.

Digging her hand into the bag, pushing past the sandwiches wrapped in tinfoil she'd hastily put together and stuffed in, alongside a sandy bottle of sun cream, she located the key and swung back round. As she did so, she knocked into Beau's rucksack and it made the clinking sound of what she thought were bottles knocking into one another. Olivia's heart sank. She'd smelled alcohol on Beau's breath recently. Whereas other, calmer mothers would sit down and talk through the dangers of alcohol in the rational manner that parenting manuals advise,

Olivia had flown off the handle and plugged straight for night-mare stories of liver failure, blackout and death.

'Beau!' she said now. 'What's that in your bag? I hope it's not alcohol!'

Beau slowly removed the earphones from her ears. 'What?'

'What have you got in your bag?'

'Nothing,' said Beau. 'Leave me alone, will you? What are you accusing me of now? You're always on my case. You're so unbelievably controlling!'

Olivia opened her mouth to reply but shut it before she said anything. She had the ridiculous urge to cry.

That's right, taunted Oscar's voice from the dim and distant past, *turn on the tears*.

'Come on,' said Hattie, 'leave her be. Let's get this over with. I want to get back home.'

'But this is for you... and Jesse,' said Olivia quietly. 'It's almost the anniversary of his death. It's taken me this long to convince you to come back to the beach.'

'I know that, for heaven's sake!' said Hattie, gripping the box on her lap. 'I just prefer being at home these days. I'm rather more of a hermit now.'

'I'm not going to let you become a lonely old recluse,' said Olivia. 'I know you don't really like being on your own. You used to love meeting people on the beach.'

'I'm a happy hermit,' said Hattie, looking thoroughly miserable.

'Shall we get going? I've got to meet someone,' said Beau. 'No offence, Granny. Sorry, Mum, for snapping just then.'

Olivia gave her a small, well-practised 'it doesn't matter' smile.

'No offence taken,' Hattie said. 'It's too busy here for my liking and I'm keen to get home too, for a cup of tea and a garibaldi. My one pleasure in life.'

A speed-walking woman carrying weights in each hand

zipped past, but apart from that, it was quiet. Olivia stared at them both, open-mouthed.

'We haven't even got out of the van yet!' she said, her face flushing with heat. 'A show of enthusiasm would be nice, please!'

Hattie's shoulders sagged and she turned to Olivia, an apologetic expression on her face. 'I'm sorry,' she mumbled. 'I'm just... scared. Being here, it brings it all back. But part of my stupid brain is imagining that I've dreamed the whole thing and he'll be there, on the beach, setting up the deckchairs, chatting away to anyone who'll listen.'

Olivia's heart contracted. 'I know,' she said, leaning towards Hattie and giving her a hug.

TWO

Today was a big day. They were taking some of Jesse's ashes to the beach to scatter at his favourite place, the beach hut. The rest had been scattered in the garden, with some kept in pride of place on the mantlepiece, next to the jar of Michael's ashes, which had emerged from the shoebox in the bottom of the wardrobe since Jesse's death. 'My two husbands can keep each other company,' Hattie had said without a note of irony in her voice.

Hattie had on new sandals for the occasion, which had been a fiasco to order and had involved Olivia driving to a retail park thirty miles away to collect. Unfortunately, the straps were rubbing her heels despite the plasters Olivia had provided, so progress along the promenade was slow.

Hattie and Olivia walked arm in arm, with Beau just behind, kicking at pebbles with her Doc Martens. Olivia wished she could find new words to comfort Hattie. She'd experimented with so many this last year, but they felt like platitudes that had belly-flopped hopelessly into Hattie's heart.

'Hard to believe it's been a year,' tried Olivia. 'Has it got any easier for you, Mum? Perhaps the summer will help?'

'It actually gets harder,' said Hattie, shutting Olivia down. 'Because with every day that passes, it's even longer since I last saw him. It's a physical pain, right here.' She pointed to her heart.

Olivia fell horribly silent and scanned the surroundings. She'd hoped for good weather to at least soften the edges of the day – calm seas and bright-blue skies – but the sea roared at the top of its voice and foamed at the mouth. She hadn't been back in the water since the accident, and she wondered if she ever would.

Despite the weather, there were a few brave families trying to enjoy the beach, sun tents wobbling in the breeze, jumpers pulled on over T-shirts, shivering children with blue-edged lips. A boy tried to fly a dragon-shaped kite, but it repeatedly nose-dived into the sand. Seagulls yelled at the tops of their lungs, fiercely warning potential predators to stay away from their chicks. Olivia's head pounded with stress, and she was acutely aware of Beau's phone repeatedly going off.

'Are you going to answer that?' Olivia asked, more abruptly than she'd intended.

Beau screwed up her nose and lowered her eyes, made cat-like with black eyeliner. 'In a minute,' she said, pausing to pick up a discarded plastic bottle and hand it to Olivia. 'Do you know there's eight million tonnes of plastic in the sea?'

'Is there?' said Hattie, coming to an abrupt halt. 'What sort of plastic?'

'Fishing rope, nets, plastic bottles, cups, all sorts,' said Beau. 'Mostly down to Mum's generation wrecking the planet.'

Olivia closed her eyes and inhaled deeply. The phone continued to whistle. Finally, Beau answered it, pulling back a few metres behind Hattie and Olivia, putting up her hood as she muttered into the phone.

'We've lost her to one of her pals, I'm afraid,' said Olivia, giving Hattie's arm a squeeze, aware of how pin-thin her mother had become this last year. Olivia cooked for Hattie regularly and put high-calorie puddings in her basket when they shopped for groceries together, but Hattie's appetite was meagre. It was better than it had been at the beginning, when she'd survived on nothing more than the occasional humbug, but it still didn't stretch far beyond cheese on toast or tea and biscuits. She said she couldn't see the point in cooking a proper meal for one.

'We're almost there now,' said Olivia. 'Do your feet hurt? Are you alright?'

The closer they got to the beach hut, the more tense Hattie became.

'Since you ask, no, I'm not alright,' Hattie said. 'It's not as if the hoover broke, is it? Is anyone *alright* after killing their husband?'

Olivia's stomach twisted. A man walking his Labrador nearby stopped walking and gaped at Hattie. The Labrador quietly studied a 'no dogs on the beach' sign.

'You did not kill your husband,' Olivia said calmly, smiling at the man. She raised her voice to say, 'She did not kill her husband! Come on, Mum – it wasn't your fault in any way whatsoever.'

'It was,' Hattie said. 'I was the one who told him to help the boy. I should've known he'd try to be the hero. So it's my fault. Even Alec said so.'

At the mention of Alec's name, Olivia's heart plunged like a stone in a glass of water. He was Jesse's son from his first marriage, Hattie's stepson, and Olivia's stepbrother. He'd always refused to acknowledge Hattie as his stepmother and would only see Jesse away from their home on 'neutral territory'. He'd caused horrible heartache over the years and Olivia disliked him intensely, a feeling which had only been exacerbated at Jesse's funeral when he'd asked Hattie near the buffet table, in earshot of the entire funeral party, whether she blamed herself for Jesse's death. Olivia wasn't proud of tipping the silver platter of egg-and-cress sandwiches into his lap, but something had to be done.

'Take no notice of Alec,' said Olivia, stopping herself from going into a full rant about him. 'Look, I think the sun is going to come out. Isn't that great?' She pointed at a break in the clouds.

'I think a downpour is imminent,' Hattie replied, her voice quivering. 'How can I not take notice of Alec.' It wasn't even a question. 'He's Jesse's son, I have to love him.'

'You don't have to love anybody,' said Olivia, turning towards her mother.

'That's where you're wrong. He's all I have left of Jesse, so I want to love him!'

'But he hardly even speaks to you. He treats both of us with contempt. When his inheritance is through, I doubt we'll see him again.'

'I hope that's not true,' said Hattie, her voice cracking.

Her chin-length hair was tucked into one of Jesse's caps. Usually styled in a smart blunt bob, her hair was tangled and wavy because she'd stopped blow-drying it. Her ordinarily dark, bright eyes were pink and puffy from sleepless nights, and her pockets overflowed with tightly scrunched damp tissues like clusters of woodland mushrooms. Before now, Olivia had never really believed that someone could die of heartache when their partner died, but watching Hattie fade like this over the course of a year, it seemed a real possibility.

'Remember how Jesse always wore socks with his sandals, even in summer?' said Olivia, trying to lift the mood.

As soon as she said the words, an image flashed into her head of him taking off his sandals and socks before he'd entered the water that day. She swallowed.

'And that red waistcoat!' she said cheerfully. 'Looked like a garden gnome!'

'I remember,' said Hattie. 'He used to get those dreadful tan lines on his ankles. He looked like he was wearing white socks to bed. I liked the waistcoat. In fact...'

Hattie stopped walking and unbuttoned her cardigan a little so Olivia could see that she was in fact wearing the red woollen waistcoat over her dress. It drowned her tiny frame.

'In his honour,' she said.

Olivia smiled and reached for her mother's hand. It felt soft and childlike. Increasingly, Olivia had felt their roles reversing. Grief had diminished Hattie. Everyday things floored her. Online banking passwords, booking her car in for an MOT, opening tightly screwed jars of jam – these things could reduce her to frustrated, despondent tears and fraught phone calls to Olivia. The thought made a hard lump form in her throat.

'Are you coming, Beau?' Olivia called back to her daughter, who was still on her phone, trailing further and further behind them.

Beau stiffened and raised her palm as if to say 'wait'.

Olivia couldn't help but feel annoyed – it seemed that these days there was always someone else somewhere else who needed Beau's attention.

Eventually, holding her phone against her chest, Beau called over to Olivia and Hattie. 'Is it okay if I go? I need to sort something out. I'll see you later. Sorry, Granny.'

Before Olivia could respond, Beau dashed over to Hattie and gave her a quick kiss on the cheek, leaving a faint red lipstick mark, before turning away.

'But...' called Olivia into the breeze. 'I thought you were going to be with us. I was hoping you'd want to spend—'

'What did you say?' asked Beau, turning and lifting her hand to her ear.

Olivia sighed, the energy draining out of her.

'Let her go,' said Hattie, giving Beau a wave. 'She doesn't want to be hanging around with old ladies.'

'Old la*dy*,' Olivia corrected.

'I remember when you were a teenager,' said Hattie. 'Revising for your exams so studiously. You were such a good girl, never put a foot wrong. I was always waiting for you to rebel.'

'Yes, well,' said Olivia, feeling a pang of sorrow for her conscientious, people-pleasing younger self.

She watched Beau run up the cliff steps away from the beach, swallowing the feeling of disappointment and concern rising in her throat. She felt as if she was holding on to Beau with the finest of threads, that if she pulled any harder, the thread would snap, and she'd be lost. It was hard, sometimes, to conceal her fears. She wished she could yell like the seagulls did, to protect her chick.

Olivia and Hattie reached the beach hut. It had been locked up for most of the year, bar the few times Olivia had come down to check it. Beach huts had been on Milton-on-Sea's promenade for almost a century, updated and repainted by new lease-holders over the years. When their doors were open, passers-by would peer in to catch a glimpse of the interior: glass floats in nets, driftwood signs, pans of sizzling sausages, gin and tonics. On the grassy cliff behind the huts, clumps of sea pinks quivered, and yellow gorse filled the air with its coconut scent.

Even though she'd been to the beach several times since that dreadful day, Olivia felt a blow to the stomach at the memory of Jesse collapsed on the sand. But returning here and ensuring that memory was not the prevailing one was important – key – Olivia believed, to Hattie's ability to move forward.

'Here we are then,' said Hattie, her voice quivering.

The deckchairs, previously stacked up together in a sheltered space near Hattie and Jesse's beach hut during the summer months, had been put into winter storage. There wasn't a piece of striped canvas in sight.

'It's as if our business never existed,' said Hattie quietly. 'By now, we'd have the chairs out and ready to hire. Poor Jesse... if only I hadn't been the one to spot that boy—' She stopped short, breaking down into a sob, before searching for a tissue in her pocket. 'Silly old woman. I want to go home,' she added, noisily blowing her nose.

'You and Jesse were a part of this beach for years,' said Olivia encouragingly. 'Jesse adored being here. Imagine how many holiday photographs you've been in the background of? You'll be in so many family albums.'

A tiny half-smile crept across Hattie's lips at the thought.

'Your deckchairs have welcomed thousands of bottoms over the years,' Olivia added. 'Bottoms from John o' Groats to Land's End.'

'Little and large,' said Hattie.

Olivia grinned.

The enamel sign, white with navy-blue lettering, which read 'Deckchairs for Hire' had come loose, hanging off a nail on the wall near the hut. Olivia tried to straighten it, but it immediately swung onto its side.

'That just about sums it all up,' said Hattie, her half-smile vanished. 'It's all over.'

'The beach hut is still here, and your memories are still here,' said Olivia, relentlessly optimistic, opening the hut's padlock, swinging open the door. 'And, look, your deckchairs are here.'

Olivia dragged out the two deckchairs, banging them against her knees as she did so, her hands trembling as she battled to put them up. Inside the beach hut, Jesse's towel and a pair of his sandals were in the shoe basket, as if he'd just popped to the sea for a swim.

'I'm quite lost without him,' said Hattie quietly as she discreetly opened the box of ashes and sprinkled some around the beach hut. 'I sometimes set two plates out at dinner time out of habit or make him a cup of tea in the morning. I'm losing my marbles.'

'You're not. Why don't you sit down for a minute?' Olivia said, pointing at the deckchair. 'Maybe you can start coming down to the beach again this summer. You both loved it here so much. You were a permanent fixture.'

Olivia was desperate for something to spark Hattie's interest in life, to keep her connected to the life she'd loved.

Hattie sat down and stared out towards the sea. 'I could,' she said quietly.

Holding her breath, Olivia straightened her back with hope, meerkat-like.

'But what would be the point?' Hattie continued, gesturing to the empty deckchair beside her with a floppy hand.

Olivia's shoulders sagged.

'Who would I talk to?' said Hattie. 'I've lost my best friend. Jesse was everything I had. It'll never be the same again. It's all pointless now. Oh, Liv, please take me home. I just want to go home and be on my own.'

Olivia swallowed the childish feeling of hurt that sometimes crept in when Hattie spoke about the pointlessness of her life now that Jesse was dead. *What about me and Beau?* she felt like yelling but never did. The feeling ran deep. It was an old hurt that she was well practised at suppressing. *What about me?*

'But we need to keep Jesse company,' Olivia persisted, glancing at the ashes on the ground. 'Just for a little while. Let me get us a cup of tea while we're here. I've brought some garibaldi biscuits with me.' She held up the packet in her hand and smiled.

Hattie blinked. 'I hadn't thought of it like that,' she said, her voice softening. 'Poor Jesse. Didn't he have a lovely singing voice? The bungalow is so quiet without him. I can hear things I never heard before, like the fridge humming, the radio from next door through the wall, even the woodworm munching the floorboards.'

Olivia let out a puff of laughter. Yes, he'd had a lovely

singing voice. He'd had a wonderful rendition of 'Singin' in the Rain' while holding a beach parasol. He'd been a lovely, gentle man who could talk to anyone and who listened well, with big eyes full of unspoken emotion. And despite the situation with Alec they'd had to deal with over the years, he'd treated Olivia as his child.

Thinking about Alec made Olivia tense and she rotated her head in small circles, wincing at the pain in her neck. 'I'll just be a minute,' she said, feeling for the purse in her bag and walking towards the beach café to order two teas.

'Ginger for sore throats, green for bloating, chamomile for anxiety or white for detox?' said the woman behind the till. 'Or ordinary?'

Olivia needed them all.

'Chamomile, please,' she said, her eyes resting on the café's noticeboard. There were several notices pinned up: paddle-boarding safaris, a guide to the lifeguard's flags, a swimming group, a warning about weever fish, yoga sessions at sunrise.

She glanced back at Hattie sitting on her deckchair, all alone with her arms folded across her chest, the fabric of Jesse's empty deckchair beside her, flapping in the breeze. Olivia felt suddenly desolate, struck by a memory of Hattie sitting alone in the living room of Olivia's childhood house, the curtains closed at midday, after Olivia's father had died. Of herself, as a small child, perched on the bottom stair of the staircase, looking at Hattie through the open living-room door, not knowing how to help her.

And there was another dreadful feeling that made her shiver; that when she looked at Hattie, she was staring at an image of her future self, equally alone. She couldn't let that happen. She had to *do* something. Something drastic. There had to be another chapter, more to the story. Hattie needed a friend, something or someone to lift her spirits.

Olivia's eyes swept over the 'Deckchairs for Hire' sign sadly drooping towards the ground on the wall behind Hattie. A crazy idea struck her.

'That'll be four pounds,' said the woman behind the till, handing Olivia two cups.

'Thank you,' she said. 'Can I borrow a pen and a piece of paper, please?'

The woman tossed them to her. Resting the cups of tea on a table, her mind buzzing, Olivia drew a little illustration of two deckchairs, wrote a note underneath it and handed it back to the woman.

'Could you put this up on that noticeboard, please?' Olivia asked, a burst of hope striking in her heart like a match.

The woman nodded and tucked the paper in her apron.

'Eight pounds for a month,' she said. 'Ten pounds including a mention on our social channels too.'

Olivia quickly handed the woman a ten-pound note before heading back to Hattie, clutching a paper cup of hot tea in each hand. For the briefest moment, the sun came out from behind the clouds, turning the grey sea aquamarine. Some optimistic holidaymakers took off their jumpers. Olivia felt the sun on her skin – after the cold wind, warmth.

DECKCHAIR FOR HIRE

Do you have an hour to spare? My mother, Hattie, lost her husband, Jesse, last year. You might have seen them sitting in their deckchairs outside beach hut 236, where they ran a deckchair-for-hire business. I'm looking for friendly people to hire out Jesse's deckchair, for an hour or so this summer, for conversation and friendship. Any donation will go to a local befriending charity, to help fight social isolation.

Email me at oliviafryer@hotmail.com

THREE

'Welcome to the "sandwich generation", my friend,' said Olivia's closest friend, Isla, stabbing her fork into a slice of coffee-and-walnut cake.

Olivia had just finished telling Isla about her plan to cheer up Hattie. They were sitting in the snug kitchen of Olivia's mid-terrace house where, Olivia noticed, all the pot plants needed watering, the dishwasher needed refilling with salt and a bag of food shopping sat, unpacked, on the tiled floor. Her sketchbooks, full of her coastal-themed textile designs, were in a pile on the kitchen counter near the fruit bowl, gathering dust.

'That's what being in your late forties and early fifties is all about,' continued Isla, tucking her wild mane of long blonde hair behind her ears. 'You're stuck in the middle of trying to care for elderly parents, while working full-time and looking after teenage kids. Nightmare.'

'I wouldn't say "stuck" exactly,' said Olivia. 'Or "nightmare". Well...'

'I would,' said Isla. 'It's all about self-sacrifice. We're last on the list of priorities. Look at you – you've always put Beau first, of course you have, and now, not only are you putting Beau first, but your mum is also jostling for the top spot.'

'I'm all Beau's got,' said Olivia. 'And now I'm all Mum's got too. I want to be there for them both.'

'And that's what you're doing. Hey, at least you haven't got a husband who snores like a warthog all night, leaving you sleep-starved as well,' said Isla. 'He puts out the bins at least – I'll give him that.'

Both women laughed, but Olivia's laugh was tinged with sadness. Isla had been happily married to Hugh for years, and they had five gorgeous children, but marriage had eluded Olivia. It wasn't an institution she necessarily aspired to belong to, but not having a partner to love who loved her was something she deeply regretted.

Bringing up Beau had made dating difficult. There had been a couple of men she'd been out with, but as soon as she made it clear to them that Beau was her priority and that, because she was a lone parent, she didn't have much free time to date, the men had lost interest. They wanted more attention than she could give, so after a while, she gave up trying.

There had been Oscar of course, before everything with him went wrong. He was the only man she'd loved, but when they broke up, she'd told him she wanted a clean break, that she never wanted to see him again. They'd made a deal – he'd get on with his life, she'd get on with hers. She couldn't deny there was always a chance he'd come back – and it had played on her mind over the years – but after the way he'd treated her, she'd hoped he would respect her wishes and leave her alone.

The news of his return last year, then, had come as a stomach-churning shock. And the thought that he might now be in the UK, and close by, made her feel horribly cornered.

'Has there been any more word about Oscar?' said Isla, as if she'd read Olivia's mind.

Olivia shook her head. 'Only what I heard last year – that

he was planning to come back for a new restaurant opening or something,' she said, shrugging, pretending to be unconcerned.

'Well, he wasn't interested in supporting you all those years ago,' said Isla, 'so I doubt he'll come rushing back into your life now, unless he realises what an idiot he was and wants to make it up to you.'

Olivia blushed. She hadn't even told Isla the whole truth.

'Hopefully he's forgotten all about me,' she said.

'Nobody could forget you!' Isla said. 'You're beautiful, clever, talented and you make great coffee cake.'

Isla rose from her chair and gave Olivia a hug – she was a good friend.

'Look, I better go,' she said. 'I've got to walk the dog, cook for eight thirteen-year-olds for Sam's birthday and then go to a roller disco, before popping round to my dad's flat to make him his Ovaltine.' Isla sighed heavily, dropped her shoulders in a comical way and hobbled into the hallway.

They both cracked up laughing and Olivia let Isla out of the front door, closing it behind her. She picked up some official-looking post from the mat and called up the stairs to Beau, who was in her bedroom with her music blaring.

'Isla's gone,' she called. 'I'm down here if you need me.'

There was no reply, so Olivia flicked through the post, opening the letter she knew to be from the solicitor who'd dealt with Jesse's estate.

'Brilliant,' she said in a tone that meant the opposite, a flutter of palpitations ripping across her chest.

As an executor to Jesse's will along with Hattie, it had been left to Olivia to distribute the part of his estate he hadn't handed over to his wife. There were savings and another property he'd held on to from a previous life. It had been complex and taken some time waiting for probate to be granted. He'd left a generous sum to Alec, who'd initially contested the will, claiming he should receive a bigger share of Jesse's assets. He'd sent Olivia several terse and cold-hearted emails, 'chasing' her up, and a handwritten letter where the biro had almost gone through the paper from how hard he'd pressed, writing words such as *unnecessary delay* and *utterly incompetent*. She'd drafted many vitriolic replies but deleted them all in favour of emotionless, factual communication.

'You'll finally get what you want, Alec,' she muttered, shoving the letter back into the envelope and moving through to the kitchen. 'A big wad of cash to buy your boat or flashy watch or designer brogues.'

On the one occasion Olivia had been to Alec's home, to break the news about Jesse's death in person, she'd been startled by the stark, minimalist decor. Even the doorbell had been hard to locate – until she'd pressed a button and realised it was a high-tech video doorbell. From what she could see from the hallway, the interior couldn't have been more different to her house. Nothing was out of place. The only possessions she could see looked wildly expensive; everything was remote controlled, possibly even Alec himself.

'Thank you for informing me,' he'd said, opening the door by typing something into his phone, so Olivia could take her trembling voice, watering eyes and snotty nose and leave five minutes after she'd arrived. She'd waited on the doorstep, clutching a tissue to her nose, to see if he'd make any sound when she left, but all she'd heard was baffling silence. Perhaps he'd watched her through his video doorbell, waiting for her to drive away, before he'd fallen to his knees and reacted to the news of his father's death.

Alec's grudge against Hattie and Olivia for 'stealing' Jesse was lifelong. His refusal to come into their home since Hattie and Jesse had got together almost forty years ago had deeply affected them all. When he was a child, they'd tried all manner of temptations: a newly decorated bedroom with a drum kit, a trampoline in the garden, a ginger-and-white kitten. But Alec wouldn't budge.

Olivia remembered the time Jesse had brought Alec to see the kitten but he'd refused to get out of the car. Olivia had waved from her bedroom window and pushed a piece of paper with 'Hello!' written on it in colourful bubble lettering onto the glass, but he'd given her the V sign and stared at his lap, making Olivia's cheeks burn with embarrassment. Jesse had taken the kitten out to the car, to Alec, but it had escaped into the steering-wheel column of his brown VW Volvo, trapped and terrified until a mechanic had freed him.

I hope you never come back, Olivia had thought, scrunching the piece of paper into a ball, when Alec was driven away again, like a royal prince. But the rejection hurt, and she knew that all Hattie wanted was for Alec to accept her and for them all to be a family. Why else would she bake a Victoria sandwich, dress in her smartest clothes, clip on her pearl earrings, buy a crisp new *Beano* magazine for Alec and wait at the door for him to arrive, only to sag with disappointment when he didn't come in, yet again.

And each time she was disappointed, Hattie would tip the cake into the dustbin, pull off her earrings, slump into the doldrums and snap at Olivia as if it was all her fault.

Jesse would try to console Hattie, muttering things Olivia couldn't quite hear. Cross words would be exchanged. Doors would slam.

Olivia would frantically try to rectify the mood in the house – paint Hattie pictures, write poems and make necklaces out of colourful beads to make her mother feel better. She'd tried to do more. To be more. She'd tried to fill the space that Alec's absence left by getting better at the piano, running faster in the races and scoring A grades at school, so Hattie had no choice but to smile. So that Hattie wouldn't care about Alec. But despite not ever being there in person,

Alec was *always* there. Not just an elephant in the room, but a whole herd of elephants. Two herds. A parade of the damn things.

Now though, Olivia didn't have to pretend not to dislike him. There were a handful of times when their paths had crossed as adults – family events – where Alec would arrive in his flash car and expensive suits, say no more than a few, curt words and drive off again, his polished brogue slamming down hard on the accelerator as if he couldn't get away fast enough.

Olivia would complain about him to Hattie, but her mother would remain tight-lipped, give a slight shake of her head and pat Olivia's wrist to stop her from bad-mouthing him further. 'Jesse adores him,' she'd say, as if that trumped Olivia's feelings.

'I expect we'll never hear from him again after this,' muttered Olivia to the empty room. 'Good riddance, that's what I say.'

She meant what she said but was left with a bitter aftertaste. She always felt defeated where Alec was concerned. He was one of those people you could never get the better of, a narcissist who never said sorry or, as Isla often said: 'a total arse'.

Olivia looked around in dismay at the general debris in the kitchen. A pile of laundry. A bag of clothes that needed taking to the charity shop that had been there for at least six months. A collection of old shoes of Beau's that she was meaning to sell on eBay but hadn't quite got round to. The pot plants. The dishwasher. Spending so much time with Hattie meant Olivia's house was sorely neglected. She felt guilty and told herself she must do better. The house had been a good home for her and Beau, and now that she had no plan to move, she needed to look after it.

The house was small enough for her not to feel too lonely on the many nights she'd spent alone while Beau was growing up. Those evenings were why she'd started to volunteer with a befriending charity, where she had phone conversations with isolated older people. There were so many people, living alone, who benefitted from a good chat. Just like Hattie would now.

Her thoughts were disturbed by a sharp knock. There at the window was the candle-wax-white face of her neighbour, ninety-seven-year-old Donald. The sleeves of his blue shirt were pushed up to his elbows, exposing the whitest arms known to man, and the waistband of his grey trousers was pulled up high over his egg-shaped belly.

'Have you seen what she's done now?' he said, his voice muffled through the glass.

'Come round to the door,' Olivia mouthed, pointing at the door and muttering, 'What now?' under her breath.

'Do you want to come in, Donald?' she said loudly. 'I have home-made coffee cake.'

He wavered. His hand on the door frame to steady himself, he looked beyond her into the kitchen, his watery eyes scanning the surfaces for cake. 'Did you bake it today?' he asked.

'A couple of days ago, but it's still good. It's in the fridge to keep the cream-cheese frosting fresh.'

'No thank you then,' he said. 'Have you seen what Beau's done to that garage door on Avenue Road? You'll be lucky if nobody calls the police. They probably have already. When I was a lad, nobody would dream of doing such a thing. Only those who ended up in borstal.'

Olivia's heart sank. She longed for the days when going down a slide in the park or finding a worm in the soil was enough of a thrill for Beau. Now, she'd entered that teenage stage where she was more secretive and spending more time with her friends than at home.

'What's she done that's so terrible?' Olivia asked, unable to prevent defensive irritability from entering her tone. Her stomach grumbled loudly, and she pressed down on it. Behind her, the bag of shopping toppled over. Apples rolled across the floor.

'She's graffitied it!' he said. 'Thinks she's Bagsy or whoever that lad is! Nobody else is washing it off – she can! How dare she? She's a crackpot, your Beau. When I was a lad, my dad would've given me the slipper. Mind you, there's no father figure for Beau, is there? Maybe that's the problem. You unmarried mothers are all the same!'

The colour drained from Olivia's face. Graffiti?

'What are you talking about?' she asked, trying to gather her wits. 'I can't imagine Beau ever doing that. Did you see her with your own eyes? And all that stuff about unmarried mothers is absolute rubbish. Where there's an unmarried mother, there's an unmarried father somewhere.'

'I don't care what you say,' he said. 'It's vandalism. My mother would have a fit if she could see Beau! Blue hair! Has she got a job? Get her under control! And, yes, I saw her with my own eyes. I gave her a piece of my mind. When I was a lad, we knew right from wrong. Sort her out!'

Donald left his accusations on the doorstep and left.

'When you were a lad, children were sent up chimneys!' Olivia called after him. 'And women weren't allowed to vote! And it's Banksy, not Bagsy!'

She slammed the back door shut, shoving her shoulder against it to make it close completely, then rested her hand on her pounding heart. Graffiti.

'BEAU!' she shouted at the top of her voice, marching towards the stairs. She shivered with a red flash of anger.

When there was no answer, she paused and told herself to calm down. Massaging her temples, she thought about what she should do. She needed to talk to Beau but knew if she approached her with all guns blazing, her daughter would shut down and tell her nothing.

Olivia was stricken with worry. The last year had been turbulent for Beau and now she'd got in with a crowd Olivia didn't know. Were they influencing her? Olivia had suggested

Beau bring them home for dinner – she'd cook lasagne or get a takeaway pizza – but Beau had laughed.

'You wouldn't understand them,' she'd said. 'You belong to a different era.'

Olivia wasn't sure where she belonged anymore.

Glancing at the clock, she realised she couldn't deal with Beau now; she had to ring Winnie Alexander, one of the befriending contacts she spoke to once a week. Olivia took a deep breath to calm her pounding heart.

Winnie must have been waiting by the phone because she picked it up before it even rang. Olivia imagined Winnie perched on her telephone chair in the hallway of her home, her hand hovering over the receiver. She'd seen a photograph of her; tall, with short grey curly hair and huge round spectacles that magnified her eyes.

'Is that you, Olivia?' Winnie asked.

'It's me, Winnie,' said Olivia. 'How are you today?'

'Still here, dear,' she said. 'Still here. Sorry I'm a bit croaky – I haven't spoken to anyone since last week apart from shouting at the politicians on the radio. Not even a funeral to go to this week!' Winnie let out a bark of laughter.

'We'll make up for it now,' said Olivia, her heart cracking.

'Oops, hang on a minute,' Winnie said. 'I've wrapped the telephone cord around my fingers. Did you know they're phasing out these landline phones soon? The young people don't use them apparently.'

Olivia waited for Winnie to sort out the phone cord.

'Now, that's better, I'm back. How are you, dear?' asked Winnie.

'I'm well,' Olivia replied. 'How has your week been? Did you get out for a walk?'

'Let's talk about me later. You sound a bit tired,' said Winnie. 'Is it the perimenopause? Nobody ever talks about the perimenopause, do they? I think there should be a school subject in it. That and birth. There's a reason it's called "labour", you know. Nobody ever talks about that either. I wish I was in charge of the school curriculum; I would introduce a lesson called "The Things Nobody Tells You About". Anyway, dear, tell me how you are. I'd love to know.'

Out of nowhere, Olivia felt her bottom lip quiver. She slapped her hand over her mouth, closed her eyes and bit the inside of her cheek. She was supposed to listen to Winnie, not the other way around, and chat about everyday things.

'I know you're thinking you should be cheering me up,' said Winnie. 'But you know how much I like to help. I used to love helping my daughter Sophie, until she passed away. She would be about your age. We used to speak on the phone for hours. She'd have me booming out of the speakerphone in her car as she drove to work every day! She said I was better than her playlist. Oh dear, now I'm going to cry. Hang on, dear, I need a tissue.'

Olivia waited and listened to the sound of Winnie putting the receiver down, blowing her nose and picking the phone back up again.

'Do you need to take a minute, Winnie?' asked Olivia. 'You must miss Sophie so much.' She swallowed. The thought of losing Beau was unbearable.

'No, no, I'm alright now,' said Winnie. 'It just takes me by surprise sometimes. Like a cricket ball in the face – hard enough to give you a nosebleed. I was in the supermarket two weeks ago, choosing a melon – they're so expensive these days but they do come halfway around the world, I suppose – and I had a memory of Sophie which floored me. It was a silly thing, just the thought of her as a girl pushing her feet into her little white ankle socks with frills on the top, would you believe? I slipped to the floor, right there near the melons. A young man helped me up, thought my knees were dodgy. Talked at me in a loud, slow voice as if I had half a brain. When I told him I used to be an air hostess, I could tell he didn't believe me. How are you?'

'Oh, I'm alright,' Olivia said. 'I've seen a lot of my mum, trying to help her find a new interest.'

'Yes, poor her, I know how she feels,' said Winnie. 'And your daughter? How is she?'

'She's busy being a teenager!' said Olivia, forcing a laugh, her mind going to Donald's words. 'I think she might be going through a bit of a rebellious stage. Was your daughter like that? Mine doesn't seem to want to spend much time with me at the moment. I know it's natural, but, well, it...'

'Hurts?' said Winnie. 'One minute we're their heroes; the next, we're contemptuous.'

Olivia swallowed, feeling heat spreading over her chest and rising in her cheeks. She pulled off her cardigan. They'd been so close when Beau was growing up. It was just the two of them and they'd been happy like that. But over the last year, Beau had been asking questions about her father again, and Olivia knew Beau suspected she wasn't telling her the whole truth.

'The same thing happened to me, dear – it's very normal,' said Winnie. 'Sophie was quite wild for a time! She learned to smoke when she was fifteen and came home one day stinking of tobacco, complaining about the people in the park who were smoking near her – of course it was her! The devil. She climbed out the bedroom window when I told her she was grounded for a week. It's not easy being a mother, or a daughter for that matter. Talking is the answer. It always is.'

The call lasted just over the allotted half an hour. Winnie's throat was hoarse from talking when the call ended. They agreed to speak again in a week, in which time Winnie was going to go to the library and sign up for a creative writing class.

After the call, Olivia stood at the bottom of the stairs and yelled up to Beau, who, after turning off her music, came out of her room clutching her phone. She had on denim black shorts, a black vest top and black high-top boots.

'Beau, we need to have a talk,' Olivia said. 'A serious talk.'

'Mum, I thought you didn't use social media!' Beau replied.

'I don't,' replied Olivia, frowning. 'I never have and never will. Now, listen, Donald came round and told me about the garage door. About the graffiti. Beau, this is really serious and counts as criminal damage. Why would you do such a thing?'

'Then why has this message, from you, via the beach café, gone viral?' Beau asked, totally ignoring Olivia's words. 'It's about hiring out Granddad's deckchair. It's been viewed thousands of times! There are loads of comments.'

'What?' Olivia said, taking the stairs two at a time and peering over Beau's shoulder to look at the phone screen, her entire body flaming with heat.

Beau jabbed the screen with her finger. 'Look! There's a comment here from a local newspaper journalist who wants to do an interview with you,' she said, an amused smile on her lips.

Olivia's hand flew to her mouth. Behind her fingers, she said: 'How on earth has that happened? I only pinned a piece of paper to the noticeboard at the beach!'

'It's social media, Mother,' said Beau, rolling her eyes. 'Once it's out there, it's out there. And, by the way, don't worry about Donald. He's got it all wrong.'

FOUR

The emails came thick and fast. And with every new email, Olivia felt increasingly like lying down in a darkened room and never emerging. She hadn't expected this response *at all*. One or two older people looking for friendship maybe, but not this. Hattie would never agree to this.

To make matters worse, Beau persuaded her to agree to the newspaper interview before she'd had time to think it through – arranging for her to meet the reporter at Hattie's home. Pacing up and down the kitchen, she twisted the chunky silver ring she wore on her index finger round and round.

'I haven't even told Granny!' she said to Beau, who was scrolling through the emails on the laptop. 'What's she going to say? She's never going to agree to do an interview with the local paper. She won't even go to the chemist! And what about all these people?'

'You've tapped into the zeitgeist,' said Beau.

'Loneliness,' said Olivia. 'Not much of a zeitgeist.'

'Are you lonely, Mum?' asked Beau. 'You don't seem to see your friends that much.'

Olivia flushed red. She hated it when Beau put her life

under the magnifying glass and identified all her weaknesses and flaws. She was always so irritatingly accurate.

'I guess since Jesse died, I've spent a lot more time with Granny,' Olivia answered. 'I have to make sure she's not getting too isolated. You and Granny are my priorities.'

'Do you wish you had a partner?' asked Beau. 'I could put one of these signs up for you!'

'No, thank you,' said Olivia. 'I'm fine on my own, and I've got you and Granny to worry about. Talking of which, we need to discuss this garage door. What did you mean when you said Donald's got it all wrong? You do realise the police could get involved?'

Beau pulled a face. 'The police won't get involved! Why can't you trust me? I told you not to worry about it! Why would you believe dozy Donald over me?'

'I don't,' said Olivia. 'But you're my daughter – I just want to know what you're up to.'

'Up to?' said Beau. 'You make me sound like a child, Mum. Stop worrying! I'll tell you all about it later. I think you need to stop focusing on me and concentrate on your life. Maybe you're the one who's lonely, not Granny?'

'I like being on my own. I'm *fine*,' said Olivia, feeling heat rise in her cheeks.

'You should look at those dating apps – there are lots of different ones for all age groups,' said Beau. 'It's crazy really that there are lonely people in the world, when there are so many people.'

It wasn't just a matter of statistics though. Loneliness wasn't the same thing as being alone. She knew very well that you could be in a packed room, chatting away to a group of people and still feel lonely. You could be in a relationship and feel as though you'd been abandoned on an island with no means of escape. Was loneliness more of a question that was folded deep into a person's heart?

'I don't have time for dating apps,' said Olivia, crossing her arms over her chest. She wanted to change the topic. 'Especially now! Look at all those emails!'

Beau's gaze returned to the screen. 'Look, there's a medium who says she communicates with deceased people,' she said, pulling a horrified expression.

Olivia rolled her eyes.

'And a man who's training to swim the English Channel,' said Beau. 'Look, he's sent a picture in.'

Olivia peered at the picture – a giant of a man wearing goggles and a swimming hat.

'There's a man here who collects moths, walking the south-west coastal path, who'd like to book the chair. Oh, and one here from Alec!'

'Alec?' said Olivia. 'What does he want? Maybe he's had a personality transplant and wants to get involved.'

Olivia leaned over and scanned the email from Alec.

Olivia. Why are you renting out my father's deckchair, without even consulting me, for this mawkish purpose? Rather a surprise to see his photograph in the newspaper. He would not have approved. Is this deckchair one of the collection I am to inherit? If so, it's rightfully mine and I think I should have been consulted, but yet again you make decisions without notifying me, i.e. funeral buffet. Please reply promptly.

Olivia's blood boiled. 'Delete it!' she said quickly. 'I can't believe Alec. You'd think he'd be grateful I organised that bloody buffet.'

'Forget about him,' said Beau. 'He'll come round.'

Olivia shook her head. 'He's never going to change.'

'Anyone can change,' said Beau. 'Even the worst people can change.'

'That's the optimism of youth speaking. We're going to need

to answer all these emails and set up a fundraising page, so it's all done properly. I think it might all be too much for Granny, so I'm going to have to limit it to every Saturday for a month and if people aren't invited to the deckchair, perhaps they can donate to the charity if they'd like to.'

'There's one here from a man called Harvey,' said Beau. 'He says a few years ago Granny and Granddad helped him when he was down on his luck. They gave him the coat and shoes Jesse was wearing, because his own were falling apart, and they let him stay in their caravan for a few nights. She's never mentioned that. I wonder what else she hasn't told us. Perhaps all mothers have secrets.' Beau was staring intently at Olivia, her mood visibly darkening.

She was so changeable, like coastal weather. You didn't know if you needed your raincoat or your sun hat.

Olivia exhaled a lengthy sigh. 'It's not unusual for people to keep a few things to themselves,' she replied, turning away from Beau's penetrative glare. 'They're not necessarily secrets. Speaking of, time's up – tell me what's going on with this garage thing.'

'I will!' said Beau, returning her gaze to the screen and continuing to look through the emails.

'There's a woman who does sunrise swims and paddleboard yoga,' she said. 'And a lady who runs a mobile cocktail bar, who recently divorced her husband.'

'Beau, you can't keep ignoring me,' said Olivia.

'It's not unusual for people to keep a few things to themselves,' she replied mockingly.

Olivia opened her mouth to reply but was stopped by a knock at the door.

It was a community police officer. Donald had made a complaint. Unless Beau could prove she had permission from the owner, the officer was giving them a day to clean the graffiti off or paint over it, or they'd have to officially follow it up. Olivia clutched the door and forced herself to be polite, promising to clean the garage, and apologising profusely.

She closed the front door then shut her eyes for a long moment, before returning to the kitchen, where Beau was stuffing her coat into her bag, ready to take off.

'You're not going anywhere,' said Olivia, 'unless it's to remove that graffiti. It's private property, Beau. You can't just do what you like to it.'

'Why are you thinking the worst of me?' Beau was trembling with anger.

She'd always had a temper, ever since she was a little girl. It reminded Olivia of someone she'd rather not be reminded of.

'Where do you think you're going?' Olivia demanded.

'Out,' said Beau. 'I've got things to do. I'll see you later.'

'But... We need to talk about this!'

'I can't be bothered,' Beau shouted. 'I was going to tell you about it, but I wanted to do it my way. I wanted to surprise you and take you to see what I've done, so you could be happy and take notice of me! But you don't listen, and you're so wrapped up with worrying about Granny, you just snap at me whenever I see you! I miss Granddad too!'

'Oh, Beau, I know you do, and I do take notice of y...' said Olivia, but her words trailed off as the front door slammed shut.

Suddenly it was silent. A beam of sunlight shone through the porch window and made the dust particles in the air sparkle. She waved her hand around to bat them away.

Back in the kitchen, she leaned against the edge of the table and massaged the stress knots in the back of her neck. She felt light-headed with worry, her heart racing. The 'Things to Worry About' list was growing ever longer.

She noticed a tortoiseshell butterfly trapped inside the kitchen, beating its red-and-black wings against the glass. She opened the window to release it, but it stayed where it was on the windowsill, unsure of what to do next.

. . .

Hattie's front door was painted green and had a glass panel in the upper half, which was covered by a white lace curtain drooping a little on a sagging curtain wire. The house numbers – two nines, ninety-nine – were set at an angle like closing speech marks. A pot of geraniums stood by the doorstep, their perfume filling Olivia's nostrils.

At first Hattie didn't answer the door when Olivia knocked their code: four knocks, rest, four more knocks.

'Mum?' Olivia shouted through the letter box. 'It's me.'

Peering through the letter box, she saw Hattie's slipper-clad feet emerge from the bedroom. Slowly, her mother opened the front door, blinking like a mole in the sunlight. In her hand she clutched a cloth and a spray bottle of glass cleaner.

'I was hiding,' she said. 'In case it was the courier.'

'He won't come now,' said Olivia. 'That was ages ago! What are you doing?'

'I've been cleaning the photographs,' said Hattie. 'In the back of my mind, I think if I rub the glass hard enough, Jesse will come back, like the genie in the lamp. I miss him, Liv.' She pulled a tissue from her sleeve and dabbed her eyes.

'I know you do,' said Olivia, gently rubbing Hattie's arm. 'So do I. Can I come in then?'

Hattie opened the door, and Olivia walked into the hallway, taking a moment to adjust to the dark after the bright outdoors.

Moving through to the kitchen, she clocked the two cups of tea at the table – one empty, one full and stone cold.

Hattie picked up the full mug, took it over to the sink and poured it away. 'Jesse wasn't thirsty this morning,' she said with a little embarrassed laugh.

'Oh, Mum,' Olivia said.

She looked around the room. It was a small, sweet kitchen. The units were pine, the splashback tiles a pale blue, and above the sink, a window looked out over the back garden, crammed with plants Jesse had once tended. The windowsill was crowded with vases and pots, and a row of hooks hung near the sink draining board for a selection of multicoloured mugs. A shelf on one side of the kitchen held jars full of pasta, flour or grains. It looked like they hadn't been opened in a long time. In fact, the whole room was tidy and seemed mostly undisturbed. Olivia had the feeling that Hattie was only using the kettle, one mug and one plate.

On the table was a collection of framed photographs of Jesse.

'No wonder you're missing him,' Olivia said, 'all these photos...'

She lifted the calendar off the wall; it was open on the month of March, three months ago, and each day was blank. Turning it to August, she cleared her throat.

'I'm fine,' said Hattie, visibly gathering herself. 'It's just when I saw you, I got emotional. If I go too long without seeing someone, I get lost in my thoughts. The quieter it is in the house, the louder my thoughts get.'

'I might have an answer for that,' Olivia replied. 'Imagine if lots of the boxes on this calendar were filled up with the names of people who wanted to meet you.' She gestured towards the calendar.

Hattie frowned. 'What? Why would I imagine that? I can't think of anything worse.'

'Imagine there were people, like you, who wanted to find a new friend to meet and talk with,' said Olivia.

'I don't want a new friend!' said Hattie, throwing the cloth on the floor. 'What are you talking about, for God's sake?'

'What if people were interested in finding out about you? What if the newspaper wanted to speak to you?'

'Have you lost your mind? You're talking in riddles! Why on earth would the newspaper want to talk to me?'

Olivia's heart was pounding. Why had she ever thought it was a good idea to do this?

'Just hear me out,' said Olivia. 'I'm going to rent Jesse's deckchair in hourly slots on Saturdays, throughout August, to people who'd like to come and sit with you and talk.'

'You've done what? What do you mean, you've rented his chair?' Hattie demanded.

'So people can sit for an hour to have a chat with you.'

'Liv, I'm speechless. Why would you do such a thing? Have you gone mad? Why would anyone want to talk to me, let alone pay to talk to me? An hour with Hattie Fryer doesn't have much of a ring to it,' she said. 'I don't need anyone but you and Beau. I certainly don't need strangers. I wouldn't have a clue what to say. Jesse was the talkative, sociable one. Oh, Liv, tell me you're joking.'

Hattie's cheeks were bright spots of pink. Her dark eyes were watering.

Olivia was going to have to think fast. What were the magic words Hattie would be unable to refuse?

'It's for a good cause,' said Olivia. 'It's not about you specifically. It's to raise money for charity. I just thought you'd be happy to help. You know how much Jesse used to do for charity. I know you can't say no to a good cause – you're too kind; you care too much. I know you can put your grief aside to help other people.' She was laying it on thick.

Hattie curled her fingers around the top of the chair and narrowed her eyes at Olivia. 'Oh?' she said, her eyes darting about the room, her interest reluctantly piqued. 'What good cause exactly?'

FIVE

The journalist, Paul Woolly, was a young man on his first assignment for the *Echo*. He looked as if he was wearing his father's suit and blushed wildly whenever he spoke. Even the whites of his eyes seemed to blush.

'He's little more than fifteen,' hissed Hattie when he popped to the bathroom with his messenger bag still slung over his shoulder, probably to get away from Hattie's intimidating glare and give his reflection a motivational talk. 'Do you think he's on work experience?'

'He's at least twenty-one,' Olivia replied. 'Just relax. You're making him nervous!'

'I *am* relaxed,' said Hattie with a sigh, rearranging her string of pearls for the hundredth time. 'Shall we sit outside instead? The gladioli are wonderful, but the grass is long. Do you think he'd mind? I mean, he might have hay fever, I suppose. Everyone has allergies these days.'

'Let's stay here. He'll want to do a photograph at the beach, but here is fine for the interview.'

'You know best,' said Hattie, pursing her lips. 'Or at least you think you do! That's why we're in this ridiculous situation!'

They were in the living room of Hattie's bungalow, waiting
for Paul to return. The room was filled with sunshine – with a
window that looked out towards the sea beyond the front garden.
The decor was traditional – a tweed-style sofa and two
armchairs, all arms protected with plastic slipcovers that Olivia
could never comprehend, a thick blue rug over a cream carpet
and a low mahogany coffee table with a glass centre, in case you
wanted to look at the carpet. On the back wall was a shelving
unit that held books and board games and more framed
photographs of Jesse and Hattie on holiday, looking happy. The
lamps on the side tables had pleated shades, and there was a big
vase of flowers on a side table, hastily picked from the garden by
Olivia that morning to freshen up the place. On the mantelpiece
was a tin with the remainder of Jesse's ashes, alongside Michael's.

'It's nice and quiet in here, that's all,' Olivia said, trying to
break the tangible tension. She wished Paul would hurry up
and get on with it before Hattie changed her mind and put a
stop to the whole thing.

Just as she spoke, the toilet flushed, not once but twice, and
Hattie and Olivia exchanged a wide-eyed stare. Olivia felt an
inappropriate bubble of laughter growing in her belly. She
cleared her throat, standing up when Paul was suddenly back in
the room, drying his hands on his trousers. She gestured to an
armchair for him to sit in.

'Sorry, nerves,' he said, blushing again as the chair squeaked
when he sat down. 'Thank you. Do you mind if I record this?
I'll take notes too.'

'Feel free,' said Olivia, watching his hands tremble as he set
up his phone to record.

After what seemed like ten more minutes but was probably
only two, he turned it on. 'Testing, testing,' he said into the
microphone, fiddling with the buttons and wiping his palms on
his trousers before finally looking up at Hattie and smiling. He

had a surprisingly sweet smile, punctuated with two dimples, like commas on each cheek.

'I apologise profusely for the delay, Mrs Fryer,' he said. 'I've been trying to think of a way to say how sorry I am about your husband. My granddad died last year too, and I miss him. We used to have dinner together every Friday – and now I'm at a loss about what to do on those evenings. I used to complain about having to go, but now I miss it. How are you getting on without your husband? I imagine it's a difficult time for you.' He blushed deeper red and said the words stiffly, as if he'd rehearsed them in the toilet.

Hattie visibly softened. 'In all honesty, it's as if someone has ripped out my heart and replaced it with a stone,' she said quietly.

Paul swallowed.

'I'm sorry about your granddad,' Hattie added.

He smiled his sweet smile again, cleared his throat, opened the notepad and took the lid off his pen. 'When did you get together with Jesse?' he asked.

'About thirty-five years ago.'

'He was Mum's second husband,' interrupted Olivia. 'She was married to my father, Michael, but he died. He was knocked off his bicycle and killed by a drunk driver, and then, in the years after, Mum got together with Jesse.'

'Yes, I've lost two husbands,' said Hattie quietly. 'Some would call me careless.'

'Oh no, I'm sorry to hear that about your first husband,' said Paul. 'Was the driver jailed?'

'Yes,' said Olivia and was about to carry on, but Hattie interrupted.

'We don't need to tell the whole world every minute detail, do we, dear? Nobody wants to know my inside leg measure-ment. Please don't write about Michael. It's private. The person who killed him has been out of prison for a long time. I don't want to bring it all up. Do you understand?'

Paul's ears turned red. He nodded and cleared his throat. 'Okay, so could you tell me about your husband, your current husband – I mean the recently deceased husband's deckchair, please? I understand you're renting it out, and that people are already coming forward, wanting to meet you.'

'I didn't rent it out,' said Hattie crossly. 'My daughter here thought it was a good idea, for some craz—'

'Yes, we've had dozens of replies so far,' cut in Olivia. 'I haven't checked my email for a few hours, but I expect there are more. We've had all sorts of people. A Spanish exchange student wanting to practise English, dog walkers who say they could do with a chat as part of their routine, a man who collects moths, a psychic medium, one or two of Mum's old contacts.'

'How does that make you feel, Hattie?' Paul asked.

'Pretty bloody terrified,' she replied, glaring at Olivia. 'How would it make *you* feel?'

Paul opened his mouth and shut it again.

'It's for a good cause,' Olivia cut in.

'Yes, it's for a good cause,' repeated Hattie, quickly nodding. 'We're raising money for the befriending charity my daughter volunteers for. Lots of oldies like me out there with nobody to talk to. We don't want you to feel sorry for us though, thank you very much. Once upon a time we were dancing on tables and rushing around, just like you young people.'

Hattie glared at Olivia again, who smiled back encouragingly.

'It must be an ego boost,' said Paul. 'If I was in the deckchair, I'm not sure anyone would want to come!'

'Oh, I haven't thought about it like that,' said Hattie, rolling her shoulders back once and lifting her chin a fraction higher.

'And who would you most like to see in that deckchair?' Paul asked. 'If you could choose anyone?'

'That's like the dinner party question,' said Olivia. 'The one about if you could invite six guests—'

'Dead or alive?' interrupted Hattie. 'Because obviously I'd like Jesse back, if I could have anyone.'

'Alive,' Paul said, his pen hovering over his notepad.

'Well now, there's a question,' Hattie said wistfully, picking at a loose thread in the chair. 'Gosh, if I could talk to anyone—' She stopped, looked suddenly very sad, and gave a quick shake of her head. 'Oh, nobody,' she said, drawing in a breath. 'Ignore me – I went off on a trip down memory lane. Sorry, not very exciting.'

Olivia was curious. Hattie was very private about her past. She would share occasional stories about Michael, like wrapped gifts, but they were few and far between.

'I'd be pleased to meet anyone who's generous enough to donate to the befriending charity and I'd love to hear what they have to say,' Hattie said, snapping back into the present. 'And everyone has a story to tell, don't they? I bet you've got a story, Paul.'

'I don't think I've got anything very interesting to say,' he said with a strange laugh. 'And anyway, I'm supposed to be interviewing you.'

'Everyone has something to say – you just have to dig a little deeper or allow a little more space and time with some people,' said Hattie gently. 'That's what I've learned over the years.'

'Can I quote you on that?' Paul asked.

'You certainly can,' she replied, relaxing into the conversation a little now, the awkward moment left behind. She picked up a cup of tea from the tray and a garibaldi biscuit.

There were four cups on the tray – one for Jesse, Olivia realised.

'What else would you like my opinion on, dear? I've got lots of opinions,' said Hattie. 'Ask me what you like. I could tell you my thoughts about a recent attempted identity-theft incident if you like? In my day, there was no such thing.'

'And when was *your day*?' Paul asked. 'If you had to pinpoint a time in your life?'

Hattie narrowed her eyes a little, as if sharpening her focus. 'My day,' she mused. 'Maybe that would be when I was in my twenties, or thirties, I suppose, although some of those years were tough. Made me resilient, I suppose.'

'Maybe your day is "now",' said Olivia. 'Don't rule anything out.'

Hattie erupted with a short bark of laughter. 'Maybe.'

For a second, she seemed a little bit like her old self. Olivia felt a flurry of hopefulness in her belly.

Olivia had expected a photographer to accompany them to the beach – someone with a vast canvas bag of lenses, but it seemed Paul wasn't only the reporter but also the photographer, using his phone's camera.

'Humans will have phones instead of a beating heart before too long, won't they, Paul?' said Hattie.

Beau, who'd reluctantly joined them for the photograph on the beach, sighed. 'Embarrassing,' she muttered.

Paul shot her a smile.

Olivia pulled the deckchairs from the beach hut and put them into position. Hattie sat on her deckchair, while Olivia and Beau stood stiffly beside her. Paul took a couple of photographs then stuffed his phone in his pocket.

'It should be up in the next couple of days, so keep an eye on the website,' he said.

'Will it be in the proper newspaper?' asked Hattie. 'You know, the one you can hold?'

'Online is the proper newspaper,' he said. 'The print edition was ditched long ago.'

'Oh,' said Hattie, frowning. 'Another thing down the pan. Real money, letter writing, newspapers, receipts, tickets – all gone.'

'Granny!' said Beau. 'It's not that bad. What do you need receipts for anyway? It just means more trees being chopped down.'

'For keeping in my ledger accounting book,' Hattie replied. 'Jesse and I used to do all our accounts that way. I have drawers full of old receipts, going back decades. All my old letters, my old school reports, everything.'

'Times have changed,' said Beau.

'I know,' Hattie replied, 'and not for the better. My generation is rather invisible now.'

'No, you're not,' said Beau. 'You're about to be in the paper!'

A day later, Paul messaged Olivia to tell her the story was online. Sitting in Hattie's garden, the three women crowded around Olivia's laptop to read Paul's article. There was a photograph of the three of them too.

WISH YOU WERE HERE

The family of a grieving woman are tackling her loneliness by hiring out her late husband's deckchair to find her a new friend. Hattie Fryer has lost two husbands – the first was killed by a drunk driver; the second, Jesse, died a hero last year, trying to rescue a local surfer in distress. The family, Hattie's daughter Olivia and granddaughter Beau, hope the deckchair will become a place for Hattie to meet new friends, while raising money for a good cause.

'Everyone has a story to tell,' said Hattie, and she's looking forward to hearing yours this summer.

To hire out the deckchair, or simply make a donation to a local befriending charity, email oliviafryer@hotmail.com with the subject 'deckchair for hire'.

Olivia scrolled down further, where there were already several responses in the comments section. She read out the first one: *Bit OTT? Can't they just talk to her?*

And the next: *Tinder for old people?*

And another: *This is sweet. I'll send my granddad down. He goes for days without speaking to anyone.*

And another: *Lost two husbands? Why can't people just say the word 'dead'?*

And another: *There you are.*

Olivia frowned and reread the last comment. The author's 'name' was just a mixture of letters and numbers. Maybe it was nothing, but her scalp tingled.

'It's been shared on Instagram and Twitter too,' said Beau. 'Granny, you're not invisible – you're famous. We all are.'

'Oh dear,' said Hattie, 'I should have worn something nicer.'

'You look lovely,' said Olivia. 'I think I'll ask Paul to turn off the comments. They're unnecessary. Why does everyone need to have an opinion?'

She checked her email and her heartbeat quickened. There were ten new unread messages, entitled 'deckchair for hire'.

'Wow,' she said. 'More people have written in already.'

She scrolled through the names, feeling light-headed with a sudden sense of dread. *There you are.* She knew what was going to happen before it happened, and as her eyes scanned the names, she knew his would be there.

Sure enough, there it was: Oscar Gregory.

Heat travelled up her throat and into her mouth. She bit down on her top lip and flicked her eyes up and in the direction of Hattie and Beau, who were pointing at a squirrel running along the fence. They would surely be able to hear her heart pounding in her chest.

Her breathing was shallow, her thoughts fragmented. Tiny shapes shifted and fizzed behind her eyes in a kaleidoscope of memories. Oscar laughing. Oscar crying. Oscar shouting.

The years between their relationship ending and this moment seemed to shrink to nothing more than a few days. She'd kept a low profile all that time, dreading him coming back into her life, paralysed by the prospect, and now, here he was.

Feeling the need to put physical distance between herself and his name, she pushed the laptop away from her and leaned back in her chair, staring up at the vast blue sky, wishing she was in it, on board a plane, flying to the other side of the world.

'Are you alright, Olivia?' asked Hattie. 'You've gone very pale. Do you feel unwell?'

Olivia gave a vague nod and pulled the laptop back towards her, hovering her shaking finger over the keypad before deleting Oscar's email.

'I'm fine. Just some spam,' she said, before closing the laptop and placing her hands flat on the table. 'It's junk. Nothing.'

The lightness she'd felt earlier was gone. Oscar was back.

SIX

Olivia heaved two carrier bags filled with tea, coffee, milk, sugar, crockery, sun hats and sun cream down the path to the beach hut, the plastic bag handles digging into her wrists and almost cutting off her circulation. She walked quickly, with Hattie on her heels, muttering about her blisters. The arrival of the first visitor to the deckchair, a woman called Elaine, was imminent, and thanks to Hattie suffering a dramatic case of cold feet about the whole idea and Olivia having to gently coax her out of her bungalow, they were very late setting up.

It was a sunny morning, with a breeze that should have felt warm and feathery on the skin, but Olivia shivered with the gnawing fear that, after she'd ignored his email, Oscar would contact her again. Every time she received a message notification on her phone, she felt sick.

'I've been waiting half an hour,' said a woman standing beside the beach hut, a half-smile, half-grimace on her face. 'Thought you'd stood me up! I'm Elaine. I hope you're expecting me. I made quite a generous donation!'

The woman was in her sixties and wore black jeans, a green T-shirt and black sandals, exposing a couple of silver toe rings.

She had a battered leather rucksack slung over one shoulder and a reusable coffee cup in her hand.

Olivia bit her bottom lip, took a deep breath, dumped the carrier bags on the ground outside the beach hut and extended her hand to Elaine. They shook briefly and looked towards Hattie, who'd just reached the beach hut and was taking off her sandals.

'I'm so sorry to keep you waiting,' Olivia said, smiling broadly. 'It's so kind of you to come down and donate to the charity, thank you. This is my mum, Hattie. We were... a little held up. Mum, this is Elaine, your first visitor! I'll get the deckchairs set up and make you a drink. Would you like a tea or coffee?'

Hattie smiled, raised her hand in salute, took off her sun hat and flapped it in front of her face. 'Sorry to keep you, Elaine,' she said. 'Tea please, Olivia.'

'Tea, thank you,' said Elaine. 'Two sugars. How are you, Hattie? I must congratulate you.'

'Congratulate me?' said Hattie. 'What on earth for?'

'For being brave,' said Elaine. 'Doing this – it's a brave thing to do.'

'Oh, I'm not brave,' said Hattie quietly. 'I'm the opposite of brave.'

'Mum was a bit reluctant this morning,' said Olivia, unlocking the beach hut and pulling out the deckchairs. 'She had an attack of the nerves.'

'This wasn't my idea and... though it's a lovely idea, I felt this morning that I don't really have much to say,' said Hattie, struggling to find her words. 'What I mean is... since Jesse died, I've lost quite a lot of confidence.'

Olivia paused for a moment while she was putting up the deckchairs and gave Hattie a small smile. She gestured for her mother and Elaine to sit down.

'What you mean is, you'd rather hide under the duvet and

shut the world out,' said Elaine curtly. 'Been there, done that, know how you feel.'

Olivia hurriedly organised the drinks and the two women sat down on the deckchairs, looking out towards the sea.

'But you did get out from under the duvet so you *are* brave,' said Elaine. 'And getting out and about is the best way to navigate grief.' She took a sip of her tea and gestured towards the sea.

'Is this the beach where your husband had his accident?' she asked. 'From what I read in the newspaper, he did a very brave thing too.'

Hattie stared searchingly at Olivia, who gave her a supportive smile.

'Yes, this is the beach,' Hattie said, her voice cracking. 'I don't like to think about that day, I'd rather put it out of my mind.'

'He was a hero, by all accounts,' said Elaine. 'That's something to be proud of. Some people do nothing remotely courageous their entire lives. He made a brave decision.'

Olivia watched Hattie closely, her heart in her mouth. She half expected her to burst into tears.

'I feel quite responsible for his death,' Hattie said quietly. 'I told him to check on the boy in the water. As I said, I don't like to think about it. If we carry on talking about it, I'm going to get upset, and I really don't want to start crying.'

'There's nothing wrong with crying,' said Elaine. 'Cry if you feel like it. Don't mind me.'

Hattie pulled a tissue out from her sleeve and dabbed her eyes.

'So,' said Olivia quickly, trying to bring the conversation down from the emotional precipice it was on, 'what brings you here, Elaine? What made you want to come down?'

Elaine watched Hattie compose herself. 'You know you

mustn't brush difficult things under the carpet,' she said. 'There leads the road to madness.'

Olivia immediately thought of the email from Oscar she'd deleted and wondered where he was. Heat spread across her chest.

'I've learned that it's better to face tough things head-on. Headbutt them, in fact. Like this.' Elaine demonstrated a head-butt. 'I've headbutted a few things in my life. It's part of the road to acceptance.'

Hattie gave Olivia a sideways glance and Olivia internally sighed. She'd hoped for a light-hearted conversation to kick-start the deckchair meetings, but Elaine clearly had a different plan.

'You're a natural at that – isn't she, Mum?' said Olivia with a gentle laugh, planning to end this line of conversation and steer it onto neutral ground. 'Do you live locally? It was good of you to hire out the chair. What made you do it?'

'I read what you said, Hattie, about everyone having a story to tell and I thought I'd tell you mine,' said Elaine. 'I'm here to tell you that things do get easier, in time, and if you're tough enough to face things.'

Olivia's thoughts shot to Oscar. The last thing she wanted to do was face him.

'Years ago, and I'm talking decades now, my heart was shat-tered,' said Elaine. 'I was literally walking down the aisle towards my fiancé when he took one look at me in my wedding dress and legged it out of the side door of the village church. I realised when I heard the crunch of car tyres on gravel and him screeching off down the lane that he'd changed his mind. There were hundreds of guests there, all of them staring at me, some thrilled with the drama of it all, while I wished for the ground to open and swallow me up or for a meteor to fall to Earth and smash the church to smithereens.'

Olivia and Hattie gasped.

'That's awful,' said Olivia. 'Poor you.'

'Yes, poor me. That's certainly how I felt,' Elaine continued. 'We'd been together for years. Childhood sweethearts. Grown up in the same village. Anyway, I went home, put my wedding dress in the dustbin, packed a bag and left the village. I moved in with a friend at the other end of the country and spent what felt like years under my duvet. I felt utterly sorry for myself, blamed myself and blamed him. I just couldn't accept that it had happened, which stopped me moving on with my life. My poor friend didn't know what to do with me. She kept trying to convince me there was life after being jilted at the altar, but I let it define me. It wasn't until a decade later that I went back to the village and confronted him and accepted it.'

'What did he say?' asked Hattie. 'Was he sorry?'

'Not especially,' said Elaine. 'He said I'd bullied him into getting married in the first place.'

'That doesn't sound fair,' said Olivia.

'That's his side of the story, so I can't just deny it,' said Elaine. 'But the reason I felt compelled to come here and tell you this was because I felt like I'd gone through a bereavement, and for a long time, I couldn't face it. I know grieving is personal and denial is self-protection, but I missed out on other things, other people, other experiences. My advice to you is to keep on living a full life, even if you don't feel like it, because being out in the world will help, and the pain will lessen. Also, you'll find that most people have something difficult in their past and can relate to how you feel. Realising that helped me no end.'

'Yes, I guess we've all got things in our lives we wish hadn't happened, or skeletons hanging in our cupboards,' said Olivia quietly.

'The things you run from always catch up with you in the end,' said Elaine. 'That unresolved relationship, an argument you regret, something you did you know you shouldn't have, a feeling of guilt you can't forgive yourself for. It's impossible to move forward without making peace with the past. That's what I found anyway.'

Olivia swallowed noisily.

'I'll never be able to move on from Jesse,' said Hattie. 'I don't really want to.'

'No, and you don't have to,' said Elaine, 'but maybe in time, you can enjoy other things in life.'

Hattie's eyes started to leak tears.

Olivia cleared her throat. 'Thanks for sharing your story with us, Elaine,' she said awkwardly. 'Can I get you another tea? I don't have much else to offer you.'

Elaine shook her head. 'About that... do you know what would improve this place?' she asked, leaning forward in her chair.

'Um, what?' said Olivia.

'Some food. A cream tea, and not one from a supermarket either,' said Elaine. 'The tea is nice, but a home-made scone, clotted cream and strawberry jam would be a great touch. People relax more when there's food around. The beach hut could do with a lick of paint too and that sign there, the "deckchairs to hire" one – could you fix it to the wall properly? It looks a bit sad like that. You could provide a headrest cushion for this deckchair too.'

They all looked at the enamel sign. Hattie put on her sunglasses and fell silent.

Olivia forced a smile. 'You're right and I meant to do that this morning. I'll make scones for the next visitor. You're our first, so it's all a learning curve. The emphasis is on having a chat really, rather than a...'

'Rather than a dining experience,' said Hattie, raising her eyebrows.

'Understood,' said Elaine, standing up and stretching out her back. 'But I like to give feedback. I always leave a review wherever I go. It's been good to meet you both. Hattie, I wish you well for the next part of your life, and I hope things get easier.'

'Thank you...' started Hattie, then almost in a whisper said, 'but you can't force these things.'

Elaine put her rucksack onto her back and began walking away from the beach hut. When she was out of earshot, Hattie pushed up her sunglasses and stared at Olivia with wide eyes.

'Well,' she said, her tone indignant. 'How dare she tell us the beach hut needs painting? And how could she say "congratulations" to me, after I've lost my Jesse?'

'It *does* need painting,' said Olivia, glancing at the hut. 'And she said she thought you're brave, which you are, and she's trying to get you to think about things differently. You should be proud of yourself for doing this. She had a point, didn't she, about some of the other things too? Skeletons in cupboards and so on. Shouldn't we talk more about the things we don't want to talk about?'

'No,' said Hattie, her voice wobbling and her tone uncertain. 'I think everyone is different – everyone deals with things differently.'

Olivia knew she was provoking Hattie. They'd never really been ones for talking about painful things.

Both women fell silent. Hattie put her sunglasses back down and turned her attention to a group on the beach playing a rowdy game of rounders, while Olivia watched Elaine in the far distance, walking away. She thought about the undeniable skeleton in her cupboard, the skeleton that had stopped her moving on with her life, the skeleton that was currently shaking the cupboard door and threatening to burst out.

Oscar.

SEVEN

Olivia had met Oscar at a colleague's wedding. Well, *ex*-colleague, since it was held soon after she'd quit her job as a teacher of textiles at a secondary school. She was twenty-seven and quitting her job was the first time she'd done something that felt remotely reckless. She'd been tipped over the edge when, on almost the last day of term, a group of her students had taken scissors to the projects they'd been working on for months, laughing as they did so. She'd swept up the shreds of fabric on the art-room floor, tears splashing onto her lanyard. Her colleagues had dismissed the act as teenage stupidity and told her she needed to develop a thicker skin to survive in teaching. But the destruction had felt personal. Too violent. Everyone had a limit, and that had been hers. She would do something else with her life and her thin skin.

'But *what?*' Hattie had asked at the time, disappointment written across her face in capital letters.

'I'll be a vintage and antiques dealer,' Olivia had replied, surprising herself. 'And don't ask me what I know about vintage and antiques.'

'What do you know about vintage and antiques?' Hattie had said anyway. 'You've lost your way.'

I haven't even found my way yet, let alone lost it, Olivia had thought.

She'd fallen into teaching after leaving university because Hattie had convinced her it was a good path to follow. She'd dreamed of designing textiles in her spare time, but with the teaching workload, those dreams had gradually faded.

The wedding was held one hot August day at a spa hotel in Dorset. There were almost two hundred guests, marquees on the lawn and a converted camper van serving ice cream. And a lot of wasps. Olivia marvelled at how one couple could know so many people. It prompted her to write a list of potential invitees to her future wedding on the 'order of events' card. There were twenty-one, twenty-two including Alec, whose name she'd put a line through as soon as she'd written it down.

She'd accepted the wedding invitation through gritted teeth. Another of her peers had seemingly fallen into the arms of their soulmate at exactly the right age, while she herself remained resolutely single and now jobless too, albeit by her own hand. Despite the vast number of guests, she didn't know many people there. The one woman she did know was heavily pregnant and had talked non-stop about her birthing plan. She felt rather uncomfortable in her floral dress, hurriedly bought from Miss Selfridge, and had been seated next to ageing Uncle Lionel and his companion pug for the dinner.

The hands on the clock she watched stood still. Nothing happened; nobody had tearfully swept in at the last moment with a reason the couple shouldn't exchange vows; there had been no brawls between feuding family members or a bridesmaid seducing the married best man. Olivia felt that all the excitement in life was happening elsewhere.

'And now,' the groom stood up to announce, banging his glass with a knife, 'there's a few people I'd like to thank.'

There was a long, long list. A nice trait in a groom, she supposed, but after twenty minutes of flower girls and stags collecting hairclips and cufflinks, the guests were sliding down their chairs and running out of claps, the bride's mouth set in a grim smile. The last on the list to be thanked was the chef at the venue. The groom insisted on thanking him personally for the best wedding food he'd ever tasted.

Cue Oscar entering the room. He was clean-shaven with short dark hair with a slight quiff at the front, high cheekbones and a thick scar across his cheek. There was something of a pirate about him. He was tall, athletic-looking and very slim, with broad shoulders, and wore a serious, concentrated expression, which entirely changed when he smiled, like sudden sunshine on a cold day. He owned one of those loud, frequent laughs that made other people jump, or worry they weren't enjoying themselves enough.

While she cringed on his behalf at the groom's deference, Oscar wasn't at all embarrassed. In fact, he accepted a glass of champagne, which he swallowed in one gulp, after which he waited for a refill. He then sat at her table and asked everyone what they thought of the crème caramel dessert. His question was met with vigorous praise and enthusiasm, which he accepted as if it was entirely expected.

Oscar's bold manner piqued her interest, but Uncle Lionel started telling her about his classic car, so her attention was forcibly diverted, until later, when people had dispersed and she remained at the table. Oscar had tapped her on the shoulder and held the order of events card she'd written her list on in front of her eyes.

'Is this your hit list?' he asked, smiling. 'Why has this poor guy Alec got a line through his name? Is he an ex? Is he still alive?'

Oscar had a New Zealand accent. He smelled faintly of fresh mint.

Olivia blushed madly. 'He's my stepbrother,' she said. 'We don't get on. You know, family stuff. It's just a list. I write a lot of lists.' She took the card from him and stuffed it into her pocket.

'My family are on the other side of the world,' he said. 'I've found that really works well for getting on with them.' He grinned and raised his hand to shake hers. 'I'm Oscar and you are...?'

'Olivia,' she said.

'Hello, Olivia. You have the word "live" in your name. Do you?'

'What?' she asked.

'Live. Because if you don't, this conversation ends here.'

She frowned and he laughed.

'I'm joking,' he said. 'But it's true, we only get one life, one chance to live it, one chance to prove ourselves. Life isn't a dress rehearsal and all that!'

Olivia was taken aback by his intensity, but it excited her. So many conversations she had with people were bland and unmemorable.

'Of course I live!' she said with a laugh but quietly wondering if that was true. She often felt she was waiting in the wings of life. That she was the understudy, poised to rush on stage and stand in the spotlight when she was called to, only nobody ever called. She decided against mentioning that to Oscar.

'Although I think I'm going to struggle to survive the night,' she said. 'Looks like it's going to be long.'

Her eyes moved to the DJ, hauling his equipment into an adjoining room, where paper honeycomb garlands were stretched across the ceiling and a balloon centrepiece quivered in the breeze. In one corner of the room, a woman was setting up an old-fashioned sweets stall, carefully displaying striped bags of sweets, from flying saucers to liquorice tornados.

Oscar walked over to her, said something Olivia couldn't hear and brought back a bag of coconut mushrooms.

'I hope you like these.'

Olivia nodded. 'Yes, thank you.' Even though in fact she didn't like them.

'Come outside. There's something I want to show you.'

'Sounds ominous,' she replied, clutching hold of the bag of sweets and following him out onto the lawn, where guests were standing in groups, holding drinks and talking, children darting around between them. Fairy lights had come on, though it wasn't yet dark. A photographer was doing the rounds and snapped her and Oscar, who sloped his arm casually over her shoulder.

'Do you like honey? You must like honey,' he said.

She nodded again – genuinely now – and followed him into a kitchen garden area bursting with rows of growing vegetables and herbs. Beyond the allotment were two beehives. While she waited under an apple tree, Oscar pulled on a beekeeper's hat and billowed smoke into one of the hives. 'To make the bees mellow,' he said.

With bees now buzzing lazily around him, he calmly took the honeycomb from the hive and broke off a small section into a jar. He scooped out a spoonful of liquid honey and honey-comb and passed it to her. She accepted it and put the spoon into her mouth. Every taste bud on her tongue jumped to attention.

'Honey is really good for you – for inflammation, wounds, your heart. We have a lot to thank bees for, but I'm telling you things you already know. Why don't you tell me something I don't know? And then I'll do the same.' He crossed his arms over his chest and waited.

'Do you need to get back to work?' she asked, trying to change the direction of the conversation. 'I mean, are you cooking again today?'

He laughed and shook his head. 'I'm off duty. Come on, out with it – tell me something about you.'

'I can't think of anything,' she said, frowning, surreptitiously licking the honey from her lips.

'You have to,' he replied with a warm smile. 'What's the thing about your life so far that pops into your head? The main thing.'

The main thing. Olivia didn't hesitate.

'My dad died when I was six,' she said, surprised at her candour. 'He left on his bike and never came back. He loved cycling. He thought we should all cycle, not drive. He even ran a "bike bus", for kids at the school he worked at, and they all cycled in a long line together. He was killed by a drunk driver. My mum would never let me go on a bike again, even though I loved my bike more than anything. It was pale blue and had these purple ribbon streamers on the handles that flew up in the wind when I cycled. I loved them! My dad had taught me how to ride without stabilisers when I was three. My mum doesn't know, but I've got a bike now, just a second-hand one, that I keep well hidden in my flat.'

'I'm sorry,' said Oscar softly.

'What about you?' she said. 'What's your main thing?'

He shrugged and kicked at a stone in the grass. 'My mother left home – well, abandoned me – when I was thirteen and has never contacted me, my dad or my siblings since,' he said, his voice cracking very slightly. 'She left a note, saying she was leaving, no explanation or anything. I spend a lot of time searching for her online, but she seems to have disappeared. She taught me to cook. We were close, or at least I thought we were. One day I'll find her and cook for her, show her who I've become. She'll be sorry she left. I plan to make her feel guilty as hell.'

Oscar's expression had changed. His tone had gone from gentle to aggressive in a flash. Olivia swallowed; his pain was clear to see and she felt sorry for him.

'You must have missed her when you were growing up,' she said.

'I did, but now I want to find her to prove a point,' he replied. 'I want to tell her exactly what I think of her. You can't just walk out on a kid's life. I would never do that. Not ever. Would you?'

Olivia shook her head.

They talked for hours. She was struck by Oscar's determination and certainty. He talked about his life goals. Work for a Michelin-starred chef. Become one himself. Open his own restaurant. All before he was forty.

'Success is the only option,' he told her. 'I'm not interested in being Mr Mediocre.'

He said these things with a smile and laughter in his eyes, but she could tell he meant them, and there was something exciting about that. His energy gave her energy. His self-belief made her wonder if she should believe in herself a bit more.

They watched the sun set, drenching the sky with colour. Olivia wasn't sure whether it was the champagne, the honey or something else less definable, but she felt incredibly mellow, like the bees. She took off her shoes and wriggled her toes in the fresh grass. The muted sound of music from the disco drifted from the hotel in the distance, the scent of flowers and honey filled her nose and, when Oscar offered her his hand, to pull her from sitting to standing, she felt the distinct possibility of love burst into her heart.

EIGHT

It was the beginning of an intense relationship. Olivia felt bewitched by Oscar; as though he'd taken hold of her hand and was running really, really fast, and she was trying to keep up behind. But she didn't want to let go, because Oscar squeezed the juice and the pips out of life. When he wasn't cooking, he was reading about cooking, and when he wasn't cooking or reading, he was testing ingredients. And when he wasn't immersed in food, he was immersed in something else – exercise, the city, music, nature.

'Take your hood down!' he said one day when they were out on a walk by the sea and it had started to pour with rain.

Olivia had immediately pulled up her hood to protect against the rain, while Oscar had tilted his face up towards the sky, opened his mouth and stuck out his tongue to catch the raindrops. She did what he said and felt the cold rain on her face, laughing at how drenched she was getting, secretly hoping the dye in her jeans wouldn't run.

'Let's climb this tree,' he said another day.

The sun was setting, and she was worried about how far they had left to walk before they would reach the car. She also had a fear of heights. 'I can't climb a tree,' she said, staring up.

But Oscar showed her how, and when they were really high, he put his arm around her waist to hold her securely on the branch. The view was beautiful, and they were hidden by the leaves. Out of his pocket, Oscar pulled a small bottle of rum, a bottle of Coke and a lime. They had a sip from each bottle and then sucked the lime. She tried not to let her fear show.

'I used to spend a lot of time in the tree at the bottom of my garden after my mum left,' he told Olivia. 'I'd wait and wait, thinking that if I waited long enough, maybe she would come back and call my name. I'd hear her voice sometimes, in my dreams.'

He fell silent, then looked Olivia directly in the eye. 'Maybe one day, we can give a child what we didn't have: two parents. What do you think?'

It was just the two of them up a tree, balancing on a branch, two little birds, and the rum had gone to her head.

'Is it a possibility?' he said. 'A maybe? A must?' He looked at her with such dedication, devotion, scrutiny, she had to answer.

'It's a definite possibility,' she said, kissing him.

'A must then,' he said, kissing her back.

On her birthday, he secured his place in her heart by giving her a beautiful new bicycle. On the handlebars, he'd tied purple ribbon streamers which flew up in the air when she cycled.

Their first weekend away together was a trip to Paris. A room in a small hotel near the Jardin du Luxembourg. The room had French windows and a tiny balcony with ornate railings. Beneath the window, Parisian life buzzed. Cars honked their horns. People talked and walked. The smell of French cigarettes wafted from the street into the room.

Oscar had introduced her to the joy of thin shards of the

darkest chocolate in fresh, crusty French baguette, accompanied by strong black coffee. He'd taken her to food markets where they bought huge, fragrant velvet-skin peaches, which they ate in the street, not caring about the juice dripping down their chins and fingers. They'd eaten steak tartare in bistros, crêpes washed down by pastis. Oscar was relentlessly enthusiastic – order this, eat this, look at this, read this, listen, let's go here, let's try this – and Olivia was happy to succumb to his enthusiasm.

But on their last night in Paris, his mood shifted. He seemed to lose energy and was brooding over something Olivia couldn't put her finger on.

'Is that a new dress?' he asked when she came out of the hotel bathroom after spending nearly an hour getting ready to go out to dinner.

Olivia nodded, struggling to suppress her smile. She held out the skirt of her new blue silk dress and did a small twirl. She knew it would cheer him up.

He was sitting on the edge of the bed, dressed in dark jeans and a shirt, reading. He glanced up from his book. 'I like your black dress better,' he said.

Olivia's eyes burned with embarrassed tears. 'Oh,' she said. 'I bought this... I mean... Should I...?'

'Change?' he said. 'It's up to you. I just really like the black one.'

A small voice in her head told her to keep the blue one on; she'd spent ages choosing it and it was expensive, but another voice told her that it was a compliment, really, that Oscar was taking an interest, wasn't it?

'Yeah,' she said quickly. 'So do I actually. I'll change. Won't be a sec.'

'Take your time,' he said. 'You could put your hair up too, if you want.'

In the bathroom, she looked at her reflection. Her cheeks were bright pink and a red rash had crept up her neck. She splashed cold water on her face and changed into her black dress, carelessly tossing the blue one over the towel rail, as if it wasn't important, as if it didn't matter. And though she hated herself for doing it, she put her hair up too.

'That's better,' he said, when she came out of the bathroom for the second time. 'Good decision.'

Olivia wondered if he was talking to himself but didn't say anything – she wanted to enjoy their last evening.

As they walked across the gardens towards the restaurant hand in hand, Olivia relaxed, watching people playing boules, sitting in deckchairs, and talking. In the restaurant, Oscar raved about the menu and recommended what she should have. When she tried to order, she struggled with the French.

'You sound so English,' he said, in front of the waitress.

Olivia bit her lip and looked down. 'I've never been good at French. This one, please.'

'You can't point at the menu!' Oscar said, barking with laughter. 'That's so "Brits abroad". Brits are so unsophisticated.'

Olivia didn't laugh. She blushed madly and smiled apologetically at the waitress.

'Your French is better than my English,' said the waitress kindly.

When the waitress left, Oscar reached for Olivia's hand, but she pulled it away.

'Have I upset you?' he said. 'Do you feel like I'm criticising you?'

'Nobody wants to feel like a fool,' she said. First the dress, now her French. She had a good mind to get up and leave, but was she overreacting?

'I think it's constructive to criticise a little bit,' Oscar said. 'How can we develop as human beings if nobody ever tells us what we could do better? Why don't you tell me something I could do better? I want to be the best. Come on – tell me.'

'I wouldn't want to upset you and, anyway, there isn't

anything,' she said, pausing to have a sip of her wine. 'I'd rather focus on the positive things. I don't want to be mean.'

'I can take it,' he said. 'Come on – tell me something. One thing. I know I'm not perfect.'

'There's nothing.'

'I don't believe you.'

'Okay then. You asking me to criticise you is the thing I don't like.'

'There,' he said, grinning. 'I knew there was something. You're not a total angel after all. I'm glad. I was worried there for a minute.'

Olivia was confused. She wasn't sure what he was trying to say or how she felt, but the food had arrived, and it was delicious, the wine wonderfully crisp and cold, and the restaurant romantically lit.

'I know I can be a bit direct, but it's good that we can be honest with each other, don't you think?' he said. 'Why don't we move in together when we get back?'

'Really?' She blanched. 'I'll need to think...'

Her words trailed off as Oscar stared at her with mock shock, eyes wide.

'What's with the hesitation?' he asked. 'This is a one-time offer that expires in about ten minutes. Come on – we're great together! What are you scared of?'

They'd only been together for a couple of months.

'There won't be another one like me,' he said, grinning.

To some it might have sounded arrogant, but Olivia thought the way he acted was something else – a vulnerability perhaps. People with true self-belief probably didn't need to promote themselves or dish out deadlines.

Oscar was everything she wasn't. Impulsive. Ambitious. Unpredictable. In the short time she'd known him, he'd turned her world upside down and given it a good shake. She'd reviewed her life's goals, tried to be more like the current and less like a piece of driftwood. Perhaps he was right and they were a good match.

'You have to grab life with both hands, Olivia,' he said. 'Or settle for being ordinary.'

She looked out the restaurant window at the people walking by on the streets, the couples hand in hand. 'I'm not scared of anything,' she said. 'And I'll never settle.'

He poured her another glass of wine and raised his to hers. 'That's why I like you so much,' he said. 'Let's drink to that.'

And so she did.

Their rented flat was on the top floor of a three-storey house. From the living-room window, if you stuck out your head and craned your neck, you could glimpse the sea. Sometimes, when the sun was setting and there were no waves, the water shone like a sheet of tinfoil. Back inside, the kitchen was small but well equipped. In the bedroom there was a skylight, which Olivia loved to stare up at and identify the clouds.

They lived above an old lady who watched TV with the volume on so high, they could hear every word. Beneath her was a young dad, Kris, with two small children, whose wife had left him for another man. Oscar took great interest in Kris and talked to him at length about the fact his mother had walked out. They didn't seem to be able to believe a female would be capable of leaving her own children, that they must be particularly bad examples of women.

'You think it's worse, don't you?' Olivia asked one day not long after they'd moved in. 'You think it's worse for a woman to leave her family than for a man to leave his, which incidentally happens all the time.'

Oscar didn't hesitate. 'I do,' he said. 'Children need their mothers.'

'They need their fathers too,' said Olivia, enraged.

'Ideally they have both. But life's not ideal, as you and I know. I'll never understand how my mum could walk out on me. I'll never forgive her.'

'There must have been a reason. I'm sure she had a reason.'

'Nothing could be a good-enough reason!' he said, almost shouting. 'Nothing! Christ, Olivia, think about what you're saying!'

She was surprised by his sudden anger but also sorry her words had upset him. 'I'm sorry.'

'Don't say things like that then!' he said furiously, before sighing and softening his tone. 'I just find all the stuff about my mum so hard to accept.'

'Come here,' she replied, holding out her arms.

He stayed where he was, so she wrapped her arms around him, but he was tense, stiff as a post.

At first they were happy. They enjoyed making a home together. They painted the walls bold, dark colours that you'd find at the bottom of the sea and filled the shelves with plants. Oscar cooked experimental dishes for Olivia. When she tasted his cooking, she would pretend to be a restaurant reviewer, always giving him five stars. The praise made his eyes shine. She saw in Oscar someone who wouldn't admit it, but who desperately wanted to be loved and approved of. And, at first, she was happy to love him.

After a few months, Oscar got a job in an exclusive restaurant, working for a renowned chef in Sandbanks. It was a demanding, highly stressful role. While she took on a part-time job as a technician in a sixth form college art department to fund her new business venture as a seller of vintage items, he worked eighteen-hour shifts. While she surrounded herself with beautiful old things – foxed mirrors, trunks covered with faded labels that told of far-flung travels, vintage biscuit tins and crockery, copper pans and teapots – he created meticulous plate after meticulous plate of food, driven by his ambition to be the best.

Sometimes Olivia could go for days without seeing Oscar – he'd have a few beers after his shift and go straight out to the early food markets to secure the best produce, napping in the office at the restaurant when he could. She realised she was spending quite a lot of her time looking out of the window, waiting for him to come home. When he did come home, he rarely slept. Or, on a day off, he'd sleep for twenty hours straight and she'd tiptoe about the place, careful not to wake him.

She tried not to complain that she never saw him, but when she once did, he confronted her.

'You're just making me more stressed! Maybe you should stop waiting for me to entertain you and get busy yourself?' he snapped. 'I thought you were going to start some big business. What a joke!'

She didn't have an answer for that. She was happy, she insisted, working as a technician while she sourced her vintage pieces from charity shops and junkyards and sketched ideas for a fabric collection with beach-themed designs.

'Hardly setting the world on fire, are you?' he said. 'Don't you want to be a success? Make something of your life?'

It was just one of many criticisms. When she objected, he would say, 'Would you rather I didn't tell you the truth?', which confused and silenced her.

It was small things at first, the criticism infrequent – she could count them on one or two hands. But then he seemed to gather momentum, and soon, criticism slipped into every day. So many things irritated him; the way she could read for hours under a blanket was 'lazy', her choice of food in a restaurant was 'boring', the things she bought to sell were 'a load of old tat', when she was sad, she was 'turning on the tears'.

She knew she should fight back, but the change in his personality floored her and she couldn't find the words.

'You're exhausted – you have such a stressful job,' she would tell him before going out for a cycle by the sea, tears stinging her eyes and blurring her vision. Exhaustion was the excuse she handed to him on a plate for the way he was treating her, reasoning that if he wasn't tired, if he was less stressed, he'd be back to his old self. *Here you go*, she imagined herself saying, *have this excuse. Please, take it.*

The head chef at Oscar's restaurant was an aggressive, bullying man – a taskmaster who continually told Oscar he had to do better and work harder, that he was useless. Wanting promotion, desperately wanting to be the best, Oscar stayed longer and later still, after service, to improve his skills, but they were never good enough for his boss. The harder he tried to prove himself, the weaker he seemed to become.

The job, the industry, took its toll. The more he struggled to keep on top of his job, the worse his criticism of Olivia became and so too his self-loathing. He started to drink even before his shift began, to pop painkillers to take the edge off the anxiety he felt. They'd been living together for a year when he eventually lost his position for being too drunk to do his job, and he became someone Olivia didn't recognise. He drowned his sorrows with alcohol, whatever the time of day. It made him nasty, and then sobriety made him ashamed.

'I'll cut back,' he'd say after having shouted at her when she suggested he should stop drinking. He'd drop to his knees and rest his head in her lap, exhausted, not even able to remember what he'd said and done.

'It's okay,' she would say, finding a twisted power in his remorse, enjoying the short period of attention he would lavish on her – the old Oscar – until yet again, he would turn to alcohol.

She tried to justify his behaviour by convincing herself that it was just the alcohol suppressing his rational mind. His chosen career was one of the most stressful there was. His boss had destroyed his confidence. He felt like his career was over. He hadn't dealt properly with his mother's abandonment. He needed counselling. She tried to encourage him to seek professional help, gave him ultimatums, hid the booze, poured it down the sink, glug, glug, glug. That made him angry, and he would pull the bottle from her hand, telling her not to waste money and treat him like a child.

'It's my money you're drinking,' she would say coolly, which made him even angrier. He would shout and slam his fist on the kitchen table, but Olivia kept her cool – believing in the Oscar she thought was still inside this angry man. But the flat was beginning to feel claustrophobic, the bold dark colours oppressive, the noise from the downstairs flat intrusive. It was beginning to not feel like a home.

One Sunday evening she cooked dinner, with the plan of talking to Oscar about how he could move his life forward and how they could get their relationship back on track. She painstakingly prepared tiramisu, his favourite pudding. But his mood was black. He stuck his fork into the chicken and banged his knife against the potatoes, like it was a hammer.

'Cardboard,' he said about the chicken. 'Cement. Overcooked mush,' he said about the green beans. He sat at the table with his arms folded and gave a horrible laugh. 'My review would be "don't eat here". Not even one star.'

She stared at him. 'Oscar, I...' she began, her eyes pricking with tears. 'How can you say that?'

'Come on – it's just a joke,' he said. 'You have no sense of humour. But, really, haven't I taught you anything about cooking? I'm a chef for God's sake! Why would you serve me this? I'd rather have a takeaway.'

She carried the plates through to the kitchen. Her hands

trembled as she put them down roughly into the sink. 'It wasn't funny, Oscar,' she said. 'Your so-called jokes never are.'

Realising he'd wound her up, suddenly Oscar was right behind her. She twisted round and pushed past him, but he stopped her, grabbing one arm so tight, she winced.

'You're hurting me,' she told him. 'Get off me. Stop it! You're upsetting me, can't you see?'

'No,' he said. 'Why are you in such a bad mood? You always twist everything. Turn everything sour. You need to develop a thicker skin. You wouldn't last a second in the kitchen I worked in!'

It wasn't the first time she'd been told she needed to develop a thicker skin, but if thick skin meant she would accept people being horrible to her, did she want it?

'I can't do this anymore,' she said. 'You can be so cruel. You've changed. You criticise me all the time, you seem to despise me sometimes and I... I... don't want to... be despised by the person who's supposed to love me.' She was struggling not to cry.

'That's right,' he said. 'Turn on the waterworks.'

'Oh, shut up, Oscar!' she said. 'I'm... I'm done with this.'

'What?' he demanded, furious. 'So you're leaving me, just when things are going badly for me? You're as bad as my bloody mother! Kick me when I'm down, why don't you?'

'Don't lump me in with your mum,' said Olivia. 'Do you know what? I'm pretty sure you have a problem with women.'

'I don't have a problem with women,' he said. 'They have a problem with me.'

'No wonder!'

As soon as she saw the way Oscar was looking at her, she wished she could push the words back in her mouth.

'No wonder what?' he yelled in her face. 'No wonder my mum left?'

'No, no,' she said. 'I didn't mean that at all. I meant no

wonder people have a problem with you when you're so irra-
tionally angry. Look. You – we – need to calm down.'

'No, hang on, SAY IT!' he screamed. 'You were going to say,
"No wonder your mum left," weren't you? Oh well, that's
fucking great. Fucking brilliant, you bitch.'

'Stop!' she spluttered. 'Just stop, Oscar! I said "no wonder"
and that's all, nothing more! You're putting words into my
mouth!'

But it was too late. Oscar pushed her up against the kitchen
wall. A hook jammed into her back, and she cried out.

'How dare you!' he snarled.

'I didn't say anything! Get off me – get off me, please. You're
hurting me!'

Suddenly he let go of her and swept his arm across the
kitchen counter, sending the glass bowl of tiramisu flying onto
the floor. The intricate layers of cream and sponge lay in a
messy puddle at her feet.

Crying, she forced her legs to carry her to the hallway. She
put her helmet on and moved towards her bike, which was
leaning against the wall.

'Where are you going?' he shouted. 'Don't you dare leave
me like this.'

'I'm going for a cycle,' she said as calmly as she could. 'I
need some air.'

'No, you're not,' he said.

He kicked the spokes of her wheel so hard that they bent,
and the wheel buckled. The bike fell over. He looked momentarily ashamed before he stormed into the bedroom, slamming
the door behind him, leaving Olivia trembling in the hallway,
watching the wheel spinning, her bike helmet perched on top of
her head.

'You shouldn't have said that!' he shouted from behind the
bedroom door, his voice muffled by the duvet he was hiding
under.

'You shouldn't have done that!' she shouted back.

Opening the door, she went out into the night, gulping the icy air. She would go and stay at Isla's.

'I have to end this,' she said, her body convulsing with sobs. She whispered into the wind: 'It's over!'

And that's when she discovered she was pregnant.

NINE

It was him. For one, dreadful, heart-stopping moment, Olivia thought the person sitting on Jesse's deckchair, staring out to sea, was Oscar. Her entire body flushed with volcanic heat, and she had the urge to run in the opposite direction and never stop. Squinting in the low, bright sunlight, she swallowed hard.

'Is that...?' she said, stopping and grasping hold of Hattie's arm.

'Yes, it's Alec!' Hattie replied, blinking in surprise.

Olivia exhaled in relief, released her grip on Hattie and rested her hand on her heart. 'Yes,' she said, for once in her life pleased to see him. 'Alec. Of course, Alec.'

It was early morning. The air was warm and carried the smells of coffee and cooked breakfast across the beach from the café. The sand was already a hive of activity. A yoga class was taking place, and a group of swimmers were gathered near the lifeguard's hut, peeling off their wetsuits, laughing raucously after their swim. A man with a metal detector swept the sand, occasionally stopping to dig for treasure, helped by his dog.

Olivia and Hattie were on their way to the beach hut with a can of paint, to give the exterior a refresh, ready for the next deckchair visitors. After Elaine's visit, they'd decided to do things differently and had agreed that, yes, the beach hut did need a lick of paint.

As they drew closer to the hut, Alec stood up and folded his arms across his chest as if they were late for an appointment. He was slim, tall and smartly dressed for the office despite being on the beach. His freckled skin and cropped dark ginger hair made him look younger than his years, but there was weariness in his eyes. By his feet were a couple of huge bulging carrier bags from the local DIY store.

'Olivia,' he said, giving a slight nod in her direction. 'Hattie.'

'Alec,' Hattie said, taking a step towards him, perhaps to embrace him, but the moment was lost.

'We all know each other's names at least,' said Olivia. 'How can we help you, Alec?'

Hattie gave Olivia a disapproving look. 'Don't talk to him like you're a beach warden,' she said. 'Sit down again, Alec. Let me make you a tea and we can have a catch-up. It's great to see you. I haven't seen you in a while. How are you? You're looking well, very smart. Are you still going to that gymnasium?'

Olivia thought he didn't look that well. His eyes were a bit pink, and she wondered if something was wrong or he wasn't sleeping.

Noticing he was being scrutinised, Alec quickly pulled his designer sunglasses from his jacket pocket and put them on. 'No, no tea,' he said. 'I can't stay. I've got things to do, but I brought a few things down for you, and I've sanded down the worst bits of flaky paint on the hut.' He lifted one of the carrier bags and opened it up. Inside there were paintbrushes, rolls of decorating tape, cloths and more.

'You must have been here for ages!' said Olivia. 'What time did you arrive? Didn't you have any overalls or something?'

'Don't cross-examine the poor man!' said Hattie. 'I could give you Jesse's overalls though, dear, if you wanted them.'

'No need,' he said. 'I'm an early riser. The early bird catches the worm and all that.'

'The early bird catches their death of cold,' said Hattie, before pulling a panicked expression. 'Sorry, not in your case, Alec – you know what you're doing. Very sensible.'

Clearly irritated, Alec handed Olivia a can of paint – in a bright yellow shade. 'Before he died, Dad told me he wanted to repaint the hut this colour,' he said. 'He even pointed it out to me once, in the DIY store. I knew you were painting it today. I saw it on Beau's Instagram post – she seems to tell the world everything she's doing. I didn't want you to paint it with something inferior or the wrong colour. This is the best acrylic you can get.'

Olivia worried for a moment about Beau telling the world everything.

'We've got blue...' she started, raising the can of paint she was carrying into the air.

But Hattie snatched it out of her hand and put it on the ground. 'We'll paint it yellow, just as Jesse wanted. Thank you, Alec. That's thoughtful, and I know Jesse would be delighted you cared so much.'

'More of a practical thing than anything,' said Alec, clearing his throat. 'I'm not keen on this whole idea, as you know, Olivia. I'm not sure Dad would approve. You might get some unwelcome attention.'

'Oh,' said Hattie, her eyes wide with worry, 'don't you think Jesse would've liked it? Do you think we should perhaps rethink, Olivia? We've already had one guest, Alec, and it didn't go all that well, if I'm honest.'

Olivia sighed inwardly. She glared at Alec, but he avoided her gaze.

'Jesse would be pleased we're raising money for a good cause,' said Olivia. 'Thank you for the paint, Alec.'

He checked his watch. 'I better go.'

'Are you sure you won't stay?' Hattie said.

Even after all these years, she was trying to make Alec stay. But he ignored the question, said a clipped 'goodbye' and walked away, his shiny shoes too polished for the beach.

'Looks like an estate agent,' said Olivia when he was out of earshot. 'He was probably trying to find out how much the beach hut is worth so he can sell it from under your nose.'

'He can't,' said Hattie. 'It's mine until I die, then it will go to him. Can't imagine him relaxing on the beach or continuing the family deckchair business, can you? You know, Liv, you'll have to think about that at some point soon. Me going. I'm not going to last forever.'

'Let's not think about that today,' Olivia replied, watching Alec get into his car.

What goes on in that head of his? she wondered. She knew very little of his life really. He was an architect, he lived in an expensive house with nothing much in it, he didn't seem to have a permanent girlfriend. He never said anything nice.

You might get some unwelcome attention.

Olivia's thoughts shot to the email from Oscar. She told herself to forget about it. Bury it. She was good at burying thoughts – had been since her dad had died. Elaine would probably have something to say about that, but when Olivia had realised her dad was never coming back, she'd buried the horror of that realisation deep inside herself: into her neural folds, blood vessels and ventricles. She carried the loss as a physical part of herself, albeit completely hidden from anyone else's view. At the time she'd been commended for coping well with his death – she was strong and brave and helping to look after her mum, who wasn't so strong and brave.

'You're helping to fill your dad's shoes,' one of her mum's friends had said.

After that, Olivia had pushed her feet into his shoes, which were huge and clownlike on her tiny feet, and tried to walk in them, only to immediately fall over and knock out one of her front teeth.

'It's only a baby tooth – it's the adult ones you need to look after,' Hattie had said, which seemed all back to front to Olivia at the time, but she nodded along and took note.

It was the adults who needed looking after.

She was nodding along again now, as Hattie regaled her with a hundred reasons why Alec might be right about reconsidering the deckchair idea.

'What if the next person starts talking about politics and we disagree or argue, and then they complain and want their money back?' said Hattie. 'I better keep a pot of money with me in case anyone wants a refund. I thought Elaine might ask for her money back, since we had no scones!'

'You're not a commodity or a sideshow, Mum,' sighed Olivia. 'They're not paying you either! You're raising money for a charity while at the same time making friends yourself. My aim is that you'll make one new friend that you can enjoy spending time with. Elaine might not have been the right person, but she meant well. There will be others: men, women, young, old.'

'Not a man for heaven's sake!' said Hattie, hand on chest, eyes wide open. 'What if a man comes thinking I'm looking for a third husband? I'll never, ever replace Jesse.'

'They won't, and anyway, you can set them straight and tell them you're not interested,' said Olivia, watching Hattie sit down in a deckchair, the bags of DIY items at her feet and the emails Olivia had printed from people who wanted to come down to the deckchair in her hand.

'This lady, Anthea,' said Hattie, 'is a yoga expert. She wants to talk about meditation and nutrition and show me some basic moves. She has a small business. Do you think people are using me as a publicity vehicle?'

Olivia laughed. 'No. You might enjoy yoga. You can learn

how to do the handstand scorpion. You could join the group over there.' She pointed to the women on the beach, bending into positions she didn't think were possible.

'I'm not doing a handstand anything at my age!' Hattie said. 'Listen, if we're doing scones now, do you think we should hang bunting across the beach hut? Or does that make it seem like we're celebrating? I'm certainly not celebrating. I hope people won't think I'm celebrating.'

Olivia sighed. 'I think bunting is fine. Let's put some up.'

'I don't know,' Hattie muttered. 'God knows what all these strangers will think! Elaine didn't seem too impressed.'

'We're not out to impress,' said Olivia wearily. 'It's about befriending, having a conversation, that's all. Elaine just wanted to share her story and tell you that things get better. She was right about the hut needing a paint, so let's get on with it!'

Olivia laid down a drop cloth near the front of the beach hut, opened a can of paint and stirred its yellow soupy contents. She handed Hattie a paintbrush and got to work, covering over the pale blue with thick bands of bright yellow. For a few minutes, they painted together in silence.

'Can I ask a question on a totally different topic?' Olivia said. 'Who was it you were thinking of when Paul asked you in the interview who you'd most like to see in that deckchair and you went all strange and clammed up?'

'Nobody,' said Hattie much too quickly. Her forehead was splattered with paint.

'You can tell me. Was it an ex?'

'No, of course it wasn't an ex. It was a knee-jerk reaction to Paul's question. I haven't been thinking straight lately. My thoughts are all over the place.'

'Go on, please tell me,' said Olivia. 'Come on – it's only me.'

Hattie put her paintbrush down on the lid of the paint tin. 'Do you ever give up? If you must know, I was thinking about

Alec's mother, Francine,' said Hattie quietly. 'She was a good friend before everything.'

Olivia frowned. Hattie and Jesse had rarely spoken about Francine, at least not in front of her. All Olivia knew of her was that she and Jesse had had an acrimonious split.

'It was very complicated and difficult,' said Hattie. 'I thought she might come to Jesse's funeral to support Alec, that's all, but of course she didn't. Anyway, let's stop thinking about her. Remind me, who's coming on Saturday?'

Olivia made a mental note to ask Hattie more about Francine another time. She reeled off the names of people she'd scheduled in for Saturday.

'We have Miriam. Miriam is a medium,' said Olivia.

'In what? Trousers?' said Hattie with a quick smile.

'Psychic medium.'

'Oh, I don't believe in all that hogwash,' said Hattie, although she gave Olivia a sideways glance that showed she was interested.

'She sent a very nice email. And then there's Glenda, who runs a mobile bar, and a man who's walking the south-west coastal path in memory of his wife. He collects moths.'

'Moths?' said Hattie, pulling an appalled expression. 'Oh, Liv, I was happier being a hermit! Why are you doing this?'

'To cheer you up,' Olivia said, dipping her paintbrush into the tin.

'I don't need cheering up.'

Olivia swept the brush across the hut. 'To find you a new friend.'

'I don't need a new friend. I'm fine as I am.'

'To help you because I can see you're unhappy. And I hate to see you suffering. I just can't stand it.'

'For goodness' sake, I'm grieving,' snapped Hattie. 'I don't need your help.'

You've always needed my help, thought Olivia as she

continued to work her brush along the grain of the wood. *You just haven't acknowledged it.*

It wasn't just now, after Jesse's death. Olivia thought back to the weeks of fog she'd found her way through after her father's death. All Hattie had wanted to do was sit with Olivia on the sofa and watch children's TV. The jolly music and jokes had felt so wrong at the time, it had made Olivia feel sick.

She remembered Hattie taking Olivia's beloved bike and sellotaping a piece of paper onto it which said 'Free, help yourself' and placing it outside the front of the house. Olivia had been enraged when a neighbouring child had taken it and gleefully rode off, the purple handlebar streamers flowing like hair in the wind. But instead of showing her anger and upset, Olivia had tried to help. She'd made Hattie bowls of cereal. Straightened her duvet. Opened the curtains. Dragged the dustbin into the street for the binmen to take.

Once the news was out that Hattie wasn't coping, Hattie's friends had got involved – the same ones who'd commended Olivia for being brave and strong and for helping look after Mummy. They'd brought food in Pyrex dishes with tinfoil on the top; a blur of skirts and blouses, perfumed and sympathetic. Olivia had heard Hattie talking to them through tears, not realising her daughter was listening from behind the door.

'I don't think I can take care of myself, let alone poor Olivia,' Hattie had wept to her friends. 'I feel broken. I'm totally broken. I'll never be mended.'

Olivia had been struck by a thought. Her dad had been good at fixing things – he had a huge toolkit that he'd kept under the stairs – but he was never coming home. If Hattie was broken, then it was going to be up to Olivia and Olivia alone to fix her.

She'd set about trying to learn from Hattie's friends, watching which buttons they pressed on the washing machine, how to best unwrap a Dairylea triangle and spread it on a cracker, how to plump up Hattie's pillows on the days she didn't want to get out of bed. She noted the soft tone they used to talk to Hattie, the sympathetic phrases they repeated. Was one of those friends Francine? Olivia didn't know.

When Hattie took a break from painting the beach hut and went inside it to make coffee – one for Hattie, one for Olivia and one for Jesse – Olivia scribbled a note under the deckchair timetable: *Invite Francine?*

TEN

That evening, Hattie couldn't stop thinking about Francine. Snapshots of her old friend appeared in her head; moving images rolled on the back of her eyelids. Despite trying to busy herself with other tasks, she found herself gravitating towards a wooden box containing a photograph album and some old letters on the top shelf of the bookcase in the living room. It had been years since she'd last pored over them, but now, with fluttering hands flecked with yellow paint, Hattie lifted the box down, sat on the sofa and rested it on her lap.

First, she took the album from the box. Memories danced across the room as she turned to the last page – a photograph of herself on holiday in Italy. She peeled back the self-adhesive sheet and lifted out the photograph to reveal one of Francine underneath. She was in a snowy park, dressed in a ski jacket, tight jeans and fur-lined boots.

'Dear Francine,' Hattie whispered into the quiet room.

Francine looked happy in the photo. Her mouth was slightly open, as if she was laughing. In her hand she held a snowball, which she'd been about to throw at Hattie. Her fingers were bright pink with cold.

This was a time before marriages and children. They were young adults, without a clue of the chaos that was to come. Not suspecting for a moment that they would one day stop speaking to each other. The memory of Francine's voice was clear as a bell in her mind – she was always talking, always laughing. Hardly took time for a breath.

Hattie closed her eyes and dug her fingernails into the plastic coverings on the arms of the sofa. The very last time she'd seen Francine was in January 1983. The raindrops on the windscreen had been blood red. Winds in the Sahara Desert had lifted the reddish sand into the atmosphere, which had then been carried over to the UK skies in the rain. It had given the day an apocalyptic feel. Hattie had recently turned forty, ambushed with cards telling her life was about to begin, but that day she'd had a very real sense that her life as she knew it was ending. Three years earlier Michael had died, and now her best friend, Francine, was threatening to cut her out of her life.

She was losing people, left, right and centre. The reason? Jesse had told Francine he was in love with Hattie. To someone who didn't know the situation, that sounded dreadful. Without knowing all the facts, Francine's threat to cut Hattie out of her life might have seemed justified. But Hattie did know all the facts – and she felt entirely wronged.

Francine and Jesse had been married for five years but had been estranged for the last two, and unhappy for at least two before that. Francine had told Hattie she wasn't interested in Jesse; she wasn't interested in men, full stop. She'd even written letters to her about it, baring her soul in pen and ink. It was funny how people didn't seem to want to bother with the whole story. They preferred to see love in black and white. People as good and evil. They wanted to take sides, start a war.

Hattie had parked her car and reread the latest note Francine had sent her, her eyes misting over with tears.

Hattie, I'm writing to tell you that this is where our journey together ends. I never want to see you again. Francine

Hattie had immediately contacted Francine and begged her to meet her for a walk, for one last conversation. Hattie walked to the meeting point – a gate at a field at the back of a National Trust property. Her legs trembled as she waited, shivering in the cold. A herd of black cows, with clouds of steam hanging around their nostrils, watched her.

'Shoo,' she said, hopelessly flapping her arms in their direction. There were some people who thought hugging cows was therapeutic, but she'd always felt frightened of them, especially the mothers, who would lower their heads and charge at perceived predators to protect their calves.

'There's nothing left to talk about,' Francine said when she arrived at the meeting point wearing a long, impractical floral dress with tights and boots, covered with a thick brown coat and woolly hat. She had shoulder-length blonde hair and huge brown eyes. 'As I've said, I'd prefer it if we never saw each other again.'

Hattie sighed. 'Can you at least try to see this from my point of view and not a victim's perspective?' she asked. 'You owe me that. Please, can we walk?'

They started walking across the field, the cows observing their every step. The footpath led them straight through the herd, towards a gate on the opposite side of the field. Hattie slowed down.

'I don't owe you a thing,' said Francine. 'Go to hell.'

'I'm already in hell,' said Hattie. 'If only we could talk about this rationally. Please, Francine, I beg you – listen to my side of the story. Look at the facts: you've been in love with someone else for two years, with a woman for God's sake! You told me repeatedly you didn't love Jesse and wanted to separate from him, and you've been estranged for ages. How can you blame your break-up on me? It's not my fault. I've been a bystander in all of this, watching two of my favourite people go headlong into some sort of awful relationship car crash.'

'A bystander!' said Francine. 'How about an opportunist, waiting for the moment you could pounce? You lost Michael, so it's time to steal my husband?'

'No!' said Hattie. 'That's not how it is, and you know it. I have letters from you telling me, from months, years ago, you'd fallen out of love with Jesse. That you've never really loved him, that your heart wasn't in conventional marriage. And don't forget that before you ever even came along, *I* was in a relationship with Jesse. Did I make this fuss when the two of you got together? No.'

'So you thought you'd make your move now?' she said.

'No, not at all. But Jesse and I have grown close again lately. We've always been friends. I'm sorry if this is hurting you; it's certainly taken me by surprise. But I would never "steal" him from you. That's not fair to say.'

'Who's playing the victim now?' asked Francine, hands on hips.

'Francine, please. Be sensible about this. You can't blame me for your unhappiness – I won't let you. And, anyway, I've told him that I'm not interested because I can't stand all this. I've lost Michael; I can't lose you too.'

'He said he loves you.'

'That's his bloody problem. I've told him I can't do it.'

'Why not?' Francine said. 'Not good enough for you?'

'Oh, I can't win,' said Hattie, crying now. 'You know how much you mean to me.'

'I'm the one who's lost everything,' said Francine. 'You can't understand. You'll never understand! Do what you want, Hattie, but just leave me alone.'

Hattie's eyes moved to the cows who, intrigued by the raised voices, were moving closer. In seconds, the women were almost surrounded by them, but Francine calmly walked ahead of Hattie, through the cows, and hopped straight over the wooden stile into the next field. Then she began walking away. Hattie, panicking, was rooted to the spot, the cows growing closer still, until she could feel the heat from their huge bodies.

'Francine!' she called timidly, not wanting to alarm the cows. 'Francine!'

A huge cow lowered its head and made a huffing sound.

Hattie made a sudden dash in the direction of the fence, but there were too many cows in front of the stile. She looked in dismay at the barbed-wire fence surrounding the field.

The cow was following her, trotting, gathering speed.

She ran at full pelt further up the paddock, put a leg up onto the barbed wire, catching her boot laces and jeans as she went, the sharp edges of the wire sticking through the denim and into her flesh. She was stuck, caught on the wire, trying to balance. Blood started to ooze from her leg.

'Give me your hand,' Francine said gently, suddenly by her side. 'I'll help you, you silly cow.'

Hattie thrust her hand into Francine's and leaned her weight into her friend's body. Francine helped lift Hattie down from the barbed wire, and for a moment, the women clung to one another, laughing uproariously, before Francine pulled away and sighed.

'I thought you were the one person in the world who understood me, but you don't,' she said, turning and marching away, her skirts, sleeves and hair billowing in the wind around her, leaving Hattie limping along behind, the blood-red rain falling into her open palms.

It was the last time they saw each other, the last time they'd spoken.

Now, alone on her sofa in the living room, wiping away a tear that had travelled down her cheek, Hattie put away the photograph, this time on top of the holiday snap. She lifted out a handful of letters Francine had sent her when she'd been unhappily married to Jesse. Hattie's eyes darted from one emotional phrase to another – outpourings of regret about marrying Jesse. It was there in black and white, yet still Francine had turned against her.

She sighed and carried the box into the bedroom, where she took off her blouse, pale-blue trousers, and pumps that made squeaky noises on the vinyl kitchen tiles to put on her pyjamas. She'd worn black for a few months after Jesse died, but now it was summer, she'd returned to her paler clothes. She thought of how horrified her grandmother would have been at this. She'd worn full black, including black gloves, for a year after her husband died.

Running a comb through her silver hair, Hattie stared at her pale reflection and let out a gasp. Without make-up, she looked ghostlike. Old. Lack of sleep had made her eyes small and pink. She felt suddenly terrified by the shortness of life.

'Didn't I understand her?' she asked her reflection. 'I thought I did.'

Right from the word go, Hattie and Francine had understood each other. They'd met aged seventeen at a house party. Hattie had come with Jesse, her then boyfriend, before she'd gone away to teacher training college and met Michael. Francine had been making a punch from whatever she could find in the host's cupboards, holding a bottle in each hand and pouring their contents into an enormous bowl. She'd suggested they carry it around the house, offering it to the guests at the party with a straw – not a care for cross-contamination – and Hattie had immediately liked her playfulness. They went on to become best friends.

When Francine told her she had feelings for women, Hattie thought she should be brave enough to follow those feelings. But instead, Francine had got together with and married Jesse, Hattie's first love, and had Alec. For a while, both families were friends, until Michael's death, when things had started to unravel.

After the day in the cow field, Hattie refused to see Jesse for over a year. She told him that he should try again with Francine, but they quickly divorced and, gradually, Jesse worked his way back into Hattie's life. But Francine refused to speak to Hattie – and Alec, her son, followed in her footsteps.

'Was I to blame?' Hattie said, shaking her head at the fact she was talking to herself – something she was doing more and more often.

She looked away and over her shoulder, feeling as if there was someone in the room. She bent down and checked under the bed.

'Jesse, am I cracking up?' she asked, but her cat Crumpet crept out from inside an open suitcase and wound itself around her legs.

'What would he say, Crumpet? Don't be doolally, Hattie – that's what he used to say. Don't be doolally.'

Her eyes welled with tears. She missed him so much, desperately, painfully. Though she longed for him, she hadn't felt Jesse's presence at all since he'd died – despite wanting to. Other people hated the thought, but she craved a visitation, a word from the other side, a sign. She squeezed her eyes shut at night, hoping for a dream to come where she'd hear him speak again, feel the warmth of his touch. But when she did fall asleep, her dreams took her to tangled lands of searching where the past arrived in jumbled truckloads and was dumped unwanted in her thoughts, like fly-tipped memories.

'Bloody Francine,' she muttered.

A sudden fizziness appeared in front of her eyes, sending a ripple of panic down her spine. She perched on the edge of the bed for a moment, feet spaced apart, hands on thighs, and regulated her breathing.

She hadn't told Olivia about the dizzy spells. She knew she

would immediately try to sort it out. Fix it. She'd always been that way, even as a child. Throwing her little arms around Hattie's neck after Michael's death to console her, pulling her by the hand into the garden to play catch whenever she felt sad, drawing pictures for her when Alec refused to come into their home. Now, caring for her in the loving way she did.

And, to her shame, Hattie hadn't done much to deter her. Olivia was her companion – a ray of sunshine.

'You'll never be lonely now that you have a daughter,' Hattie's mother had told her the day Olivia was born as Hattie cradled her tiny newborn baby in her arms. And it was true. Perhaps too true.

Deep down, Hattie knew she should convince Olivia to pick up her plans to move to Dublin, where she would have a job, friends – not a tearful old mother to help. But every time she thought about telling Olivia she should get on with her life, the words got stuck in her throat and refused to come out. Did she love her too much? Or would some say not enough? That wasn't true.

Hattie lay her head down on the pillow and closed her eyes. Love wasn't black and white.

ELEVEN

Olivia couldn't sleep. A growing ball of anxiety in her stomach had made her restless. Tomorrow there would be more visitors to the deckchair, but it wasn't that that was bothering her.

She tossed and turned in bed, the sheets twisting uncomfortably around her body, her pillow lumpy. The moon was full and shone through a gap in the curtains like a torch seeking her out. Her mind raced with thoughts.

Earlier that evening, before she'd gone to bed, she'd written an email to Francine, via Alec, asking her to consider taking part in the deckchair-hire event to talk to Hattie. She'd written that Hattie was *desperate* to see her again. *What if it's the last chance?* she'd said, citing Jesse's unexpected death.

Wondering for the tenth time if she'd done the right thing by trying to contact Francine, she decided to check for a reply.

Her digital alarm clock said it was 3.43 a.m. She switched on the lamp and checked her email on her phone. Nothing from Francine, but she closed her eyes in dismay when she saw a new one from Oscar, sent at 2.15 a.m. Olivia's heart plunged. The subject line was: *Olivia, you can't ignore me forever.*

In the last week, the subject lines on his emails had grown increasingly impatient.

Hello from the past.

Please read this.

Another attempt to contact you.

Could you answer?

IMPORTANT: please read.

Are you deleting these?

Olivia had permanently deleted them all without reading the contents.

She sighed and rubbed her eyes. Oscar's persistence sent ripples of unease through her. Even though she'd deleted his emails, she couldn't ignore his presence and imagined she saw him wherever she went.

Angrily throwing the phone down, she switched off the lamp, lay back down on the mattress, pulled the duvet over her face and squeezed her eyes tightly shut. But Oscar was on the inside of her eyelids, the image of him filling her with dread. She didn't want to respond to him; she didn't want to have anything to do with him. But could she ignore him forever?

Forcing herself to focus on something else, she thought about something another befriending client, Edith, had said when they'd spoken on the phone the day before. She hadn't mentioned Oscar or what she was going through, but everything Edith talked about seemed to relate to Olivia's personal circumstances.

'The biggest thing I've learned in life is that even the worst times pass,' Edith had said. 'You know the famous phrase: this too shall pass? It's true. I've lived it. I speak from experience. That and a bad carpenter blames his tools. That's true too. We're all responsible for our own life, aren't we? I know people who moan about their lives and blame other people, when really, they just need to take charge of the situation, fight back a bit. Easier said than done sometimes, especially when people won't listen. I've been complaining for months about the fact that, as a wheelchair user, I can't get right down to the sea, but does anyone listen? No. It's no wonder people glue their hands to the ground or stand naked outside the Houses of Parliament. Goodness knows what would happen if I went down that route, but I'm tempted! My advice to you, Olivia, is to make yourself heard. Fight back, for heaven's sake. I wish I'd fought harder.'

Edith had a disability that meant she relied on her wheelchair and her carer's help to get out and about. She was isolated and needed more social contact than she got, yet continually surprised Olivia with her strength.

'Life must be frustrating,' Olivia had said.

'Society is frustrating,' Edith had replied. 'The high kerbs, the narrow aisles, the lack of facilities on trains. As I said, I'd like to swim in the sea, but how am I supposed to get my wheelchair across the sand? Whole sections of society are ignored. That's what's frustrating.'

The conversation had given Olivia the idea to invite Edith to come to the beach hut with her carer. They'd find a way to get her to the water's edge.

Olivia thought about the logistics of that now, opening her eyes under the duvet. Would it be possible?

She turned onto her side, pushed down the duvet and looked at the clock: 4.40 a.m. It was no good – she'd have to get up. The birds were announcing the start of the day now, breaking the stifling silence of the night with their raucous song, as if the blackbirds, wrens and seagulls knew the significance of the day ahead.

Some people would go jogging or swim lengths in the pool, but Olivia tackled her anxiety by making a batch of scones, half with raisins, half without, before putting them in the oven and going up to the attic to search for a specific vintage crockery set with a strawberry print that would be perfect for the deckchair visitors.

'Where is it?' she mumbled.

The attic was stacked with cardboard boxes, many that she'd packed up and had left so after the almost-move to Dublin.

After half an hour of searching, there were things everywhere – old maps, books, curtain tiebacks, vintage plates, a lace tablecloth, but no strawberry-print crockery set.

Reaching over to a cardboard box tucked into the corner of the attic, she pulled out an old cookbook Oscar had given her. Beneath it was the strawberry-print crockery. Finally.

She opened the cookbook and out slipped a photograph of Oscar in the kitchen of the flat they'd once shared. He had on his chef's whites and was smiling proudly, like a boy in his new uniform on his first day of school. Olivia stared at the photograph for a moment before ripping it up into tiny pieces.

'What are you *doing*, Mum?' said Beau, suddenly poking her head into the attic and making Olivia jump. 'It's the middle of the night. You woke me up, plodding around up here!'

Olivia dropped the pieces of photograph and put her hand on her heart. 'You scared me! And it's not the middle of the night, Beau, it's morning. I came up to get this crockery. I thought I'd put a picnic basket together with the cream tea. The scones are in the oven. What's that in your hair?'

Beau ran her hand through her hair, which seemed to have streaks of bright pink paint on one side. 'Oh, nothing,' she said. 'Just paint from finishing off the beach hut yesterday. You'd left a few bits on one side.'

'But the beach hut is yellow, not pink,' said Olivia. 'Oh, Beau, you haven't done any more graffiti, have you? Have you painted over the other one yet?' She'd been so busy with Hattie and all the emails coming in, she'd hardly seen her daughter to check in. 'I don't have time for this kind of thing,' she sighed. 'You're almost sixteen – it's time to start taking responsibility.'

Olivia's cheeks turned pink, and she felt too hot and claustrophobic in the attic. She wasn't sure if it was the stress about Oscar making her so short-tempered, but it seemed whenever she saw Beau recently, they clashed. She felt instantly guilty for what she'd said.

'For God's sake! There you go again, assuming the worst,' said Beau.

'But you didn't get back until so late, despite me calling you!' said Olivia. 'I was worried. And when you came in, you barely spoke to me before locking yourself in your bedroom! Did you go somewhere after the beach? I need to know where you are, especially now.'

'What do you mean "especially now"?' Beau demanded, her expression furious. 'What, now that I'm a master criminal graffiti artist? I'm going back to bed. You're not listening. You treat me like I'm five years old and you have no idea what a terrible week I've had!'

Beau's head disappeared from the loft. She climbed down the ladder, and Olivia followed quickly behind her, leaving a chaotic scene in the attic.

'What do you mean?' Olivia said. 'Is it the garage thing?'

'No, it's not the stupid garage thing,' said Beau, with one hand on her bedroom door. 'I told you not to worry about that! Why don't you go and see it for yourself and you'll understand that it's meant to be there?'

'I will,' Olivia said. 'But what's wrong then? You can tell me anything. Please, tell me what's on your mind.'

Their eyes met for a moment and then Beau frowned, staring at a couple of pieces of Oscar's photograph that had fluttered down from the attic and landed on the floorboards. Olivia picked them up without saying a word, her cheeks flaming red. Whatever it was that Beau was going to say passed by unsaid.

Beau shrugged and exhaled. 'Just stuff. By the way, I'm staying at Wren's this weekend. We're doing our art project together. Her mum said it's okay. You can call her if you want to check. And, Mum? I will break the rules if I don't believe in them.'

Olivia opened her mouth to respond, but Beau disappeared back into her bedroom, closing the door behind her. Olivia approached it and went to knock, but Beau turned her music on, and Olivia's hand dropped. Unease crept across her shoulders and down her spine – she felt a sudden sense of absolute dread.

But the smell of burning grabbed her attention.

'The scones!' she shouted, turning away from Beau's door, running down the stairs to the kitchen and yanking open the oven door.

But it was too late. There on the baking tray sat twelve burned scones, like little smoking chimneys.

TWELVE

A new batch of scones later, carefully arranged in a basket with a pot of jam, clotted cream, fresh strawberries, cutlery, the strawberry crockery set, tablecloth and milk jug, Olivia made her way along the promenade towards the beach hut. Hattie was by her side, dressed in a long-sleeved striped top, pale trousers and sandals. Olivia smiled to herself when she noticed that Hattie had painted her toenails for the occasion.

The sun was shyly peering out from behind the clouds, as if it had one hand over its face, nervous about watching the day unfold. Already, families were setting up camp on the beach: hammering in windbreaks, laying down brightly coloured towels, opening flasks of coffee and paper bags filled with steaming sausage rolls or pastries. Dogs were straining on leads and the joggers were out in force, sweating profusely as they ran along the promenade, some with weights strapped to their backs.

Wanting to be better prepared than they'd been for Elaine, Olivia and Hattie had headed down half an hour before Miriam was supposed to arrive, but although she wanted to be enthusiastic, Olivia's mind was elsewhere – on Beau's terrible week,

Oscar's persistent, irritated emails and Francine's lack of response.

'Are you even listening?' said Hattie, elbowing Olivia as they walked. 'I didn't sleep a wink last night. I'm not really in the right frame of mind to do this.'

'You're doing this to raise money for isolated people,' said Olivia. 'Loneliness can lead to depression, a weakened immune system, heart problems and even dementia. What you're doing is important.'

'I'm not sure this will make any difference whatsoever.' Hattie sighed. 'Elaine didn't seem that impressed!'

'Don't underestimate the power of a conversation. Even a hello or a smile can help. Elaine wanted to share her story and you listened, which is also important. Won't you just carry on with it, for me?'

'I suppose so,' said Hattie, suddenly stopping and staring ahead at the beach hut, which had come into view.

Olivia followed her gaze. Her jaw dropped.

'Is that...?' said Hattie, gripping Olivia's forearm. '*Me?*'

On the side of the beach hut, Beau, presumably, had painted a portrait of Hattie's face, her white hair gently lifted by the breeze. She'd painted a gold frame around the edges of the hut, making it look like a portrait hanging in a gallery wall – in this case the wall was the beach and the sky, depending on your viewpoint. It was such a warm portrayal of Hattie, but her grief was there too, in the lines around her eyes, the set of her mouth.

Olivia was speechless.

In stencilled lettering, Beau had written 'Not Invisible' underneath.

'Good heavens,' said Hattie. 'Has Beau done that? When did she do that? Must have taken hours! Is it because I said people my age often feel invisible in the eyes of her generation? She must have taken it to heart.'

Moved by Beau's huge gesture, Hattie burst into shocked

tears, and Olivia pulled her into her arms for a brief hug, awash with guilt.

It all made sense now – all those hours her daughter had been out, coming home so late. No wonder she'd been angry when Olivia had accused her of being up to no good. But why hadn't Beau just told her what she was doing in the first place, if it wasn't anything bad? Perhaps she'd wanted it to be a surprise, or perhaps she'd thought Olivia would object.

The streaks of pink she'd seen in her hair matched the colour she'd used for Hattie's lips, set in the slightest smile – neither happy, nor sad.

Olivia pulled out her phone, took a photo and sent it to Beau with a message: *Beau, the beach hut is amazing. Please can we talk? Can I buy you dinner when you're back from Wren's?*

A group of people had gathered around the hut, and as Hattie and Olivia approached, they commented on the likeness to Hattie, asking who'd done the artwork. But then the tone changed from admiration to a discussion about rule-breaking.

'The council will never allow it to stay,' said one male onlooker. 'There are strict rules about decorating beach huts. It has to be one plain colour, not a riot of colour! The last time some amateur artist did this, the hut was repainted within a day or two. It's been that way for years. Decades! I'm not sure why you think you have the right to do your own thing.'

Olivia stared at the man, feeling angry and helpless. She knew he was right, and that Beau's fantastic artwork was against the council guidelines for beach huts. She thought of her daughter's words earlier that day: *I will break the rules if I don't believe in them.*

'Think of all the work that went into this,' she said quietly. 'Not everything has to stay the same.'

'Yes, but what would happen if every beach hut was painted like this?' he asked. 'What would happen if everyone broke the rules?'

'Perhaps everyone would be in a better mood,' Hattie said. 'Would you mind giving us some space? This is my beach hut.' She pushed in front of the man, muttering, 'Bog off,' under her breath.

'I'm going to have to report this,' the man said before leaving, along with a few other onlookers.

'Do what you like, you bald egghead!' Hattie shouted, her voice trembling.

One woman from the group stayed put. She was in her sixties, wore a black cheesecloth dress with a denim jacket over the top and had a pink scarf tied around her hair, which was dyed jet black. She wore little make-up, and when she moved, her long gold earrings, in the shape of leaves, glinted in the sunlight.

'Have you got something you wish to add?' snapped Hattie in the direction of the woman. 'Because if you've got complaints, I'm not interested. As if life isn't difficult enough without all these naysayers chiming in with their unwanted opinions.'

'Mum,' said Olivia, glancing at the woman apologetically. 'Calm down.'

'Well!' said Hattie.

The woman smiled warily. Over her shoulder, she carried a huge carpet bag which clamped together with big gold clasps. It bulged with whatever was inside. Balanced on the top was a small bunch of pink roses, tied with a ribbon. In her hand she carried a piece of paper, and Olivia noticed it was a printout of an email – the one Olivia had sent her, giving her a time to arrive and the location of the beach hut.

'Oh,' said Olivia. 'I'm sorry, are you Miriam?'

'I am,' the woman said. 'Sorry, I'm a little early. That man was so rude. I think the painting is wonderful actually.'

'Welcome to our fraught family,' said Olivia, reaching out to shake hands with Miriam, whose palm was hot and clammy. 'I'm Olivia and this is Hattie.'

'But you'd know that, I suppose,' said Hattie, still smarting. 'Being psychic!'

Miriam gave a small tight smile and handed the roses to Hattie.

'My favourite,' she said. 'Thank you. How did you know? Is it the psychic powers again?'

'Mum!' said Olivia.

'Sorry,' said Hattie, quivering a little. 'Those people, that man, really got my goat, after all Beau's done!'

'We had no idea my daughter had done this,' Olivia explained. 'It was a complete surprise.'

'Yes, and it's quite something to see your face staring out at you from the side of a beach hut, I can tell you – quite empowering actually,' Hattie said. 'Anyway, Miriam, it's kind of you to come. Please forgive me. Take a seat. This was Jesse's deckchair. I'll make you a tea.'

'I'll do that,' said Olivia. 'Why don't you two get acquainted?'

'I'm sure I've got nothing of interest to say,' Hattie said grumpily. 'As you can tell, I'm quite distracted.'

Awkwardly, Hattie and Miriam took their places in the deckchairs. Miriam twice rearranged her dress over her knees. Neither spoke. Olivia felt desperately uncomfortable and regretted the whole thing once again. She missed Jesse, who could strike up a conversation with a stranger so easily.

'So what made you get in touch, Miriam?' Olivia eventually said, willing the kettle to hurry up and boil.

Miriam smiled and nodded. 'I've recently retired from my day job and seem to have a lot of time on my hands,' she said. 'I have no children, and my family are mostly gone. I've found myself increasingly alone and find great comfort in being able to communicate with the deceased. I wondered if you'd like me to try today to get in touch with the other side on your behalf, Hattie?'

Hattie glanced warily at Olivia, her face ashen. 'No, dear, thank you. I would attach too much to what you said, and I think I'd get emotional. Also, if I'm entirely honest, I'm rather sceptical about the whole thing. I think about that man, the tele-vangelist man, who claimed he was getting messages from the spirit world but whose wife was giving him information about the congregation through an earpiece!'

'Well, there are some examples like that,' said Miriam stiffly. 'But some people find it greatly comforting to hear from their loved ones who've died.'

Hattie raised her eyebrows. 'I understand that, and although sometimes I find myself longing for some sort of sign from Jesse, I don't really believe it's real,' she said. 'Sorry, Miriam.'

'I'm actually rather relieved,' Miriam replied. 'People expect the spirits to say something nice, and they sometimes don't. I'll close my ears to anything they say, but if you change your mind, just say.'

Hattie sighed. 'I won't.'

Olivia placed the tray with the teapot, teacups, small plates and cream tea on a low table near Miriam and Hattie. She poured Miriam a tea and offered her the plate of scones. She took two. Hattie and Olivia exchanged a glance.

'One for me and one for him,' said Miriam.

'Oh, I do that!' said Hattie. 'Old habits die hard. Did your husband die too?'

Miriam shook her head. 'When I was a child, my twin died. We were in a car accident. I survived. He's communicated with me ever since, so he's always with me, somewhere close by, along with all the others.'

'Aah,' said Hattie. 'I'm sorry.'

Olivia swallowed, worrying whether Miriam had a screw loose.

'I know you're thinking I've got a screw loose,' said Miriam, after biting into her scone.

Olivia almost dropped the teapot.

'Many people I meet think that my childhood traumatic experience has left me wanting to hear his voice and that I've made the whole thing up. That I've constructed this whole psychic medium thing to avoid facing the truth. That I'm just comforting myself really.'

'I wasn't thinking that,' Hattie said, looking guilty. 'Anyway, Miriam, it doesn't matter what other people think, does it? You must do whatever you have to do to get through life. If that's speaking to your twin, or if that's running thirty miles a day with a rucksack of weights on your back, then so be it.'

'Exactly,' Olivia added, swiping cream and jam onto a scone and biting into it.

'What about you?' Miriam asked. 'What do you have to do to get through?'

'Good question!' said Hattie. 'I don't have an answer. Olivia helps me. We've been through some tough times together.'

'At least you had each other. I read in the paper that your first husband was killed,' said Miriam. 'That must have been hard for you.'

'Yes,' said Hattie. 'Do you know it's all very blurred. I just had to keep going because I had Olivia and she was so young at the time. Seven.'

'Six,' said Olivia.

'Gosh, that must have been hard for you, Olivia,' said Miriam. 'Childhood trauma runs very deep.'

Olivia smiled a small smile and shrugged. 'It was a long time ago,' she said, but Miriam's words had stirred something deep in her heart.

'How did you cope?' asked Miriam kindly.

Olivia opened her mouth to reply, but Hattie thought the question was directed at her.

'I had to put on a brave face for Olivia. I tried not to talk about it too much. That's what I've been trying to do since Jesse died too. I guess it's a bit old-fashioned of me, but it's the only way I know.'

Olivia averted her eyes.

'That's not always healthy,' said Miriam. 'Suppressing emotions can give you all sorts of health problems.'

Olivia felt Miriam's eyes on her, but she turned away and busied herself with finding the sun umbrella, blinking at the tears that had inexplicably popped into her eyes.

'Is there anything that doesn't?' said Hattie, biting into her scone. 'Do you know I have this awful vertigo sometimes. Perhaps that's due to suppressing emotions.'

'Try essential oils,' said Miriam. 'Peppermint and ginger are good for vertigo.'

'Write that down, will you, Olivia?' Hattie said. 'Thank you, Miriam. Most helpful.'

Olivia nodded and typed 'essential oils' into her phone, noticing yet another email from Oscar, this one entitled: *Last chance*. Angrily, Olivia deleted it and tuned back in to Hattie and Miriam's conversation instead, meandering through the tributaries of their lives.

'I tell you what has helped me in life, Hattie,' said Miriam. 'Singing. It lifts my mood no end.'

'It's been a while since I sang,' Hattie replied. 'I used to enjoy it. What sort of songs do you know?'

They discovered they had a love of musicals in common. Ten minutes later, they were singing 'Somewhere' from *West Side Story* together, Hattie moving her open palms from side to side and swaying slightly in her deckchair, her voice gradually growing louder as the song went on.

When it was time to leave, Hattie took Miriam's hand and

shook it, inviting her to come to the beach hut to say hello whenever she felt like it. Miriam thanked her, stepped away from the deckchair and into the path of a cyclist on a trishaw, similar to one you might see on holiday, used for city tours, with an elderly lady sitting in the front compartment. Olivia had seen them before in the town – they were part of a charity that cycled elderly people around so they could still enjoy the outdoors, when they could no longer cycle themselves. What a wonderful idea!

'Hold on, Daisy!' the cyclist yelled before swerving out of the way.

Miriam's hands flew to her mouth. 'I'm so sorry! I walked straight in front of you!'

'You didn't see that one coming,' said Hattie, laughing.

'I'm not a clairvoyant,' Miriam retorted, rolling her eyes.

The cyclist had scruffy, longish hair and was very tanned, as if he spent his whole life outside. He wore a striped T-shirt and denim shorts, socks pulled up and skateboarder shoes. He was a similar age to Olivia, and over his T-shirt he had on a high-visibility tabard. Seated in the front was Daisy, wrapped up in a checked blanket, her white hair blown into messy spaghetti around her head.

'Jesus, Joseph and Mary!' she cried.

'I'm really sorry,' said Miriam again.

'Don't worry. It's not as if I was travelling at speed, so no harm done!' the cyclist said, with a gentle laugh. 'All okay, Daisy?'

'I'll live,' she replied. 'Even longer. I've managed a century already. Are we stopping for a cup of tea then?'

Olivia smiled, quickly poured Daisy a cup of tea and passed it to her, before offering one to the cyclist, who shook his head. He beamed at Hattie, Miriam and Olivia, shuffling forward on his bike seat so he could shake their hands, one by one.

'I'm Seth,' he said. 'Wonderful to meet you all. This is

Daisy, as you might have gathered. I've read about this deckchair for hire. Great idea. Yours, I assume?' He looked at Olivia, directly into her eyes, and smiled a warm, gentle smile.

She smiled back. She liked the fact that he was cycling elderly people around.

Seth ruffled up his hair then rested his hands low on his hips.

'Hang on a minute,' said Miriam, 'I can see someone. A gentleman in uniform.'

'Is it my Albert?' said the old lady, from the trishaw. 'He's been dead thirty years.'

'No, it's a beach warden,' said Miriam. 'Do you think it's about the beach-hut painting?'

'It's fantastic,' said Seth. 'We were admiring it as we cycled. Best thing I've seen in a long time. Is it your work? You look like an arty person.' He fixed Olivia with his gaze.

She found herself blushing. 'Do I?' she asked, deciding it was definitely a compliment. 'No, this is my daughter's work. I think the council's going to tell us it's not allowed.'

They all fell silent and watched the beach warden approach, but he walked straight past and headed to the café for a Mr Whippy with a flake and strawberry sauce. Daisy handed the cup and saucer back to Olivia with a thank you.

'Life is short, break the rules,' Seth said, calling out, 'That's Mark Twain!' before cycling off with Daisy, raising his hand in the air and calling goodbye.

Before Miriam left, Hattie thanked her for coming.

'By the way,' said Miriam, 'I know you don't believe in the same things I believe in, but one thing I'm sure we both share is the knowledge that, even though our loved ones aren't with us in person, they are still with us, here.' She pointed to her heart.

Hattie nodded and smiled. She apologised for being sceptical. 'I hope you don't think I was rude,' she said. 'I mean, we all have different experiences and what do I know?'

'Don't be doolally, Hattie,' Miriam said.

'What did you say?' Hattie asked.

Olivia and Hattie exchanged a look.

'Don't be doolally, Hattie,' Miriam repeated. 'Why?'

'Oh, nothing,' Hattie said, visibly shaken. 'Nothing at all.'

THIRTEEN

At noon, the moth man, Jacob Oxford, arrived. He was short with a bald head, white with sun cream he hadn't rubbed in properly. He wore walking boots, full-length walking trousers and a long-sleeved top in a khaki colour. The sun was beating down, and all around them people were in bikinis or swimming shorts, seeming almost naked in comparison. Olivia put an umbrella over the deckchairs and tried to angle it over Jacob's head while he explained that he was walking around the south-west coastal path in memory of his wife, Linda, while collecting moths. As soon as he sat down, he opened a small wooden box which contained a selection of them. The smell of rubbing alcohol preservative wafted from the box into Olivia's nose as she lingered near the deckchairs, half listening to his explanation of each species.

After about fifteen minutes of explanation in the midday sun, Hattie's eyes were half closing. Olivia gave her a gentle nudge.

'Cream tea?' she asked, placing Hattie's third cup of the day in front of her and placing a small tray of tea and scones near Jacob, who thanked her profusely.

Hattie jerked upright and opened her eyes. Immediately she beamed at Jacob's face. 'So interesting,' she said. 'You must have walked miles.'

Olivia was distracted by her phone vibrating in her pocket. Hoping it would be Beau, she checked to see who it was – Isla. She would call her back.

'I find it hard to sit still,' Jacob said before taking a sip of his tea. 'With my wife gone and being retired now, I've got no reason to be in one place for any length of time anymore.'

'When did your wife die?' said Hattie.

'Six years ago. She had a heart attack.'

'Six years! Gosh. And how are you now?'

'A lot slimmer,' he said with a laugh. 'And I've got through several pairs of walking boots. I've discovered some amazing moths. I've always been interested in them. Moths are often ignored, almost invisible to people compared to butterflies, but they're beautiful if you look closely. Some also adapt to their surroundings, which I find quite inspiring. It's important we try to adapt, Hattie.'

Olivia tried to catch Hattie's eye as she suppressed a yawn.

'Hmmnhmm,' she said.

'There's one called the peppered moth, which changed colour from light to dark during industrialisation for more effective camouflage,' he said. 'You can look at that in two ways. One is that nothing happens without having an effect. And the other is that adapting to a new reality is crucial for survival. Life doesn't stand still – it changes all the time, and we, as humans, must change too. Although I do find my new reality hard to adapt to, even after six years.'

Hattie nodded in agreement. 'I've had to adapt a few times in my life. But it takes time. I read somewhere that it can take seventy years to get over a death.'

'That's us done for!' said Jacob, with a strange laugh.

Olivia smiled at Jacob. He seemed to be a sweet man, his

glasses slightly askew on his face, his moth box on his lap, talking away to Hattie, who was nodding and smiling, albeit with her head resting in her hand.

She mused on the different ways people coped with difficulty. Some shut down, others couldn't stop moving, others still went into denial, others like Elaine headbutted it out of the way. She wondered about her own life: her father's death when she was six, her failed relationship with Oscar and now the death of Jesse. She worked hard at avoiding all of it.

Olivia poured more tea and excused herself to answer the phone, which was vibrating again in her pocket. Hurrying onto the beach, a short distance away from the hut, she sat down on the sand and answered the call. A little boy flying a kite ran past her, following the kite with huge, wide eyes.

'Hello?' said Olivia. 'Isla?'

'Be quiet, Alex!' Isla said. 'I'm on the phone. I'll come back in a minute.'

'You have your hands full.'

'Always,' said Isla. 'There are cookies in that tin, Millie. Okay, so I've got thirty seconds. Hugh saw Oscar. You're right. He is back in the UK. He saw him in Winchester.'

Olivia's heart flipped over. 'Oh God. He's emailed me, Isla, numerous times. I think he saw us in the newspaper or read my stupid deckchair advert, but I've just deleted everything he sends. If things had gone to plan, I'd be in Dublin now and not having to think about this.'

'When does anything go to plan?' Isla said. 'Margot, be careful – you're going to fall! And who's to say he wouldn't have found you in Dublin?'

'But it would have been much harder and I wouldn't still be here,' said Olivia. 'If I was there, I'd be anonymous – I'd melt into the environment, camouflaged like the peppered moth.'

'Like the *what*?' said Isla. 'HENRY, WILL YOU STOP THAT! Oh, I've got to go, I think Henry has put a piece of Lego up his nose. Reply to one of Oscar's emails and tell him to go away and leave you alone. He was quick enough to leave before and reject both you and Beau. He can't come back expecting anything from you now.'

Olivia ended the call, feeling sick, and returned to the deckchairs, where Jacob had pulled up his top and was showing Hattie a tattoo he'd had done of his wife's name across his right pectoral muscle, outlined by an illustration of a moth. Hattie had on her glasses and was leaning towards Jacob, peering at his wrinkled chest.

'You should get one,' said Jacob. 'It doesn't hurt a bit. Not compared to what we've been through.'

'Do you know what?' said Hattie. 'I think I will.'

Next up was glamorous Glenda. Tall and slim, she was dressed in a polka-dot jumpsuit and wedge heels. Her hair was slicked back, Bolshoi ballerina style, and she wore huge sunglasses that covered half her cheeks and her eyebrows.

'You look like Sophia Loren,' said Hattie, rising from the chair to shake Glenda's hand.

'And you look like the vicar's wife,' said Glenda without missing a beat, studying Hattie from over the top of her sunglasses. 'But you'll scrub up well.'

'Oh,' said Hattie with a nervous laugh. 'Vicar's wife isn't quite what I was aiming for, but I don't care so much anymore what I look like. Not since Jesse died.'

Olivia's heart cracked a little.

'Well, you damn well should!' said Glenda. 'With a figure like yours, you could wear almost anything.'

'Figure like mine!' said Hattie, hooting with laughter.

'Yes,' said Glenda. 'You're beautiful.'

'Hardly,' Hattie said, quivering with embarrassment as she played with the beads on her necklace.

Olivia cleared her throat. 'Who's for tea?' she asked, putting down a pot on the table in front of Glenda and Hattie.

At the sight of the teapot, Hattie paled. Glenda sighed, picked up the teapot, took off the lid and poured the liquid away around the back of the beach hut, before emptying the contents of a bottle of rosé wine into it.

'Just because we're seventy something doesn't mean we have to act like old bats,' she said. 'I strongly believe that alongside whatever hell you're going through, you can still have a good time. I look at it like this: there are two buckets, one which is for our sad, unhappy feelings, the other for our happy feelings. When you're sad, you have to work hard to keep the other bucket topped up, but they can co-exist and should co-exist. I run a mobile drinks van for older people's events. The line-dancing crowd are wild. Most of them are widows and widowers, and boy, do they let their hair down when they get together. Our generation needs to keep active and let off steam. We're so buttoned-up in this country. Try this, Hattie – ARGH!'

Glenda placed her hands on her diaphragm and let out a scream. People on the beach turned to stare.

Hattie reddened, smiled at her sweetly and gave a little laugh.

'Too soon?' asked Glenda.

Hattie nodded. 'Maybe later – my throat's a bit sore from singing earlier,' she said, looking at Olivia with a desperate expression.

Olivia tried to distract Glenda by asking her about her working life. Glenda said that she used to run laughter therapy workshops, which worked a treat when people were feeling down in the dumps. Olivia wondered if she could benefit from trying one herself.

'You start with literally laughing,' said Glenda. 'Even if you're not laughing at anything funny, just the act of laughing has physical benefits. You should try it, Hattie, and you, Olivia.

Life's too short for worrying – it gets us absolutely nowhere and nothing besides a wrinkled forehead. And as for a glass of wine, I think a little decadence in the day doesn't hurt anyone too much.'

'I'm not sure,' said Hattie. 'It's not really for me, drinking in the day. I prefer to be in control.'

'I dare you,' said Glenda. 'When did you last have a drink in the day?'

Olivia's palms began to sweat. They didn't have a good history with alcohol – Michael had been killed by a drink driver and Oscar... well, Oscar.

Hattie screwed up her face, thinking long and hard. 'I went through a period of drinking in the day when I was about forty,' she said.

Olivia cast her mind back and did the maths. That was after her father had died. She shuddered at the memory and quickly pushed it from her thoughts.

'That's my girl!' said Glenda.

'No, no, it wasn't fun,' said Hattie, frowning. 'I was rather depressed. I didn't have any counselling – we didn't really, back then. I just coped with it all on my own and started to use alcohol in the wrong way. I'm ashamed of myself really.'

'We've all been there,' said Glenda, leaning forward and gripping Hattie's hand with hers. 'But if you can drag yourself through your darkest day, the sun always rises. I did read about your husband. I'm so sorry. Do you miss him terribly? When my husband and I divorced and I found myself alone, I enjoyed a lot of it. Having the house to myself, eating what I wanted, not having to tell anyone where I was going, but I missed the physical side.' She leaned forward and said in a loud whisper, 'The sex.'

Hattie drained her cup of wine, the cup pressed so close to her face, Olivia could only see her raised eyebrows above the rim.

Olivia cleared her throat again.

'How did you meet Jesse?' Glenda asked, filling up both their teacups with more wine.

'I met him when I was seventeen at a party on the beach, not too far from here.'

Olivia listened as Hattie told her story of meeting Jesse, then Michael and everything that had happened afterwards.

'I think Francine poisoned her son against me,' Hattie concluded, drinking more wine.

'Bitch!' said Glenda. 'I hate women who hate women.'

'I don't think she hated women,' said Hattie. 'Just me for some reason.'

'Was it because you poached her husband?' asked Glenda with a bark of laughter. 'The woman who my partner met and married was welcome to him!'

'No,' sighed Hattie. 'I didn't poach him, as you crudely put it. I told you: I pushed him back to her twice. I told him no; I stopped all contact. I did a lot of rejecting before I stopped putting everyone else first. It was quite torturous. I don't like to think about it. I lost a very dear friend. Pour me some more wine, will you, Glenda?'

Olivia worried about Hattie drinking – she hadn't had alcohol for ages – and put down a glass of water next to her 'tea'.

Half an hour later, Glenda and Hattie were at the water's edge, Hattie rolling up her trousers to her milk-white knees, Glenda stripping off her jumpsuit to reveal a black costume.

'Is this a good idea?' Olivia asked, hovering by the edge of the sea. 'I don't think when you've been drinking alcohol, swimming is ever a good idea.'

'According to...?' said Glenda, hands on her hips.

'Absolutely everyone? Honestly, Glenda, you could have a heart attack, or drown, or anything!'

'We're not swimming, for heaven's sake; we're paddling. Relax! Don't be a fun sponge, dear. Come on, Hattie.'

Olivia watched Hattie walk unsteadily into the sea, sighed and kicked off her flip-flops, so she could hold Hattie's hand as she paddled. The water was calm, warm, the sand soft under their toes.

'Oh dear,' Hattie said, turning to face Olivia, her eyes moist with tears. 'It's bringing back memories of the day Jesse died. He must have been in such pain.' She patted her eyes with a tissue that she pulled from her sleeve.

'I don't think he knew much about it, Mum,' said Olivia, squeezing Hattie's hand.

'Right, I'm going all the way in,' said Glenda, lowering her voice to a loud whisper. 'When I'm in, I'm going to have a skinny-dip, so don't be alarmed!'

'Careful!' said Hattie. 'It's so cold! There are fish in there!'

'The cold water is good for you – have you not seen Wim Hof and all those celebrities on television?' Glenda replied, striding in up to her waist. There, she crouched down, her shoulders under the water, and peeled off her swimsuit. The sea was completely transparent, and Olivia and Hattie didn't know where to look.

Once she'd taken off her swimsuit, Glenda spun it around her head like a lasso. Olivia and Hattie stared at each other, their eyes wide. Olivia's heart was in her mouth. Luckily there was nobody else in that stretch of water.

'Would you believe the gall of the woman?' Hattie said, chuckling, while Glenda swam a few quick strokes, shrieking at the cold, before pulling her swimsuit back on and running out of the water, laughing madly.

'You could have had a heart attack!' said Olivia. 'Or given us one!'

'I could get run over by a bus, struck by lightning or get a terminal illness,' said Glenda. 'The fear of what might happen isn't going to stop me enjoying myself. In fact, the fear of what might happen motivates me to enjoy myself more. I'm trying paragliding next week. Want to come, Hattie?'

'Um,' said Hattie. 'I'm not sure about that, I have to be honest.'

'Well, why don't you come and watch me at least? Right now, though, I fancy another glass of wine. Who's joining me? Hey, I think we should make this a regular thing, Hats!'

Glenda jogged ahead of them, her slim, tall frame, youthful and strong. Hattie pushed her arm through Olivia's, and they looked at one another in alarm.

'Hats,' Hattie said, laughing. 'I haven't been called that in a while.'

'I think Glenda's got a wild streak,' Olivia replied with a smile, feeling slightly envious. Wouldn't it be lovely to let her hair down? Olivia felt it had been such a long time since she'd really enjoyed herself.

'I rather like her,' said Hattie, her eyes sparkling. 'She's a breath of fresh air, isn't she?'

A hurricane more like, thought Olivia, watching Glenda push her feet into her wedges and apply a new coat of lipstick.

FOURTEEN

Early evening, the deckchairs packed away, Olivia helped an inebriated Hattie into bed, where she collapsed onto the mattress with an enormous sigh. Olivia switched on the bedside lamp, disturbing a moth that had settled on the pleated pink lampshade. It fluttered away and landed on the wallpaper, where it was lost in the busy floral pattern.

'The thing is, Olivia,' Hattie mumbled, 'there's nothing in life so certain as death – it's the one thing we know will definitely happen, but when it does happen, it's the most dreadfully painful shock. It's hard to believe that the person you love isn't there anymore. I miss saying goodnight to Jesse, asking him if he'd locked the back door, whether the bathroom light was out – you know, the ordinary things. He used to make the bed so warm too. It's so cold now, like stepping into a fridge.'

Olivia smiled sadly and nodded, glancing at the framed photograph of Jesse on the bedside table. Next to his photo was a shell with his wedding ring inside.

'Would you like a hot-water bottle?' Olivia asked, but Hattie shook her head and closed her eyes. Her mother's white hair was camouflaged against the white cotton pillowcase, making her look as if she was just a face. In the last year, she had aged ten. Olivia blinked and gave Hattie's hand a gentle squeeze, whispering goodnight.

'Goodnight,' Hattie replied before turning onto her side and falling into a deep, snoring sleep.

Olivia glanced at the empty pillow next to Hattie and sighed. She left two paracetamol and a glass of water on the bedside table and, as she went to turn off the lamp, noticed a wooden box on the floor. Opening it, she found a photo album and a few handwritten letters.

She carried the box to the kitchen and furtively read the contents of a letter from Francine, who'd written to Hattie about how she wished she hadn't married Jesse, about how she wanted to get a divorce. Olivia wondered if she'd done the right thing trying to contact Francine – but it sounded as though they'd been through a lot together as young people, and it was clear that Hattie still thought of her often.

She closed the lid of the box and returned it to Hattie's bedside, then quickly checked every room – she wasn't sure what for – locked the front door behind her and walked out into the garden.

It was one of those lovely August evenings where the air smelled of sea salt and jasmine and sun cream and the sky was a vibrant palette of pink, blue and violet. Because she'd had some of Glenda's wine, Olivia would need to leave her camper van at Hattie's house and walk home, but she didn't mind. It was the perfect evening to be outside and clear her head.

Walking along the clifftop, she thought about the day, hoping that Hattie had enjoyed some of it, but before too long, Oscar shoved his way into her thoughts, making her stomach clench in discomfort. She imagined him in Winchester, repeatedly checking his email for her reply. He wasn't a patient man. He'd probably sent a dozen more by now, despite the subject of the last one she'd seen. Not for the first time, she wished she was miles away, starting a new life.

'Need a lift?' said a male voice from behind her.

She spun round and there, on his trishaw, was Seth – the man from earlier. He was beaming expectantly.

Olivia hesitated.

'Where are you going?' he asked. 'I know all the shortcuts. I have "the knowledge" for cyclists. Give me an address, I'll take you there.' Seth tapped his head as if inside he held all the answers.

Olivia explained she was going to walk to Avenue Road, where she needed to look at a garage door.

'Garage door? Now that sounds interesting,' he said with a laugh. 'Jump in. There's a blanket there, to keep your knees warm.'

She gave him a sideways glance. 'I'm not that old!'

'No, I wasn't suggesting that you were... I...' he stuttered. 'I think even young knees get cold.'

She laughed. 'Don't worry, I am almost fifty.' She pulled a face.

Seth shook his head. 'I don't believe it. Impossible.'

She climbed into the bicycle seat and pulled the blanket over her knees, listening as Seth cycled and talked about his own fiftieth year, where he'd promised himself he'd do fifty new things – one a week – all year, but he stopped at week four, saying the whole experiment was too exhausting.

When cycling uphill, he became gradually quieter, then silent, and Olivia sat up as straight as possible, trying to distribute her weight in the lightest way, imagining beads of sweat rolling down Seth's forehead as he cycled on determinedly.

'Are you okay? Shall I get off? I feel too guilty,' she said before they reached the top of the hill, Seth breathing heavily. 'Your legs must be like steel, all this cycling you do.'

But Seth just kept going.

They reached the top of the hill and he took a swig from his water bottle and wiped the sweat from his forehead with his forearm. 'It's the only way to travel,' he said, setting off again and taking the next left.

'Ah, we're here, Avenue Road. Any particular address?'

Olivia inelegantly climbed off the bike, saying that it wasn't far and she'd walk the final stretch. She pointed vaguely ahead towards the close at the far end of the quiet tree-lined street.

'I really enjoyed that,' she said. 'Haven't cycled for ages. I'd forgotten how much I love it. Not that I actually cycled just then, but you know what I mean.'

'Do you have a bike?' Seth asked.

Olivia shook her head, thinking of the bike Oscar had ruined when he'd stamped on the wheel. She'd never got it fixed or bought a new one.

'My mate and I run a bike shop,' Seth said. 'It's what I do for a living. You should come in and see if anything catches your eye. We do social cycles too on a Wednesday evening depending on the weather. It's all on Instagram. It would be great to see you there.' He fished in his bag for his business card and handed it to her.

She glanced at his full name. 'Maybe I will, Seth Price,' she said, tucking the card into her bag.

He dipped his hand back into his bag and pulled out a small boat, made from driftwood, with a triangle of white fabric for a sail. He handed it to her. 'They're just these little things I make from driftwood and bits I find on the beach. Often give them to the old folk, but maybe you'd like this one?'

Olivia studied it and grinned. 'Thanks, I love it. And thanks for the lift – that was fun. I better go and see this door. My daughter has apparently done some sort of artwork on it and people have complained.' She rolled her eyes and sighed.

'Like the beach hut?' he asked. 'If I had a beach hut, I'd

want her to paint mine. Maybe a bike, or a guitar, or a plate of waffles. I love waffles, with a mountain of fruit and lashings of maple syrup, even a bit of crispy bacon if I'm going wild.'

Olivia laughed and stood awkwardly for a moment, wondering whether he would go. But he didn't leave. He didn't seem to want to. So Olivia turned and started to walk down Avenue Road and he walked by her side, pushing his bike, still talking about waffles and toppings.

As they approached the garages, the one Beau had painted came into view, stopping Olivia in her tracks. Beau had painted a beautiful image of a surfer in the waves, with a huge sun setting behind him. It was fantastic but stuck out a mile against the other white-painted doors and was directly overlooked by the downstairs flat in the opposite block.

'She's so talented,' said Seth, grinning widely. 'What a great mural. Wow!'

Olivia felt both proud and desperately concerned. If Beau was doing this, without Olivia even knowing or without her even feeling the need to tell, what else was she doing?

Taking a deep breath, Olivia knocked on the door of the flat opposite and a woman around Olivia's age came to the door, dressed in denim shorts, a white sun top and flip-flops. From inside the house came the sound of children and a dog barking. Olivia explained, apologetically, that it had been Beau who'd painted the door and clenched her jaw, ready for an onslaught.

'Hello there!' said Seth, leaning in to shake the woman's hand before she could reply. 'I'm Seth. Olivia's friend. I was blown away by your garage door!'

Olivia's friend. Seth's words rang in Olivia's ears, and she wondered why she'd heard them so clearly.

'Sorry, yes,' said Olivia. 'This is Seth.'

'I'm Beth,' the woman said, a little confused, but shaking Seth's hand enthusiastically. 'Isn't it wonderful? Beau asked me if I'd like it done. She knows that my youngest son, Ralph, doesn't leave the house very much. He has a skin condition, which means he has an extreme sensitivity to sunlight, so he spends a lot of his time during the day in the summer months in this room overlooking the garages. My eldest, Matthew, is a friend of Beau's. Lovely girl. Such a talent. I did try to pay her, but she would only accept the money for the paint. Didn't she tell you about it?'

Olivia felt her eyes moisten. She felt insanely proud but also guilty.

'It was just that a community police officer came to the door...' she started to explain. 'Asked us to clean it off, so I didn't know if you'd complained and whether Beau had permission, although she told me there was nothing to worry about.' She felt Seth's eyes on her.

Beth pointed to the flat above her and rolled her eyes. 'Probably because of her upstairs,' she said. 'Complains about everything! She's got nothing better to do. But it's my garage and I'll do what I like with it. Ralph loves it. He can't get down to the sea, but he can at least look at this beautiful artwork and imagine he's there...'

Beth's voice cracked and she stopped speaking, putting the back of her hand against her lips and shaking her head a little bit, rolling her eyes at herself.

Olivia reached over and briefly touched her arm.

From the hallway behind Beth, a teenage boy emerged, six-foot at least, with black hair, piercings and a black T-shirt.

'Matthew, this is Beau's mum,' said Beth.

'Hi, Beau's mum,' he said. 'You must be the one who rented Beau's granddad's deckchair out. Cool idea. Beau's been posting about it.'

'Yes, hi,' said Olivia. 'That's right. She's at Wren's this evening.'

'Wren's here,' said Beth. 'She's Matthew's girlfriend.'

'Did someone call me?' said Wren, coming to the doorway.

'Oh, hi, Olivia.'

'Hi, Wren,' said Olivia, her scalp prickling. 'I thought Beau was staying with you tonight? I thought you were doing your art project?'

Wren's expression changed. She looked suddenly sheepish and mumbled something about their plans changing last minute but that Beau hadn't told her exactly where she was going.

The hairs on Olivia's neck stood to attention. 'So do you know where she is or not?' she snapped.

Wren shrugged and shook her head and didn't look Olivia in the eye. 'She didn't say much. Maybe she's at someone else's? She's done more of these murals. People ask her online. Through Instagram. Maybe she's doing that. She did mention a man who'd been in touch.'

'Oh God,' said Olivia, her mind going into overdrive. 'What man? If you hear from her, please can you ask her to get in touch with me?'

Wren studied her fingernails. Beth and Olivia shared a concerned glance. Seth cleared his throat.

'Can I help at all, Olivia?' he said. 'Take you somewhere on the bike?'

Olivia felt dread creep into her heart. Instantly, she blamed herself for not taking enough notice of where Beau had said she was going and failing to question her more. She'd been so busy with Hattie and with the constant anxiety she felt about Oscar turning up on the doorstep, she'd ignored her daughter.

'I'm a bad mother,' she said when she walked away from Beth's house.

Seth gave her a quizzical look. 'I doubt that. You're a great daughter – I've seen how you are with your mum, so I can't imagine you're a bad mother. They're both lucky to have you.'

But Olivia wasn't listening. She was heading quickly home, pulling her phone from her pocket and tapping out a message to Beau.

Where are you?

At Wren's.

Please phone me. I know you're not at Wren's.

I'm with another friend.

Who are you with?

I'm fine. Stop worrying.

Olivia's heart pounded in her chest. She called Beau's phone, but Beau didn't answer. She left a message telling her to call. Tried again, willing her to pick up. This time Beau answered and immediately hung up.

As she reached the front door and unlocked it with a trembling hand, various scenarios played out in Olivia's head. How many awful stories had she read about young people meeting someone online who they thought was their age and then being assaulted or worse? She couldn't help her mind going to the most awful dark places.

'Are you any good with social media, Seth?' Olivia asked. 'I need to check my daughter's Instagram account.'

'I know how to use Instagram,' he said. 'I use it at the bike shop. Do you know her passwords?'

'I think she has them saved on her laptop,' she said, going inside.

Seth hovered on the doorstep behind her. 'Should I wait here?' he asked.

'Come in,' she said. 'Your bike will be fine outside. If you wait in the living room, you can see it from the window. I'll get Beau's laptop from her bedroom.'

Seth seemed to fill the entire hallway. He knocked into the

radiator cover and sent a glass jar of loose change flying. He caught it just before it hit the floor, apologising repeatedly, coins scattering all over the floorboards.

Olivia was hardly aware of him – dread had given her tunnel vision.

Pushing open Beau's door, she moved to her unmade bed, strewn with clothing, and picked up jumpers, jeans and socks until she located the laptop buried beneath. She powered it on, then carried it downstairs and logged on to Instagram.

'Where do I find the messages?' she asked. 'Which one is it, Seth?' Olivia's hands were shaking.

Seth moved a little closer and apologised when his arm brushed against Olivia's elbow. 'That one,' he said. 'The triangular icon.'

Olivia clicked on it and scanned the messages. There were dozens, from names she didn't recognise, some of them asking about mural painting, others from friends talking about meeting and others still about the deckchair hire.

'I can't find anything,' she said, feeling desperate as she scrolled down further. 'Can they be deleted?'

'Yes,' Seth said. 'Have you checked the comments on her posts?'

Olivia scrolled through Beau's recent posts about the deckchairs and the painting of Hattie she'd done on the beach hut. There were dozens of comments – but nothing about a meeting.

Tears pricked Olivia's eyes. She leaned her head back into the sofa and exhaled.

'Does she have the Find My Phone app?' asked Seth. 'You could find out where she is from that. It uses GPS.'

Olivia frowned. 'Yes – she used to at least. Unless she's disabled it.'

She checked the app, blood rushing in her ears. The dot

moved around the screen until it settled on a street in Winchester.

'Winchester!' she shouted, leaping up from her seat. That could only mean one thing: Oscar.

'Oh Christ! Seth, do you have a car, or could you drive mine if we went back to collect it? I've had a drink – I can't drive.'

Seth also leaped up from the seat. His eyes were shining with concern. 'No,' he said. 'I don't drive – never learned. I've always gone everywhere by bike, foot or public transport. Sorry.'

'I need to get to Winchester,' she said. 'Now!'

She called Beau's number again, but it went straight to voicemail. Olivia gave a strangled sob.

Seth, utterly confused, rested a hand on her shoulder. 'What can I do?' he asked. 'Call you a taxi? Or check the train timetable? Is she in danger? Do you want me to call the police?'

'Not the police,' she said. 'I just need to get there. Now.'

He pulled his phone from his pocket and dialled the taxi firm, but there was a recorded message. He put his phone on speaker: 'Due to a driver shortage, we are experiencing high demand. Please book your journey well in advance.'

'Train then,' she said, grabbing her bag.

Seth followed.

Olivia locked the front door and stood on the pavement for a moment, feeling bewildered and trying to look up the train times, when Alec's Mercedes pulled up. He lowered a window and peered at her over his sunglasses.

'Alec?' she said. 'What are you doing here?'

'That message you sent for my mother,' he replied. 'I came to ask you to kindly refrain from trying to contact her.'

'What? What are you talking about?'

'Hi,' said Seth, holding up his hand in a salute. 'I'm Seth. Olivia's friend.'

Alec nodded briskly. Olivia rushed to the passenger door of Alec's car and opened it, sliding into the seat.

'Can you give me a lift?' she said. 'To Winchester? My car's not here and I need to get there urgently. I'll pay you.'

'But, I'm...' he started, taken aback. 'I was going to... I have an important...'

'Please, Alec,' she said. 'Whatever it is, this is more important. Beau's in trouble. I wouldn't ask unless I was absolutely desperate. I'll explain on the way.'

Alec's cheeks flushed with irritation, but Olivia didn't care. She wasn't getting out.

'If you don't drive, I'll scream until you do,' she said.

'No need for that,' he said. 'For heaven's sake!'

They left Seth on the pavement outside her house. She turned to give him a quick wave and he smiled, climbing back onto his bike.

Digging in her bag for her phone to message Beau, she sent sand flying into the footwell of Alec's immaculate car. He tutted, but Olivia ignored him. With trembling hands, she sent Beau a message: *I know you're with Oscar. Please call me.*

Then came Beau's reply: *He's told me everything. He wants you to give him another chance.*

Thoughts spun and clashed in Olivia's head. What exactly had he told Beau?

She tried to regulate her breathing. The battery on her phone was low. She took down the street name of Beau's location and tried to open her emails, so she could find Oscar's. But she'd permanently deleted them. Tears slipped down her cheeks. She didn't know how she was going to get out of this situation.

Alec looked at her from the corner of his eye. They drove in silence, but he pressed a button and the glove compartment opened to reveal a box of tissues. She glanced at him before reaching for a tissue and holding it against her leaking eyes.

He's told me everything. He wants you to give him another chance.

FIFTEEN

When they were together, Olivia lost count of the chances she gave Oscar. But despite Oscar's promises, his behaviour didn't change. He did the same things over and over, like a slot car on a loop-the-loop racing track. And each time he fell back into his old ways, Olivia's heart hardened a fraction.

She'd turned herself inside out trying to help him, to cover his back, support him, find reasons to justify his anger. But whatever she did, however much she tried to fix him, it failed. After being sure she was going to end things with him on the night he'd stamped on the bike wheel, Olivia started to worry that, if she broke up with him, he'd fall into an even worse depression, or have an episode of extreme anger and do something stupid.

'He never has to take responsibility for what he says and does,' Isla told her. 'By the sounds of things, he really lost it this time. He needs to sort out whatever's making him angry. You need to protect yourself and get away from him.'

'He wasn't like this to start with,' Olivia replied. 'I don't think he means what he says or does. His anger is the result of his frustration, his sadness, his vulnerability. He's suffering – I know he is.'

'So are you. You need to put yourself first. Your kindness won't change him. He can't use his problems to control the way your relationship goes.'

'I understand what you're saying and I do agree with you,' Olivia said, seeing Oscar with more clarity than ever before. 'I'm going to give him just one last chance, then that's it. Over.'

'He doesn't deserve one last anything,' Isla replied. 'He'll let you down.'

Isla was right – he did let her down again, this time at Hattie's birthday meal at an expensive fish restaurant in Poole. She'd planned to meet Oscar there, but before going out for dinner, she'd felt nauseous and, worried about the fact that her period was late, had taken a pregnancy test.

'Oh my God, oh my God,' she said repeatedly, her heart in her mouth.

She sat on the toilet in the bathroom, clutching the stick and staring at the bold blue lines. Positive. Her forehead pricked with sweat and her eyes filled with tears. Trying to work out the dates in her head, she realised the pregnancy must be two months in. Their usual form of contraception had obviously failed. She thought of ringing Oscar to tell him before the meal but stopped herself. For now, she needed the news to sink in. She needed time to think.

Oscar arrived at the restaurant late, just before Olivia was going to suggest they order without him. She knew immediately, by the way he flung open the restaurant door, that he'd been drinking heavily. Her face burned. She waved at him half-heartedly, despite wanting to slip under the table and hide. He staggered over, pulling out his chair so aggressively the table wobbled, and a glass of sparkling water fell over and spilled on Olivia's new dress.

'Oscar!' she cried, leaping up. 'My dress!'

'What?' he snapped. 'It's only water.'

'Don't worry,' she said, quickly recovering. 'I'm fine. I'll be fine. It's just a dress.'

'It's a beautiful dress,' Hattie said, helping to soak up the spilled water with napkins. Then she raised her hand to call the waiter.

'Another sparkling water for my daughter, please,' she said before gesturing vaguely in Oscar's direction. 'And I think we need a jug of tap water on the table, please.'

'And I'll have a beer,' Oscar said.

'Haven't you had enough?' Jesse asked.

Hattie crossed her arms across her chest, narrowed her eyes at Oscar and frowned. Olivia's heart pumped in her ears.

'I'm not a child,' said Oscar. 'Kindly don't tell me what to do.'

'It was a suggestion. Calm down, son,' Jesse said.

'I'm not your son,' Oscar said. 'Oh, hang on a minute, your son won't come out with you because he doesn't like your wife. Not surprised.' He laughed a slurry laugh.

Olivia took a sharp intake of breath and pulled an embarrassed and apologetic face at Hattie. 'Oscar!' she hissed, her eyes stinging. She pushed his foot under the table, and he kicked out at her, whacking her ankle. She bent down to rub it, noticing a muddy mark on her suede ankle boots.

'Jesus, Oscar,' she said, at which point the waiter brought Oscar's pint of beer.

He drank it down in one go. Hattie stroked an invisible mark on the tablecloth and Jesse put down his menu, his expression stony.

'I think you should go,' he said.

'What?' Oscar replied. 'I've just got here.'

'It's Mum's birthday – don't ruin it for her,' said Olivia, Isla's words ringing in her ears. 'Couldn't you for once not behave like this? I've asked you so many times, so many, to get a grip on this problem. I've had it with you. Especially now... today... when I've just...' The news almost burst out of her, but she broke down in tears before she could get the words out.

Oscar banged his fist against the table.

'Oscar!' said Jesse. 'Stop this! Just get out.'

'She's turning on the bloody waterworks again!' he said, pushing his chair back, making a loud scraping sound on the floor. 'I'm more than happy to go.'

He pushed his hand into Olivia's bag and took out her car keys, then staggered towards the door and tripped on the restaurant steps, falling over. When he raised his head, his cheek was grazed and bleeding.

A waiter came to his assistance, but Oscar pushed him away and stormed towards the car park.

'Oh my God,' Olivia said, blushing madly. 'What's he doing? He's got my keys!'

'He can't drive, bloody fool!' said Hattie, standing up. 'He's out of control!'

Jesse put his hand on Olivia's arm. 'I'll go.'

'No, I will. He's my problem – I'll deal with it,' said Olivia, her stomach in a tight knot as she ran between the tables of diners after him.

'Oscar!' she cried, pulling at his arm, but he was strong and shook her off. 'I demand you give me those keys back,' she said, gripping his arm again.

'If you get in that car,' she said through tears, 'that's it forever. We're finished.'

The image of her positive pregnancy test blazed across her thoughts. The words were on the tip of her tongue.

'I'm seeing someone else anyway,' he said, climbing into the driver's seat and slamming the door. 'I've got another girlfriend

– it's time you knew. She wants us to go to New Zealand together.'

Olivia hardly heard what he said. Memories of the day her dad died flooded her mind, and all she could think about was stopping Oscar from driving.

She stood in front of the car, hands on the bonnet, but Oscar pressed one hand down hard on the horn and left it there, so that the entire restaurant, forks in mid-air, turned to stare out at them through the windows.

Jesse and Hattie were outside now, telling Oscar to be sensible for heaven's sake, to stop, to get out of the car, for Olivia to move away, to leave him be.

A couple of waiters were asking what was going on, and in all the confusion, as Oscar turned on the engine, Olivia ran around to the passenger side and flung the door open.

She climbed inside and rested her hand on his forearm. 'Stop,' she said. 'Please, Oscar, think about this. Let me talk to you.'

She took a deep breath.

I'm pregnant, she thought about screaming. *I'm pregnant!* But again, something stopped her.

'Please. Give me the keys, Oscar,' she said. 'Remember what happened to my dad?'

Oscar shrugged and suddenly reversed out of the car park in a zigzag line. The tyres screeched on the road.

'Please!' she said. 'Pull over!'

Oscar's hands were tightly wound around the steering wheel. Nothing was going to deter him.

He started to drive too fast up the road – a quiet road, thank God. Olivia gripped the car seat and glanced out the window at Hattie and Jesse, who were clinging to each other in the car park. Jesse was getting out his phone – Olivia knew he'd be calling the police.

Tears were leaking down Oscar's face now, and his foot was pressing harder on the accelerator.

'I'm sorry, Olivia,' he wept. 'I'm sorry I'm such a waste of space. I'm sorry I got angry and wrecked your bike wheel. I didn't mean to do that!'

'You get so angry, Oscar,' Olivia said, a feeling of utter dread washing over her. 'I'm just scared of what might happen.'

'I'm sorry,' he wept. 'I would never hurt you.'

'You're hurting me now, doing this,' she said. 'Please, just stop driving.'

The speedometer needle continued to climb. In that moment, she thought she was going to die, that they were both going to die and that this was Oscar's intention.

Olivia felt utterly helpless, powerless. She realised this was how she'd felt for most of their relationship and was suddenly filled with rage.

'STOP,' she screamed. 'STOP NOW.'

'I don't care anymore!' he said. 'I don't care!'

Out of nowhere, a child on a bright-blue scooter wheeled out into the road. He was no more than four years old – a shock of blond curls, his mother hot on his heels, screaming at him to get on the pavement.

Olivia gasped then grabbed hold of the steering wheel and turned it sharply right, so that the car spun across the opposite side of the road, narrowly avoiding a lamp post. It came to a crashing halt in a hedge.

'Oscar,' said Olivia calmly. 'What the hell are you doing? You nearly killed that child!'

'Christ!' Oscar whimpered, banging his head against the steering wheel. 'I'm sorry. I'm so sorry. I just want to go home. I need to go.'

Home. He meant New Zealand.

A moment of shocked silence passed between them.

Olivia glanced behind the car. The child was fine, pulled

into the arms of his mother, who was crouched on the pavement.

Olivia had started shaking violently when Oscar suddenly opened the car door and, without looking back or saying another word, got out and ran up the road, away from the car.

'Oscar!' she cried, her voice strangled.

She waited a moment for him to return, but he didn't. He'd left. Abandoned her.

The police arrived soon after – Jesse had called them, explained that Oscar was driving drunk and given them the car registration.

Olivia was lost for words. Eventually, she said, yes, Oscar had driven the car out of the restaurant car park but that she'd quickly talked him into pulling over and letting her drive. He'd got out and she'd carried on driving, swerving out of the way when a little boy had scooted onto the road.

The police breathalysed her, but she hadn't had any alcohol. There were no witnesses other than the mother, who'd been talking on her phone when her son swerved onto the road and she hadn't seen who was driving or what had happened until it was almost too late.

'I'm so sorry,' Olivia apologised to the little boy's mother, who, also in shock, slapped Olivia across the face. She raised her hand to her cheek and felt the heat of her skin. Oscar was nowhere in sight.

She could have told the police the truth, that he'd been drink driving, dangerously, but she didn't. Even though he'd abandoned her, even though he could have killed a child, even though he'd ruined Hattie's birthday, even though he'd admitted to having another girlfriend, she'd protected him. Enough was enough. It was time to be strong. Not only for herself, but for the baby growing inside her.

. . .

When Oscar had sobered up and returned to their flat later that night, Olivia told him the relationship was over, for good. Her voice cracked with anger and hurt when she said the words, 'You're a coward and I've given you too many chances. I don't love you.'

He told her he was moving back to New Zealand.

She shrugged, catching the inside of her cheek in her teeth and pressing down on the soft flesh. 'I think it'll be easier if we don't see or contact each other ever again. For our entire lives. It's the only way I can move forward.'

'Whatever you want,' he said. 'I don't care.'

While he started to pack, Olivia lay down. The chaos of the day had caught up with her and she felt sick, trembling with what might have been.

The image of the little boy on the scooter flashed into her thoughts. She felt a rush of bile in her throat and raced to the toilet, where she fell to her knees and threw up in the loo.

Sweating profusely, she washed her face and waited in the bathroom in case she was going to be sick again. She jumped when she looked in the mirror and saw Oscar standing behind her. He was holding the pregnancy stick, which she'd buried in the bathroom dustbin, intending to empty it that evening.

'Is this yours?' he said. 'Are you...?'

Olivia looked into Oscar's eyes, scared of what she'd find. But in them she saw a glimpse of the man she'd met two years before – a spark of fire and, deeper, an unreachable sorrow. She opened her mouth to speak, but no words came out.

Oscar fell to his knees and clasped his hands together, as if in prayer. 'I can change,' he said quietly. 'Olivia, really, I can be better. You know I can. I've been a mess. I've blamed you, I know, for my mess. You're right about my mum leaving affecting me. I'm sorry. We can try again. If you have a baby, I will change, I promise you. Please give me one more chance.'

One more chance.

Olivia's thoughts returned to the wretched emptiness she'd felt when he ran away from the car. Who would do that? Only someone too frightened to take responsibility.

She shook her head. 'False alarm,' she lied. 'I've got my period. I'm not pregnant.'

It was a lie she kept going for fifteen years. She'd never told Oscar about the baby girl she'd had seven months after he'd left for New Zealand with his new girlfriend, and she'd left his name off the birth certificate. And she'd told her friends another lie; that she'd told Oscar about the pregnancy but that he'd left her for another woman and wasn't interested in having a child.

'He abandoned me,' she'd said, lapping up their comforting words, feeling on some level that she deserved them.

With Beau, she'd stuck to the same lie – her father was a man who didn't want to be a father, that he'd rejected them and left for another life overseas.

'Didn't he even want to know me or see a photograph of me?' Beau had asked when she was a small child.

It had broken Olivia's heart to see Beau feel rejected and left her feeling wracked with guilt and self-doubt, but she'd held on to the belief that, ultimately, she was protecting her daughter from the grip of an angry, emotionally manipulative coward. That the lie showed strength, not weakness.

SIXTEEN

The interior of Alec's car smelled faintly of vanilla. Olivia felt sick with worry, and the vanilla wasn't helping. She opened the window a fraction.

'Do you mind?' Alec asked, closing it again. 'It'll disrupt the air conditioning.'

Alec's phone was buzzing in his pocket, but he ignored it. Olivia wondered vaguely who it was – she didn't know anything about his life.

Her eyes were still streaming with tears. She opened the glove compartment for another tissue and scanned the contents: the car's manual, a road map, a packet of extra-strong mints and a CD. She tried to see the title of the CD – *Battling Insecurity in...* something. She moved the map to see. *Love.*

'Can we close this?' Alec said, quickly leaning over and snapping the glove compartment shut. He cleared his throat and leaned back in his seat.

She glanced over at him, noticing his pale skin turning a shade of pale pink.

'I didn't show Mum your email,' he said curtly. 'I don't think you should interfere in this situation. She decided long ago not to have anything to do with your mother.'

Olivia was staring at the speedometer. Her head swam with images of Oscar and Beau talking, of Oscar telling her what he must have worked out – that she was his daughter.

'Can't you go any faster?' she asked. 'I need to get to Beau as quickly as I can.'

'No, I'm at the speed limit,' he said. 'Did you hear what I said about my mother?'

'Yes,' said Olivia vaguely, 'but can't she decide for herself? It's only a conversation.'

Alec gave her a sharp look. 'I should have known you wouldn't understand. It's always been about what Hattie wants, with no consideration for our side of the situation. You have no idea how upset my mother has been over the years – how lonely, how heartbroken.'

'I *can* understand,' said Olivia. 'I just thought it would be good for my mum *and* your mum to put this all behind them now. Is it worth still holding on to a grudge after all these years? I've got bigger things to worry about, really, Alec.'

'The fact is that your mother stole my father from *my* mother,' he snapped. 'My mother's best friend stole her husband – it's very unsavoury. Why do you have to make demands on her now she's old, pulling on her heartstrings in your mawkish way?'

'I don't think your mum has been entirely honest with you,' Olivia replied. 'It sounds like there are things you don't know. She's told you her version of events to keep you close. Could you turn right here?'

They were close to Winchester Cathedral now, a huge 900-year-old building decorated with carvings. Olivia's stomach tensed. They were close to Beau now.

'What do you mean, her version of events?' he demanded. 'She's not some kind of conspiracy theorist!'

As he indicated right, the cuff of his shirtsleeve moved up his arm and Olivia saw a ladder of three or four pale scars on his lower forearm, each a few centimetres long. She frowned. When he saw her looking, he corrected his shirt angrily.

'Go on then,' he said. 'What do you mean by that?'

'It might be difficult for you to hear, but I discovered the other day that Francine was the one who left Jesse first. So it seems that your mum left your dad,' Olivia said. 'Then, two years later, when Hattie and Jesse got together, she didn't like it. Also – and this is interesting – Hattie and Jesse dated before your mum and Jesse ever even got together.'

'No,' said Alec. 'You clearly have this all wrong. Hattie was to blame. Who goes off with their best friend's husband? Why else would Mum not speak to either of them for the last three decades?'

Olivia sighed. 'She didn't go off with him, she actively encouraged your parents to get back together. But your mum told my mum that she didn't love Jesse. I'm sorry if this hurts your feelings, but she was in love with someone else apparently.'

'What?' Alec demanded, his fingers squeezing the steering wheel so tight his knuckles turned white.

Olivia felt, for the first time, that she had the upper hand with him. 'There are letters to prove it. I've seen them with my own eyes. And anyway, Alec, this is all ancient history. What's happening right now is far more important.'

Alec shook his head. 'Why wouldn't my dad have told me this if what you say is true? And anyway, it still wasn't a very nice thing to do, in my opinion.'

'But love is complicated, isn't it?' Olivia said, checking the map on her phone as she spoke. 'I think Hattie and Francine should talk, while they can. Please, Alec, tell her Hattie misses her. You could bring her down to the beach hut, during this deckchair thing, just once. They could spend an hour talking, clear the air.

'Could you pull up here? Beau and I can get the train back if you need to go. Thank you.'

Alec pulled into a car park, and while the car was still moving, Olivia opened the passenger door and stepped out, stumbling onto the pavement. She slammed the door behind her.

The window rolled down.

'Christ!' Alec said. 'I hadn't even stopped! Are you okay?'

Olivia lifted her hand in the air as if to say she was fine and left Alec in his Mercedes, engine purring. He looked pale and utterly bemused, but Olivia couldn't worry about him now. There was only one thing she cared about: finding Beau.

Music. The smell of food. Chatter. Laughter. The fading evening light throwing long shadows on the pavement and buildings.

Clutching her phone and following the information in the tracking app, Olivia found Beau's general location and walked briskly up and down the street where she seemed to be. She stared into the windows of the cafés, bars and restaurants, sometimes hovering in the doorway, scanning the tables. People had spilled out into the streets and were sitting around tables or standing, enjoying the warm evening.

She tried Beau's phone repeatedly, swearing under her breath when it kept going to answerphone.

The sky was a swirly mess of blue, pink and white – a giant sheet of marbled paper. On any other day, it would be a beautiful evening, but Olivia was stricken with panic, her heart heavy in her chest.

She reached a bistro, its doorway laden with a display of

hanging baskets, and at a table outside, she saw a flash of silvery blue – Beau's hair. She gasped. Sitting opposite her, grinning, gesturing with his hands about something, was Oscar. A waitress was attending to them, laughing at something Oscar had said.

Olivia forced herself to look at him. Her tongue was now dry and stuck to the roof of her mouth, and she felt faint. His once almost black hair was now greying, and the lines around his eyes and mouth were more deeply engrained, but he was tanned and looked slim under his dark-blue linen shirt and jeans. He looked exactly like Beau.

Olivia's gaze fell to the table before him, checking for alcohol, but he appeared to be drinking a coffee.

He must have sensed her standing there, staring at him, because he turned his head towards her and froze for a second, pausing his coffee cup halfway to his mouth. Beau followed his gaze, and when she saw Olivia, her body stiffened and her expression hardened.

Oscar put the coffee cup down and stood up, pushing his chair back and acquired another so that Olivia could sit down.

'Olivia, join us,' he said, beckoning her over. 'Please.' He had a tentative smile on his lips, though Beau looked furious.

The pavement beneath Olivia's feet suddenly felt as soft as marshmallow as she stepped towards them, not knowing what to say, or what Oscar had said to Beau.

As she drew closer, she blinked rapidly, completely overwhelmed by how similar they looked. Her cheeks blazed – there was no way Beau couldn't have noticed the resemblance. Their eyes were almond shaped, their noses sharp, their eyebrows perfect small arches above each eye, their hair the same shade of brown. They both had long limbs and the same way of holding themselves.

In the car, earlier, she'd been full of fury, angry at Oscar for daring to contact Beau, angry at Beau for being silly enough to go, but now, she felt drained of emotion and lost for words.

'Beau,' she managed, pushing her phone into her bag, 'are you okay?'

'Of course I'm okay,' Beau replied, but her voice was thin and tense. 'I'm a bit shocked. It's all a lot to take in.'

'What? What's a lot to take in?'

Beau looked incredulous.

Olivia turned to Oscar. 'What have you said?' she demanded, choking on her words. 'How could you contact my daughter like this and lure her away from home? You could have been anyone. A stranger.'

'I didn't lure her away,' he said. 'I've emailed you lots of times. I'm back in the UK on business, working on a restaurant opening here. And, Olivia, let's face it, I'm not anyone, am I?' he said. 'I'm... Well, it's quite obvious.' He looked her right in the eye.

Olivia remembered her words: *False alarm. I'm not pregnant.*

'I knew as soon as I saw Beau's photograph online,' he said. 'I was completely bowled over by our resemblance. It's true, isn't it? I'm Beau's father. You were pregnant when you said you weren't. All these years I've missed out on... There's no point denying it. We look the same, her birthday is a few months after I left. It would be ludicrous for you to sit here and deny the whole thing, so please don't insult me – us – further.'

'You told him the pregnancy test was a false alarm and that you weren't pregnant when you knew you were,' Beau said, her eyes glinting with anger. 'And then went ahead and had me without telling him? What kind of utterly selfish person does that?'

Olivia's throat was a hard lump. Her scalp burned and her head throbbed. She wanted to scream: *A person who was in a toxic relationship.* But Oscar was a smartly dressed, coffee-drinking restaurant owner now.

'I'm not talking about this here,' said Olivia. 'Beau, we need to go home.'

'I'm not coming,' she replied. 'I need some space. But, Mum, tell me, why would you do this?'

'I had my reasons,' said Olivia. 'Why have you come back now, Oscar?'

'Things in New Zealand...' He stopped and shook his head. 'I wanted a new challenge. Then, I was online, reading the local newspaper, and the picture of you popped up. I couldn't believe it. Everything I'd believed about my world was no longer true.'

Beau was visibly trembling. She pushed her chair back and pulled on her jacket. Oscar stood too.

'Please, Beau – come home with me,' said Olivia, resting a hand on her daughter's shoulder, but Beau shook it off and glared at her.

'Leave me alone. I can't get my head around this.'

'I'm sorry, Beau,' Oscar said. 'Thank you for meeting me. I hope we can do this again. I know it's a shock, but—'

'But what?' Olivia demanded, raising her voice. 'You thought you'd throw a sledgehammer in her life without consulting me?'

'I sent you, what, ten emails?' Oscar said, raising his voice.

'Go to hell, Oscar,' said Olivia. 'Beau, I'm not leaving without you.'

'For God's sake, Mum,' Beau said, 'everyone's looking at us.'

Olivia glanced up and saw that the people sitting at the nearest tables were indeed looking at them. She turned on her heels, willing Beau to follow her. She did. Oscar stayed at the table, his head bowed as he tried to locate his card to pay.

Once they were round the corner, Beau stopped still. 'I'm not coming with you, Mum.'

'I will explain everything,' Olivia promised. 'Come on – let's just go home.'

But Beau was shaking her head. 'All this time, all these

years,' she said through tears. 'You told me that my father didn't want me, that he wasn't interested in having a family, that he was selfish, that he rejected us.'

'He *was* selfish.'

'But I've spent my whole life thinking he didn't want me. Wondering what was wrong with me, wondering why. He didn't even know I existed!'

Olivia was crying now. She tried to pull Beau towards her, but Beau pushed her away, swiping her hand across her nose and taking a deep breath.

'I'm getting the train,' said Beau. 'I have a return ticket and I'll go and stay with Wren tonight.'

'Beau,' Olivia pleaded, 'there's so much more about this you don't know. He's a coward, a drunk, manipulative. It's getting late – let me take you home, or I'll come with you on the train and we can talk.'

Beau shook her head. 'Please stop. I liked Oscar. He's my dad, for God's sake. Don't start bad-mouthing him before I've even really met him. I can't believe you'd do this!'

'Why won't you just hear me out?' Olivia asked.

'You never hear *me* out!' retorted Beau. 'This is how it feels.'

Olivia's gut was in a thousand knots. Beau was too angry to reason with.

Watching her walk away up the hill towards the station, Olivia tried to make some sort of plan. If Alec was still waiting, she would ask him to drive her to the train station in Milton-on-Sea, where she would meet Beau off the train, after having time to work out exactly what to say. Otherwise she'd get a taxi.

Feeling light-headed, she looked around for somewhere to sit and spotted a newspaper stand, half full of free magazines. She perched there and stared at the pavement, feeling desolate.

A pair of shiny brogues came into her peripheral vision. It was Alec.

'Here you are,' he said irritably. 'I've got to go, Olivia. Do you want a lift home or not?' He looked around. 'Where's Beau? Isn't this why we made this ridiculous journey?'

Olivia burst into tears then stood up and leaned into Alec's shoulder, snot and tears leaking down her face onto the immaculately pressed fabric of his jacket. Alec produced a tissue and handed it to her, giving her an awkward pat on the back as she wept.

SEVENTEEN

A week later, after many failed attempts at talking to Beau, Olivia was back at the beach hut, putting out the deckchairs, ready for the day's guests. In her pocket was a screwed-up letter from the council that had been pushed under the beach-hut door, saying that the mural contravened council rules and had to go within a week. She would have to tell Beau, on top of everything else.

Behind her sunglasses, her eyes were puffy and pink from sleepless nights of worrying. Despite trying to coax Beau out of her bedroom, she'd only left it to get something to eat or to visit her friends. Olivia had explained, through the closed door, that there was a good reason for the lie she'd told: that Oscar wasn't all he seemed, and that when Beau was ready, she could explain everything. But Beau was too angry to listen. For the time being, it seemed Beau believed that she – and Oscar – had been wronged.

With shaking hands, Olivia put a pot of tea down on the small table near the deckchairs and poured Hattie a cup.

'Who do we have coming today?' asked Hattie. 'Glenda was

a hoot, wasn't she? She's coming back, you know, to see me. She wants to meet up regularly.'

Hattie gave her daughter a small smile as Olivia took a seat next to her. They looked towards the sea: as blue and flat today as a swimming pool. A group of swimmers were gathered near a yellow buoy, floating on their backs. Their gentle chatter drifted up the beach. Olivia sighed, envious of how untroubled they seemed.

'It's someone called Catherine, who lives locally,' she said dully. 'And then a booking from someone who's just given their initials. I emailed them back, asking for a bit more information. I'll have a look in a minute to see if they've replied.'

Olivia worried for a moment that it might be Oscar but pushed the thought from her mind. It wasn't Hattie he wanted to see.

Hattie twisted in her seat. 'Olivia, what's wrong with you today? You seem so distracted and you're very quiet. Forlorn, in fact. You ought to sing. Since Miriam suggested it, I've been singing in the shower. It's actually quite satisfying.'

Olivia stood up, went into the beach hut and busied herself with putting her home-made scones on a plate. She hadn't told Hattie about Oscar's return as she didn't want to give her mother something else to worry about. She also knew if she started to talk about it, she would burst into tears.

'Oh, maybe I'm coming down with something,' she mumbled. 'I'll be fine.'

'Have a scone,' said Hattie. 'You look like you need some calories.'

Realising she'd forgotten to have breakfast, Olivia shoved a scone into her mouth.

'Have two,' said Hattie, holding out the plate.

Olivia did as she was told.

·   ·   ·

Twenty minutes later, Catherine arrived. She looked to be in her forties and was accompanied by her teenage son, who she introduced as Jamie. He had his hands stuffed into the pockets of his shorts, his head bowed, and seemed extremely uncomfortable. The whole teenage-ness of him made Olivia suffer a flash of worry about Beau. She felt sweaty and nauseous at the thought but was distracted by Catherine's apparent tension as she told Jamie to sit in the deckchair. He glanced at Hattie from under his long fringe and perched on the very edge of the chair. The scones sat untouched in front of them.

'Jamie has something to say, don't you?' Catherine said, giving him a gentle nudge.

Jamie cleared his throat and, with his hands clasped together, looked at Hattie with a sorrowful expression. He opened his mouth to speak but nothing came out.

'Jamie,' Catherine said again.

'What is it?' asked Hattie. 'Are you okay?'

Jamie wrapped his arms around his middle and leaned over, as if he had stomach cramps. He looked close to tears.

Suddenly, it clicked. Olivia tensed.

'I'm the boy,' he said. 'I'm the boy your husband tried to rescue. A surfer pulled me in and I was taken to the lifeguard's hut to be checked over and then to hospital. I didn't see you. My dad wrote to you, to thank you for what your husband did, but I wanted to come myself. It's because of me he's not here, and I'm sorry for that.' The boy struggled to get his words out, and when he finished, his shoulders sagged forward.

Hattie's hand lurched to her mouth. She pinched her lips together with her thumb and forefinger as if to hold in the words or the emotion. She said nothing.

'I was stupid,' Jamie said, a tear rolling down his cheek. 'I shouldn't have gone out in the sea alone. I should've paid attention to the flag, but I thought I'd be okay. I thought...'

'I knew it was too rough,' said Catherine. 'I told him not to go, but he didn't listen.'

'I'm so sorry, Mrs Fryer,' said Jamie. 'I feel so guilty.'

Olivia willed Hattie to speak, but she was just shaking her head a little bit.

Jamie's face was turning a deep shade of red. Olivia felt his pain as if it was hers.

She put her hand on his shoulder. 'Don't feel guilty,' she blurted out. 'Honestly, don't – it wasn't your fault. Nobody blames you. You didn't ask Jesse to get in the water. I told him not to get in, but he wanted to help. You didn't know the board would hit him. Guilt – misplaced guilt – can eat you up for years. You must let this go, okay?' Olivia said the words with so much conviction, spittle flew from her lips.

Catherine gave her a grateful smile.

'Absolutely,' said Hattie, finally breaking her silence. 'And it was me who spotted you in the water. I didn't stop Jesse from going in to help you. I thought he'd be fine. He was a strong swimmer. I could have stopped him. We could have waited for the lifeguards or alerted the coastguard. If anything, it was my fault, not yours.'

'It wasn't anyone's fault,' said Olivia.

'Without Jesse, Jamie might not even be here,' Catherine said. 'I wanted to tell you, to your face, that we know that and think about that every day. The letter we sent, it never felt enough, and then we saw this in the newspaper and thought coming here would be a way to reach you in person, to apologise face to face.'

Hattie, struggling not to cry, nodded.

'I made you something,' Jamie said. 'When Jesse swam out to me, I'd already swallowed a lot of water. He helped me back onto my board, told me to relax and that he would push the board in. That all I had to do was hold on. I was so scared, I was hyperventilating. I have asthma so it was difficult to breathe.

Jesse took a shell out of his pocket and told me to hold on to it for him. He told me what sort of shell it was... I kept hold of it. I know he was just trying to distract me. It was still in my hand in the hospital, and I've held on to it ever since. I made you this.'

Jamie pushed his hand inside his pocket and pulled out the shell, which he'd drilled a tiny hole through and put onto a fine gold chain. Tentatively, he handed it to Hattie.

She held it in her palm and stared at it. It was a pale brown common cockle shell.

'Thank you,' Hattie said. 'It's beautiful. Really – thank you. I'm grateful.'

Jamie gave an awkward smile and glanced at Catherine, who was wiping the corners of her eyes with her fingertips.

'May I ask how you are, Mrs Fryer?' Catherine said.

'It's difficult, dear,' said Hattie, sucking in her breath. 'It was the shock to begin with. There was no lead-up to it, no illness, no time to prepare, but I've adjusted. You have to, I suppose. There's a moth, Jamie, the peppered moth, that changed colour during the industrial revolution, from white to black. It had to adjust to its new surroundings in order to survive, so that it was disguised from predators. I heard that recently and it's a good thing to keep in mind. You never know what's going to happen, so you can't prepare, but you need to be able to adapt once whatever happens happens. Easier said than done, of course.'

The emotionally charged conversation ended, and before Catherine and Jamie left, Catherine commented on the painting Beau had done.

The thought of Beau made Olivia's stomach turn over and she typed out a message, asking if she was ready to talk. But there was no reply.

Distracted by the sight of Alec striding towards her, she left Hattie, Catherine and Jamie to say goodbye and walked towards him. He held a clear plastic bag containing a lipstick slightly in front of his body, as if it was contaminated. She blushed as she remembered breaking down on his shoulder in Winchester. He'd been kind to her then, breaking the habit of a lifetime, but by the expression on his face, he'd returned to normal.

'I don't know how you managed to lose this,' he said. 'Your bag must have holes in it. It was in my car. Who are they?'

Olivia took the lipstick and stuffed it in her pocket. She quickly explained who Catherine and Jamie were – and about the shell necklace.

'I don't think a necklace is any kind of replacement for my father,' he said.

'It's a token,' Olivia sighed. 'He's been feeling awful since the accident. He's blamed himself, but of course it's not his fault.'

'But where does the blame lie?' said Alec. 'Isn't it the fault of the idiot who does something dangerous? The people who climb mountains in terrible weather, or who go out on the sea without life jackets – don't they have some culpability? Shouldn't people take responsibility for their actions?'

'When someone's in dire need, it doesn't really matter how they got there, does it? Everyone can make a mistake or judge a situation incorrectly,' said Olivia. 'They need help, and those courageous people with big hearts, like your dad, they go to help. It might not be the most sensible thing to do, but could you stand on the beach and watch a young boy drown? What if it were you? Wouldn't you want someone to help?'

Alec looked bored and checked his watch. 'Have you finished? Because I've left my mother in the car.'

'She's here?'

'Yes. You asked – sorry, begged – me to bring her down, remember? I booked a slot on your ridiculous deckchair-for-hire page. I asked her about the letters and, given her reaction, I guess what you said has a grain of truth in it. She agreed to come, but now that we're here, she's reluctant – and by reluctant, I mean refusing – to get out of the car.' Alec exhaled deeply, his expression weary. He suddenly seemed drained of all energy.

'Let me talk to her,' Olivia said.

Alec sighed again and shrugged, before pointing to the top of the hill, where he was parked.

Through a small gap in the car's passenger window, Olivia tried to convince Francine's profile to come down to see Hattie.

Francine maintained her stance, looking straight ahead, until Olivia stopped talking, then she turned her head in Olivia's direction, lowered the window a couple of inches and pulled her sunglasses to the end of her nose. She was an attractive woman, her brown eyes shiny and her skin smooth. She looked well maintained. Her hair was blonde shot with grey and cut in a blunt bob. She wore light make-up, honey-coloured earrings and a number of rings on her fingers.

'You have no idea,' said Francine. 'You're completely clueless, just like your mother.'

'Please,' said Olivia. 'I know she's missed you.'

'What do you know?' Francine snapped. 'Absolutely nothing!'

'Mother,' said Alec, 'as I told you, Olivia has read the letters you sent to Hattie, and you said you'd talk to her. Will you please just get out of the car?'

'Don't tell me what to do! I've changed my mind.'

'You've spent my whole life telling me what to do!' Alec said. 'And you can't change your mind now!'

Olivia frowned. Alec and Francine both seemed to be furious with the world.

'What if this is the last opportunity you get to see her?' said Olivia patiently. 'What if the difficult conversations are the most rewarding?'

'Is she ill?' Francine said.

'No,' said Olivia. 'But neither was Jesse. She's finding being alone difficult, I know that. She's lonely. She could use a friend.'

'My heart bleeds,' Francine said, pursing her lips together. She fell silent for a while, then closed the car window.

Olivia glanced at Alec, who raised his eyebrows.

Just when Olivia was about to give up, Francine opened the car door and swung her legs around to get out.

'Help me then, will you, for heaven's sake?' she snapped at Alec. 'These seats are ridiculously difficult to get out of.'

He rushed to her side and offered her his hand.

She straightened up, elegant in a long dress and long cardigan. 'Perhaps it's time Hattie heard the truth,' she said. 'I'll need a coffee first, Alec. A strong one.'

She started walking, briskly, in the direction of the beach café.

Alec sighed, muttering, 'Yes, ma'am,' under his breath, before half jogging a few steps to catch her up.

Olivia turned towards the sea and, though it must have been the direction of the sun, for a split second she imagined the water had parted.

EIGHTEEN

Olivia almost tripped over her feet as she ran back to the deckchairs. She had to warn Hattie about Francine. Prepare her. But she was mid-conversation with Seth and an elderly man who was travelling in Seth's trishaw.

When Seth saw Olivia, his face lit up with a huge smile.

'You look in a hurry!' he said, moving away from Hattie and the elderly man. 'Did you find your daughter the other night? I've been thinking about you, hoping you're okay.'

Olivia swallowed hard – she didn't want to be reminded of that right now. She forced a smile. 'Yes, I did, thank you, Seth. I'm sorry for dragging you into all of that.'

He widened his eyes and shook his head. 'I enjoyed it!' he said. Then made a face and clarified: 'I mean, I enjoyed being with you. Sort of thing.'

Olivia found herself smiling at Seth's compliment but was distracted by the knowledge that Francine would soon be walking in their direction; that she needed to talk to Hattie, quickly.

'Sorry, Seth, I need to speak to my mother,' she said. 'See you another time?'

Seth looked a little crushed. 'Yes,' he said. 'I'd like that.'

'So would I,' Olivia replied quickly, surprising herself.

Seth grinned, climbed back onto his bike and cycled away, lifting his hand in the air behind him in a goodbye salute.

'What a lovely young man he is,' said Hattie, her hands on her hips. 'I think he has a thing for you, Olivia. He told me he never used to cycle this way, but now his route seems to take him past our beach hut. Funny that! He could do with a haircut, but otherwise he's quite handsome.'

'He's just one of those chatty, helpful types,' said Olivia, aware of heat rising to her cheeks. 'Look, Mum, something's happened that I need to talk to you about. Urgently.'

Hattie immediately sat on the deckchair and held her hand over her heart. 'What now?' she asked. 'Why do you look so furtive? Is it Beau? Is she okay?'

Olivia checked over her shoulder, curls escaping her clips and hanging around her jaw. She tucked them behind her ears and took a seat on the deckchair next to Hattie.

'I emailed Francine,' she said. 'Alec gave me her address for the funeral invitations. After what you said about maybe wanting to see her again, I emailed her and asked her to come down. Then I saw those letters from her that were in your bedroom and... it just makes sense for you to see each other. She's on her way.'

Hattie gaped. She put her hands flat on her thighs and straightened her back. Her face had turned as white as her hair. 'Francine?' she said quietly. 'On her way *here*?'

'Yes,' Olivia said, trying to read Hattie's expression.

'But how? She hasn't spoken to me in years – decades. What did you say to get her to come? Does Alec know?'

Olivia nodded and chewed the inside of her cheek, biting so hard her eyes stung.

'But he would never want her to come here either,' Hattie

said. 'They've always been so separate to me. They've not wanted me to be in their lives. I don't understand.'

There were tears in Hattie's voice, and Olivia felt terribly guilty all of a sudden. Had she gone too far?

'I told Alec about the letters,' said Olivia as calmly as she could. 'His entire life he's blamed you for something that wasn't your fault. I didn't like that, Mum. It wasn't fair.'

'You told him about the letters?' said Hattie, almost inaudible.

'Yes. I thought he ought to know the truth. I don't know why you didn't tell him earlier. Maybe if you had, we wouldn't have been held to ransom all those years.' Olivia thought back to her childhood – the many times Hattie had been so wounded by Alec's refusal to accept her.

Hattie put her hand over her face and lowered her head. 'You shouldn't have done that,' said Hattie. 'Jesse never wanted that.'

'Why?' said Olivia. 'Why wouldn't he have wanted that?'

'Because Alec wanted to believe everything his mum told him,' Hattie said. 'What kind of parent would Jesse have been to tell Alec his mum was lying?'

'A good one? One that thinks it's important to be honest?' Olivia dropped her eyes from Hattie's glare, all too aware of her hypocrisy.

'No,' said Hattie. 'You don't understand. When Jesse and Francine broke up, Alec suffered terribly. He fell apart. It was awful and very worrying, Olivia. He started to hurt himself, to cut his arms. He was in dreadful emotional pain and for some reason seemed to blame himself for the break-up until Francine transferred the blame to me.'

Olivia remembered Alec pulling at his shirtsleeve in the car, the faint lines of old scars poking out from beneath his cuff.

'Jesse was desperately, desperately worried about him. The

only person he felt safe with was Francine. They were terribly close. She told the story of their break-up in a way that portrayed her as a victim and Alec felt so angry about it, he wanted to blame someone. Jesse didn't want to tell Alec that his mum hadn't told him the true version of events and leave him not being able to trust anyone. After a while, the subject became too difficult to approach and it was easier to keep us all separate. They had a scapegoat – me.'

'What?' said Olivia, incredulous. 'So your happiness was sacrificed?'

'No,' said Hattie. 'I *was* happy. I had you and Jesse. And I did feel guilty about Francine, so perhaps I deserved their ill feeling. Maybe it was wrong of me to marry Jesse. Maybe I should have avoided him completely. Moved to the other side of the world and joined a goddam circus.'

'But you were with him before Dad, and they'd been separated for years before you got together,' said Olivia. 'If anyone was in the wrong, it was Francine.'

'What's this then,' said a female voice behind them, 'the lonely hearts beach club?'

Hattie and Olivia turned to find Francine standing a few steps away, Alec close behind her, his forehead glistening with sweat. Olivia tried to meet his eyes, but he avoided her gaze. Hattie leaped up from her deckchair, gripping hold of the back of it. Her knuckles were white.

'Francine, oh heavens, it's really you,' Hattie said, her mouth audibly dry.

The two women looked at one another for a long moment.

'Please, will you sit down with me?' Hattie's voice was heavy with emotion, her eyes shiny with tears.

Francine held herself stiffly, seemingly bracing herself for what was to come. Then she lowered herself into Jesse's old deckchair, and Hattie sat down in hers. Alec's expression was thunderous. The sun ducked behind a cloud, casting the beach into sudden gloom, but Olivia left them to it, leading her reluctant stepbrother off down the promenade.

NINETEEN

An enduring friendship – that was what Hattie had believed she would have with Francine, so when their friendship collapsed, Hattie had felt the loss deeply. To have Francine here now, by her side, in Jesse's deckchair, was overwhelming. She found it impossible to find the right words. Or any words. She opened and closed her mouth, but all that came out were little puffs of air. She swallowed repeatedly and looked at Francine out of the corner of her eye. Francine seemed equally uncomfortable, staring at her hands – wrinkled but glistening with hand cream and peppered with age spots – and splaying her fingers, adjusting her rings, spinning one of them round repeatedly, as if she was unscrewing a bottle.

A tiny bubble of happiness rose in Hattie's belly. She marvelled at how well Francine had aged; she obviously hadn't spent days getting weathered at the beach. Her skin was smooth, her cheekbones sharp, her Cupid's bow lips carefully painted with lipstick. Her bleached hair was straight and down, tucked under a sun hat. She wore a long brightly coloured floral dress, nipped in at the waist, and flat gold pumps – Francine had always had great style.

Hattie glanced at her own clothes – pale trousers and blouse bought from a catalogue – and blushed. Glenda was right: she could try harder. She wished she'd had time to prepare for this meeting – she would have liked to have made the effort to look a bit more glamorous.

'I like your earrings,' Hattie said, eventually breaking the tense silence. 'Are they amber?'

As soon as she'd spoken, she wrinkled her nose – what a hopeless way to open their conversation.

Francine quickly turned towards her. Was that a slight smile playing on her lips? Hattie cautiously returned it.

'Glass,' Francine said. 'Actually, Jesse bought me them, years ago.'

'Oh,' said Hattie. 'He had good taste.'

They shared a glance. The fact Francine had chosen to wear those earrings today felt provocative to Hattie. She had no idea which way this conversation was going to go – she couldn't rule out a blazing row.

'I'm sorry for your loss, Hattie, for Alec's loss,' said Francine. 'Typical of Jesse to die thinking he could rescue someone. He was always trying to solve things. Couldn't solve me though.'

Hattie mulled that over and frowned. She felt suddenly irritated that Francine was talking about Jesse as if she knew him better than anyone, when, in actual fact, their marriage had been short-lived and unloving. And if Jesse had been such a significant part of her life, why hadn't she come to his funeral?

'I thought you would have come to his funeral,' said Hattie. In her head she added, *Or at least sent a card, or flowers, or made a phone call.*

Francine shook her head. 'I decided it was best I didn't. You don't want the past reappearing at a funeral, do you? Everyone staring and pointing, thinking you're the wife that was left, the reject. No thank you.'

'You've reappeared now,' Hattie said. 'And you were never the reject, Francine. *You* rejected Jesse after your very brief marriage. I wish you'd tell the truth.'

'I was emotionally blackmailed to come here by your daughter.'

'I think that's a bit strong, isn't it? She's only trying to help.'

'She told Alec that everything he believed as a child wasn't true,' Francine replied, her voice tremulous. 'So Alec felt there was no choice but to ask me to oblige Olivia's request and come here. She wasn't very subtle.'

'Olivia saw your old letters,' said Hattie. 'And decided she'd go to Alec. I didn't ask her to. But surely he's grown-up enough now – what is he, fifty? – to understand that life's a bit more complicated than it seemed when he was a child.'

Francine shrugged. 'It caused a bit of an outburst. Unusual for Alec – he's normally so controlled.'

'Why did you never tell him the full story?' Hattie asked, her voice tremulous. 'I mean, you didn't even love Jesse – you told me so many times. Why did you have to cut yourself off from us so dramatically? I've tried to put myself in your shoes over the years, hundreds of times, and I can understand you not liking it much, me marrying your former husband, but if you didn't really care for him, I don't understand why you were so hurt. Was it more the fact that things hadn't worked out the way you wanted them to?'

Francine didn't say anything for a long moment.

'It wasn't Jesse I was bothered about,' she said in a quiet voice. 'Or the loss of our marriage.'

'What then?' asked Hattie, exasperated. 'Did you feel excluded? Couldn't we have remained friends, as I wanted us to? I told Jesse to go back to you, to try to make things work, but you'd moved on to someone else, so why did you care so much?'

A young woman and her greyhound walked past, and the dog sniffed Francine's ankles then jumped up at her lap.

'Get down, Bobby! Get down!' the young woman said. 'Naughty boy. Don't worry, he's friendly. Just a bit enthusiastic! Beautiful day, isn't it?'

Francine sighed and moved her knees sideways so the dog slipped down. Hattie wished the woman would go away and glared at her. After a moment, she got the message and dragged the dog along the promenade, his paws skidding on the concrete.

'Some people,' Francine said under her breath.

'I know.'

'I mean, it's obvious we're talking.'

'I know! Some people have got nothing but air whooshing between their ears!'

Hattie rose from her deckchair and retrieved a jug of water from the beach hut. She put it on a tray between them, with two glasses, and filled both. As she took a sip, she noticed her hands were shaking.

'You were about to tell me what motivated your exile,' said Hattie, bringing the conversation back to the point.

Francine let out a snort of laughter. 'My exile!'

'Well, whatever you want to call it then,' Hattie replied. 'As far as I understand it, you wanted to divorce Jesse anyway and were in love with someone else, yet you held a grudge against me and Jesse for decades and turned Alec against me, despite me trying to reach out to you several times. I'm sorry to sound repetitive, but why?'

Francine corrected her sun hat and twisted in her seat, so she was facing Hattie full on. 'You don't want to know.'

'Oh, bloody hell, Francine,' said Hattie. 'I do! We used to be such good friends. We were so close.'

'Exactly!' said Francine, her cheeks flushing pink. She sighed. 'You know I said there was a woman I loved?'

Hattie nodded. She'd been totally supportive of Francine

when she'd told her she was in love with a woman, even though she'd known Jesse would be hurt.

'That woman,' she said. 'That woman... well, Hattie, that woman was... bloody hell... it's crazy to be saying this out loud after all these years, but it was you.'

Hattie blinked. Not once had she expected Francine to say that.

'Are you joking? Because if you are, it's not very fun—'

She didn't get to finish her sentence. Francine got up and stood in front of Hattie, towering over her.

'No, I'm not joking,' she said, her voice quivering. 'Why would I joke? This is the first time I've said those words out loud and you think I'm joking? For God's sake, have a heart.'

Francine kicked at Jesse's deckchair, and it fell over, landing awkwardly on its side. Hattie struggled to her feet and put the deckchair back up.

'Calm down,' she said, reeling in shock and not knowing what to say. 'I'm sorry.'

'No, I won't calm down. You don't know how I felt. You never have! You always got it so wrong, thinking it was all about Jesse.'

'Why didn't you ever tell me? I had no idea! Sit down, Francine.'

Francine did. 'When we first met, I liked you straight away and I knew we would be friends. I realised, as time went on, that I had deeper feelings for you than friendship, that it wasn't platonic. It was so confusing because I'd had relationships with men and I still liked men. But when I met you, everything changed. I had to review everything I thought about myself.

'You married Michael, and Jesse seemed to be at a loose end without you. In a strange way, I knew how he felt, and so I got together with him. We had Alec, and I got by as I was, keeping you close as a friend. I thought that was enough. Then, when Michael was killed, it made me incredibly aware of the fragility of life and I thought I had to act, to say something to you, get out of the marriage I wasn't happy in. I told you repeatedly that I wanted to leave Jesse and that I was in love with a woman. And what did you do? You got together with Jesse!'

'But I had no idea you were talking about *me*! And I got together with Jesse ages after you broke up,' said Hattie, wracking her brains, trying to recall their old conversations. 'Honestly, I had no idea, Francine. And what would I have done anyway? I didn't feel that way. I loved you as a friend – my best friend.'

Francine let out a small, sad laugh. 'I know. I know, I know. And that's what I've dealt with my whole life. Unrequited love. It's a desperate curse, an awful thing, horrible. The only way I could get through it all was to have total separation, a huge divide and to think that I would never see you again. The easiest way was to hate you. I blamed you for my sadness. You broke up my marriage, but not in the way people thought. I wanted to punish you, Hattie. I certainly didn't want my son to slot into your life with Jesse and for everyone, except me, to have your love!'

Hattie's stomach was heavy, her head aching with Francine's revelation. 'Did you have a relationship with anyone else?' she asked.

Francine shook her head. 'No. I have friends of course, but nobody has ever quite lit my heart like you did. It's difficult to explain to people who haven't experienced it, but it was you or nobody. I got over you eventually. Time will do that.'

Hattie tried to rearrange her memories now that Francine had explained how she felt. Perhaps she'd been stupid not to realise.

'Why didn't you come out and say it?' said Hattie. 'We could have cleared the air back then. Years ago. I wish you'd just been honest. All this bad feeling could have been spared.'

Francine shrugged, and tears slipped down her cheeks. 'I

suppose I knew what you'd say. It was easier to batten down the hatches. I felt embarrassed. Very silly. Someone once told me that you can't really be in love with someone if the feeling isn't reciprocated. That it's infatuation or something else. I don't know. I just know that I made an awful mess of everything. I hurt Jesse, I hurt Alec, I hurt and lost you – I blamed you when it wasn't your fault. I was fighting a battle that didn't even exist.'

Francine broke down, apologised and grabbed a tissue from her bag. She wiped her eyes and regained her composure.

Hattie reached across the gap between the deckchairs and rested her hand on Francine's. Tentatively, she wrapped her hand around Francine's fingers.

'I'm sorry,' Hattie said gently. 'I'm sorry you suffered in this way and that I wasn't clever enough to realise how you felt. I've missed you so much over the years. Wouldn't a friendship have been enough?'

'Not back then,' Francine replied, shaking her head. 'Back then it was all or nothing. I was young – I had no concept of how short life is or how friendship can be as valuable as love.'

'I've always thought that friendship *is* love,' said Hattie, her voice choked.

Francine gave a slight nod and briefly squeezed Hattie's hand before letting go.

TWENTY

Alec and Olivia had walked towards the pier. The sun emerged from behind the clouds, and more people were arriving at the beach – adults carrying bags and beach tents; children dragging bodyboards and buckets across the sand. Alec continually checked his watch and sighed. Olivia was distracted by thoughts of Beau and what to do for the best. Part of her was desperate to tell her daughter everything about Oscar, but he'd already made an impression on Beau – a good one. And so many years had passed – maybe he wasn't the same anymore.

'I'm going back,' said Alec, suddenly stopping. 'They've had long enough to say what they need to say.'

Olivia stopped too. They were next to an ice-cream shack, where a long queue was forming. The teenage assistant blushed profusely as a ball of ice cream he was trying to squash into a wafer cone toppled off onto the floor.

'What are you so worried about?' asked Olivia. 'We could leave them for longer, couldn't we? Or do you have plans? I can get you an ice cream if you like?' Absent-mindedly, she scanned the ice-cream list.

Alec shook his head. 'I have an appointment,' he told her, checking his watch yet again.

'An appointment with a yacht dealer perhaps?' she teased. 'I'm sure you must need something shiny and new now you have your inheritance.'

Alec shook his head gravely. 'Actually no. It's with a bereavement support group. I missed the first one when I took you to Winchester, so I was hoping to get there today.'

Olivia was stunned. 'Oh,' she said. 'Sorry. I mean, I didn't think that was your style – you seem so...'

'Repressed?' he said sharply. 'Cold-hearted?'

'Well, no. But... closed. Have you found this last year difficult?'

Alec nodded. 'I thought after this long, the grief would have gone away. But it hasn't. After a particularly bad few days, I went to my doctor, and she directed me to this group. Said talking to others in the same boat might help. I don't have high hopes. I'm not the type of person who enjoys talking about how I feel. But I'll give it a go. One go.'

Olivia was quietly surprised that he had any feelings at all but then scolded herself. Everyone had feelings. Nobody was straightforward.

'You can talk to me,' she said gently. 'If you ever want to.'

The corner of Alec's mouth twitched upwards very slightly, which Olivia decided to take as an acknowledgement that he understood she was there, if needed.

'I miss him,' said Alec. 'He understood me, like nobody else. He was the only one in my life who I could relax with and enjoy being with. My mother – she can be difficult. She's been kind of angry with the way life worked out.'

'I'm sorry,' Olivia said. 'Is there anyone else you're close to? A partner? Someone you can talk to?'

Alec shook his head. 'There was someone for a while, but she said I had too many *issues*.' He mimed quote marks with his fingers. 'Insecure, clingy or something insulting like that. What nonsense!'

Olivia remembered the CD in his glove compartment and her heart softened towards him.

'It's just me,' he said. 'Me, myself and I.'

Olivia briefly rested her hand on his forearm sympathetically, and at the same moment, someone tapped her on the shoulder. It was Seth, smiling broadly and brandishing a bunch of rhubarb.

'Seth,' she said. 'Hello again.'

'This is for you,' he said, handing it to Olivia. 'I meant to give it to you earlier. It's why I came, and then I forgot. It's from my garden. It's late in the year, but it's still good. Sorry to disturb you. And who's this? Oh, the man in the car. Is this your' – panic passed across Seth's face – 'husband?' he asked.

Olivia let out a loud laugh. 'This is my stepbrother, Alec. Alec, this is Seth.'

Seth put his hand out towards Alec, who took it limply.

'I don't think I've ever been any kind of brother to you,' Alec said, before checking his watch for the umpteenth time. 'I really must get back.'

Olivia was speechless. It was the first time Alec had hinted at any kind of apology for the way he'd treated her.

Before she could say anything, he picked up the pace and walked back towards the deckchairs with a purposeful stride. Clearly there was more to Alec than she'd thought. He was more complicated than she'd realised, more like Jesse than she'd given him credit for perhaps. Below the polished exterior, he was struggling.

She turned to Seth. 'Thanks for the rhubarb.'

He put his hand on his chest, over his heart. 'Thank heavens,' he said. 'He's your stepbrother! I thought for one horrible moment he was your partner. I'm just going to come out and ask: do you have one?'

'A partner?' she said. 'No.'

'That's one hurdle flattened,' he said with another of his big grins. 'So here's the question: would you like to come out with me? We could go for a bike ride. I've got a shop full of bikes. I know all the best cycle paths. Please say yes.'

Olivia blushed deeply. She liked Seth. She liked his energy, and from what she could tell, he was a kind person and wasn't bad-looking either. In fact, he was handsome in a bit of a wild way. But she had so many things on her mind at the moment.

'Life is a bit complicated,' said Olivia. 'My mum, my daughter – there's a lot going on.'

But Seth wasn't to be deterred. 'What about you? Not too busy for a bike ride? And life is always complicated! I've learned that to keep yourself sane, you need to make an hour for yourself every day. Just an hour. It's not long. Go on – give me an hour of your time, tomorrow night. I'll pick you up at your house at 7 p.m.'

Olivia found herself nodding, remembering how, after she'd met Glenda, she'd realised she didn't let her hair down often enough. 'Okay, an hour's bike ride sounds good. Great, in fact.'

'Fantastic,' he said. 'I'll see you then. Can we swap numbers?'

'Sure,' said Olivia, quickly giving him hers.

Seth thanked her, grinned and cycled away.

Olivia held the rhubarb against her nose, breathing in its sharp, fresh fragrance, and felt a shiver of excitement.

She was walking towards the deckchair, trying to gather her thoughts, when her phone rang. She almost dropped the rhubarb when she saw it was Beau and fumbled to accept the call.

'Yes, love?' she said breathlessly. 'Are you okay? You got my message? Please, can we talk?'

'I'm going to see him again,' Beau said. 'And you can't stop me. I just wanted to let you know that.'

Olivia slowed down and held her hand over her other ear, so she could hear Beau above the shrieks of the seagulls and the children playing on the beach.

'Listen to me for a moment,' she said calmly. 'I know you think you like Oscar, but the reason I never told him about you was because when I knew him, he had a problem with alcohol. He was angry and aggressive – sometimes he would lose control. He let me down, many times, and I needed to protect you. I know this isn't nice to hear.'

She waited to see how her harsh words would land in Beau's heart. She thought about the night that Oscar drunkenly drove the car, narrowly missing the boy on the scooter, but decided to spare Beau the grim details.

'No, it's not nice to hear,' Beau said through tears. 'But Oscar has explained. He said he went through a really difficult time after losing his job and that he turned to drink. He admitted he had a problem and that it made him unkind, cruel, and that he's ashamed of how he was. But he said that he's stopped.'

'Even if he has stopped, it doesn't change the way he used to be. He was controlling and also a coward,' said Olivia. 'We need to talk – properly. I know you want him to be this amazing father that's appeared in your life, but it's not like that. He's bad news.'

'Don't patronise me! I don't want him to be an amazing father, I just want to know who he is. He wants me to give him a chance to get to know him, as he is now. I want to give him a chance to explain, Mum. I believe he's changed. I think people can. He says all he wants to do is apologise and make things up to you. He says you shouldn't have done what you did, because he would have been here sooner, to be involved in my life. He says that because of your dad, you flipped out when he once drove after having a drink. He says he was young and stupid and wants to earn your forgiveness.

'He's been really honest with me, Mum, and also, he's commissioned me to do a massive mural on the side of the wall of his new restaurant. He's going to pay me £500 for it. I'm sorry that he once hurt you – I hate to think of that, I really do – but I believe he has changed. He owns a business, employs people. Do you think you can possibly leave what happened in the past?'

'I don't think I can,' she said. 'Oscar is volatile.'

'He might have been sixteen years ago,' said Beau. 'He's convinced me that he's changed. I wish you'd back off and stop telling me what to do! I'm going to see him!'

'I forbid you to!'

Beau hung up.

Olivia let out a sob. She felt utterly powerless.

She searched for Oscar's email address and immediately typed out an email in capital letters.

LEAVE BEAU ALONE! STAY OUT OF OUR LIVES!

Her whole body was shaking with anger as she walked the last stretch towards the beach hut. She took a deep breath when she saw that Hattie was sitting alone, her expression pensive, brooding.

'Mum?' said Olivia. 'How did it go?'

'Some things are best left unsaid,' Hattie snapped, without looking at Olivia. 'I wish you hadn't interfered. I was better off leaving things as they were. You can be very selfish at times, Olivia. You just do the thing you want to do without thinking about anybody else's feelings.'

Hattie stood up, clattered the water glasses onto the tray and carried it into the beach hut before slamming it down.

Olivia was bemused for a moment then felt a surge of anger power through her. 'Selfish?' she said, the blood rising in her cheeks as she followed Hattie inside. 'How can you say that?'

Hattie spun round and looked her in the eye. 'You wanted to do this deckchair thing, not me. You decided I should meet Francine, not me. You decided to tell Alec about his mum, not me. Things were better off left as they were.'

Olivia yanked her bag up from the floor and put it on her shoulder. 'Not everything can stay the same. Sometimes you have to face things to move forward.' A little part of her knew that she was talking to herself.

'There are things I don't want to face,' said Hattie. 'This morning's conversation has made me question everything. I'm exhausted. I wish you would just leave me alone in my bungalow!'

Olivia felt her entire body stiffen. Her words came out quickly and surely: 'If that's how you really feel, then you can go to hell! I've done all this for you and you only. I wanted you to find a friend, help you put old demons to rest, find a reason to get up in the morning. I cancelled everything in Dublin for you. My entire childhood after Dad died, I worried about you and put you first. I couldn't stand to watch you be so unhappy, so I put my sadness aside. I've sat here every time someone has come to talk to you. And you say I'm selfish, that I think I know best and should leave you alone? Fine!'

'Why don't you go to Dublin then, if you're so desperate to leave?' snapped Hattie. 'I'm not stopping you! And maybe you should find yourself a friend, not me!'

Hattie's words stung. Olivia swallowed the knot of tears in her throat and left without saying goodbye.

At the front door, on the mat, she found a note. Wearily, she scanned the contents. Just as she feared, it had been scribbled by Beau to say she needed space and was going to stay with Hattie.

Olivia couldn't hold her tears in any longer. She went into the front room, collapsed onto the sofa and wept.

TWENTY-ONE

When Beau arrived, Hattie had been looking through a magnifying glass at a moth she'd caught in a jar. She'd never even really noticed them before, other than when they suddenly flew into the bathroom at night, drawn by the light, and she'd flap them away with her hand. On closer inspection, they were beautiful, just as Jacob had said. The moth's intricate antique-lace wings, Olivia's words and Francine's revelation earlier made Hattie think that she'd gone through her life not looking closely enough at the world around her. It made her shiver with self-doubt. By the look of Beau's face, she was feeling similarly unsettled.

'I've just read that male moths can smell female moths from more than seven miles away!' she told Beau, pointing to the booklet Jacob had given her. 'Nowhere to hide, poor things.'

Beau smiled briefly and dropped her rucksack and a sleeping bag on the floor in Hattie's hallway with a thud. Her eyes and nose were bright red, a sure sign she'd been crying.

Hattie put the book and magnifying glass down on the windowsill. 'I'm pleased to see you,' she said, giving Beau a hug.

'But I'm also not pleased to see you. Because the reason you're here with a sleeping bag can only mean one thing. You've fallen out with your mum?'

Beau nodded, peeling off her hoodie and hanging it on the coat stand near the telephone table. The grandfather clock beside her struck the hour, followed by the chime of the clock on the living-room mantlepiece. They'd never quite been in synch. Hattie opened a window and released the moth.

'Well,' she said, 'that makes two of us. Come through into the kitchen – let's have some tea and biscuits and try to work out this muddle we find ourselves in. Do you like shortbread? I keep buying a packet every time I go shopping because Jesse liked it, but I don't eat it myself.'

Hattie opened a kitchen cupboard and studied the pile of shortbread packets there – at least two dozen acquired in the last year. Having Beau's young eyes on the place made her aware of the strange habits she'd fallen into since Jesse had died. The extra cup of tea, the shortbread, the slippers still in position by his side of the bed.

She put some shortbread out on a plate and made a pot of tea. Beau looked distracted, her eyes sorrowful and far away.

'It's so quiet here without Granddad – you must miss him,' Beau said. 'I do. I wish I could talk to him now, about what Mum's done. It might help to have a male perspective.'

'So, tell me, what's been going on?' Hattie asked.

Beau put her cup in the saucer and started to talk. Hattie watched her granddaughter's face as she described how Oscar had contacted her via Instagram, how he'd explained he used to be in a relationship with Olivia and that he'd tried to get back in touch with her, but she'd ignored his emails. Oscar had asked Beau to meet him because he had something important to talk to her about. He'd said they could meet in a public space in Winchester and that, if she wanted, she could bring a friend.

Hattie was alarmed. 'Did you mention any of this to your mum before you met with Oscar? Because you know how dangerous it is to meet adult men you don't know, don't you? He could have been anyone!'

Beau explained that she'd gone because he'd sent her several photographs of him and Olivia together, looking happy, and that's when she realised how much she looked like him and began to suspect there was more to the story than anyone was admitting. She'd told her friend Wren where she was going to be and agreed to meet Oscar in a bistro in a street she knew would be busy. She'd lied and told Oscar that her boyfriend was waiting round the corner for her.

'Still,' said Hattie. 'You took a risk. No wonder your mum was worried.'

When they'd met, Beau told her, their physical likeness had been undeniable, and after talking about her date of birth and the dates that Oscar and Olivia's relationship ended, Oscar had said what Beau already knew – that he suspected he might be her father.

'I wanted to see for myself,' she said. 'I've asked her, straight, about who my dad was, and she always told me the same thing – he didn't want to know me. She told me that when he found out she was pregnant, he left the country. He didn't want to be a father; he rejected me. But Oscar told me a different story. Apparently, he saw her positive pregnancy test, but she told him it was a false alarm and, despite him saying he would support her and be the best dad he could, she lied and said she wasn't pregnant. Why would she do that?'

Hattie's heart sank. Beau's face was pale with distress. Olivia had told Hattie the same thing – that Oscar had chosen to abandon her and return to New Zealand the moment he found out she was pregnant.

'I asked her to be honest and she admitted that she'd lied to

Oscar about the pregnancy because she was trying to protect me – well, the unborn me,' said Beau. 'She said he had an alcohol problem and had anger issues. She said she was really unhappy, but she didn't look unhappy in that photo. And, anyway, he admitted to having a problem with alcohol, but he said he's had loads of therapy and has completely changed.'

Hattie leaned forward and took Beau's hands in hers.

'Do you think he could be... dangerous?' Beau asked. 'Was he... did he... hit her? Because if he ever hurt her, I'll tell him exactly what I think of him and never, ever see him again. I couldn't accept that.'

'These are big things for you to have to think about,' Hattie said. 'From what I could tell of your mum's relationship with Oscar, it started off well. Jesse and I liked him. He was very ambitious, a real character, who had big ideas about the way he wanted his life to be. He certainly whisked Olivia off her feet. She really fell for him and they seemed to be in love. But when things didn't go as Oscar wanted, he started drinking heavily and some problems from his past came to the surface. Your mum didn't tell me everything that went on, but she was clearly unhappy.

'Her friend Isla told me that Oscar could lose his temper very quickly and he certainly had an awful problem with alcohol. It changed his personality – I saw that first-hand. Your mum was determined to try to help him – but he wouldn't listen.

'I was relieved when he left for New Zealand, and when she discovered she was pregnant and said he wasn't interested, I wasn't particularly surprised. I don't know the full extent of it, and I didn't know she hadn't told him the whole truth, but, Beau, your mum was unhappy, and Oscar was the reason why. I was pleased to see the back of him. I'm sorry, my darling.'

Beau began to cry. 'I hate to think of Mum suffering or

being unhappy, or of him being horrible towards her in any way. But I'm so confused because he says he's changed. He seems so nice, so normal! He says he's had intensive therapy, he's sober, he's a different person and he's upset by the fact that Mum never told him about me.'

'Perhaps he has changed,' said Hattie, getting up from her seat and giving Beau a big cuddle. 'People do. I've known others who've turned their whole lives around, but when your loved ones have been hurt by a person, forgiveness isn't particularly easy, or even sensible. You must tread carefully, Beau, for yourself and for your mum. She only has your interests at heart.'

Beau nodded and wiped her eyes. 'I want to believe he's changed. I want to believe that people can change, particularly if they're my own flesh and blood, the missing piece of my jigsaw. I've spent my whole life wondering who he is.'

'I want to believe that too, darling,' Hattie said, feeling very light-headed. 'But your poor mum must be suffering terribly. I had no idea he was back on the scene. And now I've added to the problem by saying some things to her I didn't mean. I bet she's worrying about you. Is that her now, phoning you?'

Beau's phone was beeping in her pocket. She pulled it out and checked the screen. 'It's her. She's asked to meet at the gallery, so we can talk.'

She stuffed her phone back into her pocket.

'Are you going to reply?' Hattie asked.

'I will. But she needs to give me some space and time to think first.'

Hattie nodded, noticing a streak of paint on Beau's forehead.

'Beau,' she said, 'I loved the painting you did of me on the beach hut. It really meant the world to me. You know that the council have told us to paint over it though? I don't think we'll have a choice in the matter, but I've asked my newspaper friend

Paul to take a photo of it, as he wanted updates on the deckchair hire. He's very good, Paul.'

Beau shrugged. 'It was a brief beauty. We'll paint over it lightly or leave a centimetre of colour visible, so we'll always know it's there, underneath.'

'Yes,' said Hattie quietly. 'The people who look really carefully will see it.'

TWENTY-TWO

'Perhaps it's a good thing,' said Isla, handing Olivia a box of tissues. 'Perhaps you could do with some space from *them*. It's hard work being in the sandwich generation, Olivia, I told you. And sometimes the sandwich filling just needs time to drop out.'

Olivia dried her eyes. She was sitting in Isla's cabin at the end of her garden – her home office, which she'd equipped with a small fridge, a kettle, a small cupboard of snacks and two comfortable chairs. Hugh had been instructed to not let any of their children near them, and after one glance at Olivia's puffy red eyes, he'd taken the request – so far, they'd remained undisturbed.

'Not like this though,' said Olivia. 'They're both furious with me.'

'Olivia,' said Isla, 'I think it's time you started to think about yourself a bit more. You've always put Beau first, and I understand why, and of course you needed to take care of Hattie when Jesse died, but this is your life too.'

'My life is meaningless without them,' Olivia said miserably. 'What if I've lost them? I told Beau I forbade her from seeing Oscar and I told Mum that she could go to hell.'

Isla sat in the chair next to Olivia and handed her a mug of hot tea. 'You haven't lost them!' she said with a gentle laugh. 'Beau's an independent teenager and is clearly determined to find out what Oscar is like for herself. You can't protect her forever.'

Olivia nodded in reluctant agreement.

'And your mum is annoyed because you've made her face something she didn't want to. A bit like you feel now Oscar's turned up. I think maybe Hattie needed to hear that from you, after all you've done for her. Maybe she needs to hear how you've sacrificed things for her.'

'She said I forced the deckchair thing on her,' Olivia said quietly.

'Rubbish!' said Isla. 'From what you've told me, she's enjoyed it.'

Olivia thought about how Hattie had said Olivia should go to Dublin if she so desperately wanted to. Did she really want to go, or was it just about running away? The job offer and the opportunities it would have brought had been tempting, but if she wanted to realise her ambitions and develop her fabric line, couldn't she do so from Milton-on-Sea? She sighed.

'That was a big sigh,' said Isla. 'Look, I think you should stop trying to control the way other people live and give yourself a break.'

Olivia sipped her tea and wondered if that was it. Maybe she had been trying to control Beau and Hattie, but only because she wanted them both to be happy.

'Glenda, one of the women who came to the chair, called me a fun sponge,' said Olivia.

Isla burst out laughing. 'That's a new one! Don't let my kids catch on to that because I think that's how they view me. Maybe they're right and we should have more fun. Relax more, go with the flow, live and let live.'

'It's hard to relax with Oscar on the scene,' Olivia replied, feeling her phone vibrate in her pocket.

She whipped it out, thinking it might be Beau. 'Talking of which, it's him now.'

'And?' asked Isla. 'Enlighten me!'

Olivia read the message out loud. 'He says: "Beau gave me your number. I want to say I'm sorry. I understand why you did what you did. I was vile to you. I want to earn your forgiveness. Our relationship, at the beginning, was the best I've ever had. There are some flowers on your doorstep. Oscar."'

'So he's trying to get into your good books,' said Isla. 'Takes more than a bunch of flowers though, doesn't it? He must feel bad, for not sticking around when you told him you were pregnant.'

Olivia's cheeks warmed. She put her cup of tea down and folded her arms across her middle. 'I didn't. He saw my pregnancy test, and I told him it was a mistake and that I wasn't pregnant. He never knew about Beau. I didn't want him to know. I wanted him out of my life forever and, of course, he and Beau feel wronged by that. At the time I felt sure I'd made the right decision, but now, seeing how hurt he and Beau are and the fact he keeps saying he's totally changed, I'm doubting that. Do you think I'm awful?'

'I don't blame you,' said Isla. 'I'd probably have done the same thing. Mothers put their babies first, above all else.'

'He says I was punishing him for the fact my dad was killed by a drunk driver,' Olivia says. 'Punishing the wrong man sort of thing.'

'No,' said Isla, 'he always had this clever way of twisting things. Concentrate on you a bit more, Liv. Oscar's truth will come to light one way or the other. You can meet with Beau and talk to her when she's cooled off – I'm sure she'll understand where you're coming from. You've always been close.'

Olivia nodded and, noticing three of Isla's children heading towards them, one of them in tears, rose from her chair.

At that moment, another text message arrived, this time from Seth. It was a beautiful photograph of the sun rising over the sea.

This is the mad rhubarb-wielding cyclist. Looking forward to our bike ride. As Albert Einstein said: Life is like riding a bicycle. In order to keep your balance, you must keep moving.

She found herself smiling. The thought of Seth was like an island she could escape to every now and then.

She pushed the phone back into her pocket, thanked Isla for her friendship and headed home.

As she walked, she called Beau and left a message asking her again to meet at the art gallery to talk.

When she approached her house, she saw the flowers – a hand-tied bouquet of blooms in golden tones. She picked them up and held them to her nose. They smelled like honey. She sighed. No matter how hard things felt at the moment, she would keep moving.

TWENTY-THREE

Olivia's befriending client, Winnie, had once told Olivia that sometimes the hardest conversations were the most rewarding. She'd been talking about something going on in her life, but her words had reached inside Olivia's heart and squeezed it. She thought about Winnie's comment now and how she'd repeated it to Hattie at the beach as she waited on a bench in the pretty rose garden of the art gallery. Thankfully, after twenty-four hours with no reply, Beau had agreed to meet her at the majestic Victorian listed building on the clifftop overlooking the sea. Olivia had arrived early and looked expectantly at everyone who came through the gates. She felt incredibly nervous, aware that she had to get this right.

'Mum?' said Beau from behind her.

Olivia swung round and stood up. 'Hello,' she replied, surprised to see Hattie there too. 'I didn't know you were both coming. How did you get here? I could have given you a lift.'

'On the bus,' said Hattie. 'I thought I should come too, after the horrible way I spoke to you, and after what Beau told me about Oscar returning. I didn't know. You must have been struggling with all of this. I'm sorry I didn't notice. When I think about it, I realise I'm guilty of not noticing rather a lot of things with you. Which isn't very good mothering.'

Hattie moved forward, put her arms around Olivia and pulled her close.

'It's okay, Mum, forget about it,' Olivia replied, hugging her back, though Hattie's words rang in her ears.

She smiled at Beau. 'I wanted to show you something, to help you to understand my decisions better.'

Olivia led Beau and Hattie to a painting hanging in a small room of the gallery. The painting, called *The Dance of Zalongo*, pictured a line of women holding babies and children at the top of a mountain edge, with some jumping to their death below. Beau and Hattie recoiled at the sight of it.

'Do you know the story of this painting?' Olivia asked quietly.

'No,' said Beau. 'I'm not sure I want to either.'

'It looks wretched,' said Hattie.

'There's also a monument in Greece on the same subject,' said Olivia. 'It was put up in 1961 to commemorate the women and children who died in 1803 in an act of self-sacrifice. The women in this painting were trapped in the village of Zalongo by invading troops, and rather than be caught, the mothers threw their children off the cliff before jumping themselves, apparently dancing and singing as they did so.'

'Oh my God, that's terrible,' said Beau, her expression dark. 'Why are you telling me that? It's so grim! I thought we were here to talk about us!'

'It was an act of bravery,' said Olivia. 'Those women were protecting their children. That's not the only example I could tell you about.'

'But the children didn't get a say in it, did they?' said Beau.

'But when children are young, their parents have to do what they think is the right thing to protect them,' Olivia replied. 'I want you to know that I believed I was doing the right thing by not telling Oscar about you and then not telling you about Oscar. I did it because I love you.'

'Bit of an extreme example,' said Beau.

'Very extreme example – it's on another level. But the sacrifice I made on your behalf was because I believed it was the best decision,' said Olivia. 'I'm trying to show you what it's like to be a mother and I want it to have an impact, to not just be my words about the things Oscar did when we were together. Mothers feel incredibly protective of their children.'

Hattie and Olivia shared a glance, then Hattie looked at her feet.

'That's how I felt about you, right from the moment I knew I was pregnant,' said Olivia. 'I wanted to protect you from who Oscar was. I had to be strong.'

'But he's not like that now,' Beau said, almost in tears. 'If you'd told him about me, maybe he would have cleaned up his act earlier. Maybe he would have come back sooner and been a dad to me.'

'Maybe,' Olivia said. 'Maybe not. I wasn't prepared to give him the benefit of the doubt. I'd already given him so many chances.'

'Did you ever love him?' Beau asked.

'Yes, of course. When I met him, I really loved him. But I didn't like the man he became. I thought I could help him, but when you came onto the scene, I had to look at it all differently and think about you. He was moving back to New Zealand and I thought a clean break was best. I didn't want him to come back and for it to start up again. For me, it was time to focus on you alone; get a job, sort out a house, be a good mother. I've found it difficult to live with that decision and I've often wondered if I did the right thing. I've always dreaded him coming back, and there've been so many times when I wanted to tell you the truth, but as the years passed, I couldn't un-tell my lie. I just thought we could keep on keeping our heads down while he was safely on the other side of the world.'

Beau looked at the painting again and sighed. 'This painting makes me feel so sad. When I paint, I want to make people feel uplifted, happier, to feel that their situation has been noticed and that they're valued. And to make other people, onlookers, ask questions about the environment they live in.'

Olivia nodded enthusiastically. 'Asking questions is really important. Thinking about the reasons people do things is important. That's what this painting does too. It asks us to think about why those women would have made such a decision. Their situation is unfathomable to us now, but the strength of their conviction, their defiance, their ultimate sacrifice is something we can relate to.'

Hattie sat on a bench in the art gallery and fumbled in her pocket for a tissue.

'I understand what you're trying to tell me,' Beau said quietly. 'But can you understand my point of view? I've always wondered about my dad, and now he's turned up and seems to want to know me. It's not that I don't trust you and believe what happened, and I'm sorry that you were unhappy, so sorry, but I want to believe he's changed. I don't want to believe he's all bad, because he's half me. If he's bad, maybe I am.'

'No,' said Olivia, 'that's not how it works. It was the alcohol – it unleashed something in him that he'd pushed down.'

'But if he's sober now, shouldn't I – we – give him a chance?' Beau asked. 'I don't think we're like these women. I don't think we need to run and jump off the side of a mountain. I think we can face him and hopefully discover that he's not the person you fear he is.

'I tell you what,' Beau went on. 'I'll meet him in his restaurant to discuss the mural and see how that goes. You can come with me if you like. Or I'll take Wren. I just want to find out a bit more about him. Please give me your permission. You've always taught me to give people the benefit of the doubt.'

'Oh, Beau,' said Olivia, 'I don't know if—'

'I'm going to do it anyway so you might as well get used to the idea.'

She walked off a few strides and started studying another painting.

Olivia felt bewildered. She would have to change tack; be brave, support Beau and meet Oscar with her, or let her go with a friend. She would have to contact Oscar and speak to him directly in a calm manner. He would probably expect her to be remorseful. She dug her fingernails into her palms at the thought and glanced over at Hattie, who'd hardly said a word.

'Come over here, both of you,' Hattie said suddenly, patting the bench she was sitting on.

Olivia and Beau moved towards Hattie and sat down either side of her.

'Look, we need to stick together, don't you think?' Hattie said. 'Do you know what families of otters do when they sleep in the river? They hold hands, so that nobody drifts off while they're sleeping. I'm not going to let either of you drift off, whether you like it or not.'

That evening, with Beau staying at Hattie's for one more night to 'think', Olivia lay on the sofa in her pyjamas feeling sorry for herself, half a baguette filled with dark chocolate on the floor beside her. When someone knocked on the door, she answered with only her nose and lips poking through the gap, to conceal the fact that she was wearing her pyjamas.

'Are you ready?' Seth asked. 'I've wheeled a bike here for you. This is a super road bike, one of our newest additions. I think you'll love it.'

He was freshly scrubbed and smartly dressed. Olivia flushed – she'd completely forgotten about the ride.

'I'm so sorry,' she said. 'I didn't realise the time. Come in and I'll be five minutes.'

Olivia flew around her bedroom, chastising herself, pulling her jeans and a T-shirt out from under a pile of laundry. She changed quickly, checked her reflection, arranged her hair and grinned at herself to check her teeth. After dabbing a tiny bit of perfume onto her wrist, she ran back down the stairs to find Seth in the kitchen, unloading vegetables from a hessian sack.

'Ready,' she said. 'Sorry about that. My mind is in a hundred different places at the moment. What have you got there?'

He turned and grinned at her. 'Beetroot and broccoli from my garden. I've got more than I can eat myself. Perhaps you'll let me cook for you one evening? You look fabulous, by the way. You're very beautiful.'

Olivia blushed a deep shade of red and looked down at her very un-fabulous outfit.

'Sorry,' he said. 'I didn't mean to embarrass you.'

She waved a hand in front of her face, laughing. 'No, no, you didn't – I'm just not used to compliments. Right, I better lock up.'

With Seth in her kitchen, she felt self-conscious, yet he seemed perfectly relaxed, quite at home. She busied herself with locking the back door, shoving it with her shoulder to get it to close properly.

'Does it always do that?' he asked.

Olivia nodded.

'I can sort that for you if you like. Just need to shave a bit off the door, I think.'

Olivia thanked him and pulled on her cardigan, wanting to leave before the house showed any more of its flaws.

While she was finding her purse, he spotted one of her sketchbooks and held it up. 'May I?' he asked.

She nodded and shrugged at the same time. 'Just some doodles.'

'Doodles!' he said. 'These are amazing! What are they for? This is where your daughter gets her talent from.'

Olivia moved to his side and looked over his shoulder. There were pages of designs, sea-themed mostly – starfish, beach huts, deckchairs, shells.

'They're designs for textiles,' she said. 'Before my stepdad died, I was planning on moving to Dublin to take up a job there managing a haberdashery shop. I'd worked for the owners before, in a shop on the high street. They'd seen my designs and said they'd help me develop them into a collection of fabrics. My own collection. It's a bit of a dream though. But everything was put on hold, you know, when Jesse died and my plans changed.'

'I'm sorry,' said Seth, glancing at her. 'Couldn't you do it yourself, without the shop's help? Design and sell the fabrics – or find a stockist?'

'I guess,' she said. 'It's just the expense and time and space really. I hand screen-print them. The store had amazing equipment because they used to run classes – well, I used to run the classes. I trained as a teacher years ago. I do have some small-scale equipment for little projects, but it's all in my attic and a bit old now.'

'There's space upstairs from my shop if you needed somewhere to base yourself,' Seth said. 'It's a great room, with a view of the river from the window. All it's being used for at the moment is storage.'

'I—' she started, then her words failed.

'Think about it,' he said. 'You shouldn't let your talent go to waste. Shall we get going?'

Olivia felt something stir in her that she hadn't felt since she'd been offered the job in Dublin. Excitement about the future? The joy of someone being interested in her?

Seth showed her around the bike he'd brought for her and gave her a helmet. 'I thought we could cycle along the river path and have a bite to eat? I've brought some bread and cheese, and a couple of beers if you'd like? Or if you're hungrier, we could get some fish and chips? They're best eaten by the sea though, don't you agree? Or is that a bit unsophisticated?' He looked suddenly worried.

'I wholeheartedly agree they're best eaten by the sea,' she replied. 'Salt in the air and on your chips. But bread and cheese are perfect. Thank you.'

Olivia felt the knots in her shoulders loosen a little as they rode. She loved the feeling of the warm breeze against her skin, the scent of honeysuckle from the hedgerows, and the freedom of cycling. The bike he'd lent her was elegant but robust, new but with a vintage shape. It was a beautiful dark red colour, with a light sparkle in the paint.

They cycled along the stony path beside the River Stour, which, to begin with, was busy with paddleboarders and kayakers, but as they travelled further away from the residential area, it became quieter, busy instead with ducks, swans and a heron, which they stopped to watch for a few silent moments. As they rode, Seth asked Olivia questions about her fabric designs and she began to feel that, maybe, she didn't have to forget her dreams.

He talked about his life too. He'd had an office job after university but soon realised he couldn't sit behind a computer all day – he had to do something active and outdoors. He'd always loved cycling and doing up bikes, and there wasn't a good cycle shop or cycle-repair shop locally, so he and a friend started one up. He was mad about cycling. There was nothing like seeing the world from the cyclist's perspective, he said – you saw so much more than you did in a car. In lockdown, business had soared, he told her, because everyone wanted a bike. The extra cash meant he'd more time to volunteer for the cycling charity – the older people seemed to love it.

'There's this one lady, with fluffy white hair, who looks like butter wouldn't melt, but crikey, the way she talks about the other residents in her care home would curdle milk,' he said, laughing. 'She's fantastic.'

He was upbeat, humble and made Olivia laugh. He checked she was okay every now and then, and when they reached a green space with a wooden bench, he suggested they stop for a drink.

'And do you have any children, or have you ever been married?' Olivia started, wondering about his private life. 'Sorry if I'm prying.'

A cloud passed over Seth's face; it was the first time she'd ever seen him not smiling, but it only lasted for a second.

'No,' he said. 'I was in a relationship for about ten years, but she decided she wanted a more conventional life. John Lewis at the weekends, a carpet, that kind of thing. Ha!'

'Conventional life?'

'I live off-grid,' he explained. 'It's a big cabin basically, on the edge of the New Forest. Solar panels, vegetable garden. I renovated an existing structure, but it took a long time. Not everyone's cup of tea as it turns out, particularly in the winter. But I love it. You should come and visit some time – I think you'd appreciate its idiosyncrasy.' He looked at her and smiled.

Olivia found herself smiling back. She was full of admiration for Seth and felt a stab of something she hadn't felt in a while – attraction.

'I'd like that,' she said excitedly.

Seth changed the subject, asking more questions about her life, which she liked about him, because so many people she met only wanted to talk about themselves. She told him about losing her dad, about Jesse and Alec, meeting Oscar and that relationship being a disaster.

'I've made some bad decisions!' she said.

'You beat yourself up a lot,' he replied. 'You should give yourself a break. Look at all you've achieved. Your daughter, your home, the deckchair rental, your artwork. I think you're amazing.'

They were sitting side by side, and Seth put his hand on the small of her back for a moment. Olivia blushed furiously, but she liked the feeling and turned to face him. Seth too had turned pink, and they both laughed a little before leaning in towards each other. It was a brief, gentle kiss, and just as quickly as it happened, it was over.

Pausing for a moment, Olivia then found herself instinctively leaning in for another, longer kiss. Seth enthusiastically reciprocated until a dog walker came past and the dog ran onto the picnic mat, disturbing them.

'Alvin!' the owner snapped. 'Sorry, guys!'

Embarrassed and not sure what to do with herself, Olivia leaped up, laughed and energetically brushed down her jeans, while Seth busied himself with packing up the picnic. It had been a long time since she'd wanted to kiss a man and the feeling both thrilled her and took her by surprise. She caught Seth's eye and they shared a shy smile.

Cycling back home, the kiss hanging in the air like a question mark, Seth talked about the places he'd been to on his bike: Switzerland, Spain, the Pyrenees. She told him how much Michael had loved cycling, about the school bike bus, the sadness she'd felt when Hattie gave her bike away after Michael's death. How long the man who'd killed him had spent in prison before being released.

'What was your dad's full name?' Seth asked.

'Michael Morrison,' she said. 'He was thirty-nine when he was killed.'

'And where did the accident happen?'

'On the Hurst Road. It was early evening. I remember because my mother was complaining that dinner would be ruined if he didn't come back soon. It was macaroni, and it stayed in the oven for two weeks after his death. I've never been able to eat macaroni since.'

From that moment, Seth seemed to lose energy. His pedalling became limp, his lips rested not in a smile but a straight line, and his tan seemed to fade. By the time they'd reached her house, he'd fallen completely silent.

'Is something wrong?' she asked, confused. 'You seem, I don't know, upset. Was it the kiss?'

'No, no, not at all,' Seth replied before asking if he could come in for a moment.

Olivia agreed.

'I've just had the most dreadful realisation,' he told her.

TWENTY-FOUR

The morning after the cycle ride with Seth, a pair of broken spectacles, in white tissue paper, were left on Olivia's doorstep. They were carefully wrapped, a sprig of lavender pushed through the string that fastened the parcel. Olivia carried them through to the living room and sat down on the sofa, where the sun cast bright stripes of light on the burned-orange velvet cushions. Carefully unwrapping the package, her eyes filling up with tears, Seth's words replayed in her head.

'I've always remembered the name... Michael Morrison,' he'd said, nervously clasping his hands together. 'My uncle had been at a family barbecue when his daughter, my cousin, was stung in the throat by a wasp and had an allergic reaction. Apparently, my uncle had had a few drinks, but because her throat was swelling up, he drove her to the hospital. He should have called an ambulance, but he didn't – thought he'd be okay. He pulled out onto the main road and knocked into a cyclist. I've realised that cyclist was your dad, and the way he fell and hit his head on the road... well, it killed him.

'My uncle served a reduced prison sentence for Michael's death, and he's never recovered from the guilt and shame of it.

He broke up with his wife and doesn't see his daughter. He lost his mind. If you've ever seen a man walking around pushing a shopping trolley full of old suitcases and bits and pieces, that's him.

'At the time of the accident, he tried to help. He picked up your dad's spectacles because they'd fallen into the road. I'm not sure on the details – I was only five – but my cousin came to be in possession of the glasses and, for some reason, gave them to my mother. She's never known what to do with them; could never throw them away. She still has them. My whole family felt terrible shame about it, my uncle's life was destroyed and of course your father was killed. I'm so sorry.'

Now, Olivia held the glasses in her hand. They were 1970s in style, with thick pale-brown frames. The lenses were cracked from where they'd hit the road.

She put them on and blinked – her dad's eyesight had been quite bad – before taking them off again and wrapping them back up in the tissue paper. She sat for a moment on the sofa and stared out the window at the plum tree swaying gently in the wind outside. She felt embarrassed about the way she'd spoken to Seth last night, immediately asking him to leave. It was a gut response; she wanted to be alone because she knew she was about to cry.

'I understand if you don't want to see me again,' Seth had said on his way out. 'I didn't want to tell you, because I like you. I like you a lot. But "truth will come to light. Truth will out" – Shakespeare. *Merchant of Venice*.'

Olivia had closed the door while he was still talking. All the emotions she'd locked away since her father had died had come rushing to the surface and literally floored her. She'd slipped down onto the floorboards and sat there, leaning against the wall, in tears, reliving the dreadful moment she'd been told about her father's death.

She didn't know how to feel. She'd always thought of the

driver who'd killed Michael as a careless, selfish man, but Seth had put the accident into context. The driver had been acting out of love for his daughter – he'd done the wrong thing, made the wrong decision, but would she do the same in a similar situation? Now that she had her father's glasses, she felt even more confused: were they a gift from the past, to better understand it, or some kind of warning not to get involved with Seth? Hadn't Miriam said something about spirits sending messages?

'Don't be ridiculous,' she told herself, leaning her head back into the sofa.

But it wasn't only confronting the past that was upsetting Olivia. What of Oscar and Beau? If Oscar really had changed, did that mean she'd denied Beau a father all these years? The possibility made her feel terribly guilty.

'Oh, I don't know what to think,' she said to the empty living room, lifting her feet up and lying on the sofa, clutching the glasses in one hand.

She closed her eyes but opened them again when she heard footsteps outside and the sound of the doorbell.

Seth? Had he come back to see how the arrival of the glasses had sunk in?

She got up from the sofa and opened the door to bright sunlight and a silhouette that could only belong to one man.

Oscar.

'Hi, Olivia,' he said. 'Did you get the flowers?'

She opened and closed her mouth, unable to find anything to say. This was the moment she'd been dreading.

She felt his eyes on her clothing and for a split second felt conscious of how she looked, before reminding herself not to care. Just as he'd appeared in the restaurant in Winchester, he looked smart, slim and healthy. She couldn't deny it – he looked good. Well.

He offered up a baguette, a bar of dark chocolate and two takeaway coffees.

'Can I come in?' he asked. 'Or is there a way I can hire out a chair to sit and talk to you?'

He laughed his big, sudden laugh, like a klaxon, which felt intrusive and too loud. She winced, and he quickly fell silent.

'I...' she started but felt lost for words. 'I don't...'

He took a step forward.

Olivia felt herself trembling. She shook her head. 'No, you can't come in. Wait outside and I'll be with you in a minute. We can walk to the beach.'

Oscar looked crestfallen for a moment, before recovering himself. 'You don't want to eat? Or have a coffee? Come on – you love coffee.'

Olivia's stomach grumbled, but she shook her head.

'No food, but coffee would be good, thanks,' she said, before closing the door in Oscar's face and, with shaking hands, locating her bag and jacket on the coat hooks. For Beau's sake, she would hear what he had to say.

A loud piercing noise filled her ears, her body's warning bell. She looked at her reflection and instructed herself to stay calm.

They walked towards the beach with a gap – an invisible person, the shape of Beau perhaps – between them. Oscar talked in a formal and upbeat tone about his new project, consulting on a restaurant opening in Winchester. He'd been head-hunted by a friend of a friend, who knew about his work in New Zealand, where he'd headed up the kitchens of a group of luxury boutique hotels. Everything was 'great', 'awesome' and 'successful'. He spoke about his career as if he'd never had a bad day at work in his life.

Olivia wanted to ask him if he remembered the months that he'd made her life a complete misery, in part thanks to the stress of his job. He asked nothing about her last fifteen years. She wondered what had happened to the waitress he'd gone off with. She noticed his expensive watch, the silk lining of his coat and thought about the times she'd struggled to make ends meet over the years.

Feeling her resentment growing as he continued to talk about his new contract, the investors and new projects on the horizon, Olivia cut in.

'I'm not interested in your CV, Oscar. What I want to know is why you thought it was okay to contact Beau without consulting me?'

He didn't miss a beat. 'And I could ask you why you thought it was okay to deny that you were pregnant with my child? You've denied me fifteen years of fatherhood.'

Olivia swallowed hard as the emotion she'd pushed deep inside her body travelled up the back of her throat and waited there, in a hard lump. She forced herself not to cry, to remain deadly calm.

'Do I really need to remind you of what you were like?' she said. 'You're talking as if nothing bad ever happened. What about the shouting, the controlling behaviour, the alcoholic rages you got into, that day when you kicked my bike wheel...? You seemed capable of anything.'

'I didn't mean for that to happen, Olivia,' he said quietly, remorseful. 'I know I was a horrible drinker and I was nasty to you, I really was. I'm ashamed. But I would never have physically hurt you.'

'What about that day in the car, when you abandoned me to face the police after you very nearly ran over that little boy?' she went on. 'I wanted you out of my life and as far away from me as possible. When I found out I was pregnant, all I could think about was protecting the baby. The very last thing I wanted was to be tied to you, the sort of person who would drink and drive, after I'd lost my dad in that way. I gave you so many chances, Oscar – I didn't want to believe you were a bad person, but in the end, I had to admit that you were damaging me.'

Oscar's face fell and the colour drained from his cheeks.

'You told me the pregnancy was a false alarm,' he said, his voice trembling. 'And then you told Beau I wasn't interested in her, that I'd rejected her. After everything I went through with my mother abandoning me and my siblings, that was one step too far. I would never reject my child, not ever. When she told me that, it really hurt.'

'To be honest, I don't care if you're hurt,' she replied. 'If you are hurting, then perhaps you'll know a little of what I went through in our relationship. I told Beau you weren't interested because it seemed the most final way to deal with it. Plus, you went off with that waitress!'

'She didn't mean anything,' he said angrily.

'She did to me! Perhaps I should have told Beau that her biological father was dead,' said Olivia. 'In some ways I wish you were, because then I wouldn't have dreaded you coming back for the last fifteen years or be in this situation now.'

'Ouch,' said Oscar. 'Wow.'

Olivia felt a degree lighter for telling him exactly how she felt. For a few long moments, they walked together in silence.

'Look, I know I've got a lot to apologise for,' he said eventually. 'As I said when I sent you those flowers, I know I was vile to you. I'm horribly ashamed. I don't expect forgiveness on a plate, but I want you to know that I am sincerely and wholly sorry for the way I treated you and I'd like a chance to earn your forgiveness.'

Olivia couldn't help but feel that these were just words. How many times had he said sorry before?

'You always said sorry when you'd sobered up,' she said. 'But it was meaningless. What's different now? Well, I guess you want something – Beau.'

'I've had treatment,' he said. 'It's been years – I've done a lot of work on myself. I've done a lot of thinking. I've had anger management therapy. I've concentrated on my career and made a success of it. When we were together, I was so angry. Angry at my boss who made my life miserable, angry at myself for not being good enough, angry at you for being so together and for expecting more of me, and angry at my mother for abandoning us.'

'So have you forgiven your mum?' Olivia asked.

'I'm working on it,' he said unconvincingly.

They walked towards the beach hut, Olivia stewing on Oscar's words. She stopped when they reached it. The deckchairs were still out from the other day.

'Do you want to sit for a moment?' he asked.

They sat down and looked out to sea. Olivia felt confused and tangled up inside. While Oscar had been busy ironing out his creases, she'd been living with the fear of his return and the worry about whether she'd done the right thing. She only had herself to blame for this, but still, it made her angry. And although Oscar was saying the right things, she couldn't just forget everything and start trusting him. He'd made her life a misery for months.

'Honestly, Olivia, I'm sorry. I know I need to prove myself to you,' he said. 'And I will. But please let me get to know Beau. She's my daughter after all. I just want to see her a bit, talk to her, make a connection. I want her to like me.'

At the mention of Beau's name, Olivia lurched to her feet. 'If you see Beau, there will be rules you'll need to follow, and if you do anything,' she said, gulping back a sudden urge to cry, 'I mean anything at all, to upset Beau in any way, shape or form, I will never let you see her again. I know that life is complicated, and people are complex and flawed, and that what you've been through in your life affected you badly, and that you're making an effort to be a better person...' She paused for breath.

'Yes,' he said, nodding. 'It's not been black and white.'

'I get that,' Olivia said. 'But when it comes to Beau, it *is* black and white. You put one foot out of line and that's it. And for this to have any chance of working, we need to be totally honest with each other, okay?'

Oscar narrowed his eyes and opened his mouth, and Olivia braced herself for some kind of dismissive retort, but he seemed to think better of it and nodded his agreement.

'Understood,' he said. 'I understand. Completely. And, Olivia? There were some good times too, right? I mean, with us. Remember those? Maybe we can reconnect. I know I'd like to, if only you'll let me in. We have a lot of catching up to do.' He faced her and smiled a small smile, the lines around his eyes creasing.

Without wanting it at all, a distant feeling from the past tugged at Olivia's heartstrings, taking her by surprise.

TWENTY-FIVE

It was a breezy, blue, beautiful Saturday, with another day of deckchair visitors ahead. Further down the beach, the life-guard's red-and-yellow flag whipped in the wind and, beneath it, a child with a weever-fish sting sat with his foot in a bucket of hot water, his mother holding his hand as she soothed him.

A good mother.

Hattie looked down at the backs of her hands and felt a pang of regret. She didn't want to admit it to herself, but she held a deep-seated fear that she hadn't been a very good mother to Olivia when Michael had died. Or lately, since losing Jesse. She'd been so consumed with grief, she'd leaned heavily on her daughter. *Too* heavily.

Hattie felt a shiver of nerves travel up her spine as she waited patiently for the first visitor, as Olivia fussed over making tea in the beach hut, clashing the cups and saucers down noisily on the tray. She was in an awful mood and looked like she hadn't slept in days but refused to share what was wrong.

Hattie knew it must be about Oscar. If only Olivia would take more notice of that lovely cyclist man, Seth. He obviously liked her. Why else would he cycle the elderly people past the hut several times a day?

Instead of trying to prise the truth out of Olivia, Hattie focused on the day ahead and how she'd arranged for Paul, the journalist from the *Echo*, to come to the hut and photograph Beau's painting before they covered it over. She'd devised a plan that she couldn't wait to share with Paul – if her idea worked out, it would be her legacy to Beau.

'It's that chap, Harvey Holmes, up first,' Olivia said, placing a cup of tea down in front of her so briskly the liquid sploshed over the edges of the cup. 'Here he comes.'

Hattie watched a magnificent bouquet of flowers walk towards the beach hut. Or at least that's how it appeared. Behind the bouquet was Harvey, a man who Hattie and Jesse had, years earlier, helped when he was going through a rough time. Hattie hardly recognised him – he'd put some weight on his bones, was well dressed and smiling broadly. Poles apart from the shivering, wretched man who'd drifted along the beach towards them one cold morning, years ago.

Hattie laughed when he threw his arms around her and held her tight, eventually pushing him off gently and inviting him to sit down, waiting while Olivia served more sloshed tea.

'I was stealing from shops to fund my drug habit,' Harvey explained to Hattie and Olivia. 'I was a horrible, selfish person, a disaster area, but a few people went out of their way to help me and now look where I am. Now I have a job, a wife and precious twin sons!'

He dug into his pocket and produced his phone, beaming from ear to ear as he showed Hattie the image of his baby boys, dressed in matching T-shirts and shorts.

'Family, jobs – they're quite ordinary things to some people, but I feel so thankful for what I have. When they're older, I'll tell my sons that whatever happens to them in life, whatever they do, whatever mistakes they make, I'll stand by them. If you've got someone to stand by you in life, you'll be okay.'

'Any mistakes whatsoever?' asked Hattie, placing her teacup in its saucer. 'A serious crime?'

Harvey paused for a moment then nodded. 'Hopefully I won't have to deal with that, but yes. I know my sons are good people. If they take the wrong path, I'll try to steer them back onto the right one. I know some people could, but I can't imagine cutting them off. People can rehabilitate, change.'

'But what about the people who've suffered at their hands?' Olivia burst in.

Harvey put his hands up, his palms facing Olivia, and she smiled apologetically.

'I know, I know,' said Harvey. 'I admit it's a difficult scenario, but I guess you've got to maybe look at the history of it all. Saying that, if my children were in any danger, I'd probably not be so forgiving. Ah, life – I still can't work it all out! But anyway, Mrs Fryer, I wanted to thank you and Jesse for what you did – that's why I'm here, to say thank you.'

'It was nothing, Harvey,' Hattie replied. 'A pair of shoes, a deckchair, a coat, some hot food, somewhere to stay. Very small things and they certainly don't warrant this incredible bouquet.'

She touched the fragrant flowers, a fabulous mix of bright blooms. The last time she'd been given flowers like this was when Jesse died and she hadn't wanted any cut flowers since then, but these were different; joyful.

'You've no idea what a difference those small kindnesses made to me,' Harvey told her. 'When people walk past you in the street or look at you like you're something they found on their shoe, being treated like a human being means so much. I'm sorry I didn't get to thank Jesse in person. I read about what he did to help that young boy. What a hero!'

Hattie nodded, thinking about what makes a person into a

hero. Jesse would never have thought of himself like that. He was instinctively good, driven by his heart.

'He just wanted to help,' said Hattie, her voice breaking. She shook her head at herself and raised her eyebrows.

'You must miss him,' said Harvey quietly. 'I hope you're not too lonely without him.'

He reached across and rested his hand on her forearm for a moment, in consolation.

Hattie blinked back the tears then nodded and shook her head all at once. 'I was lucky to have him for as long as I did,' she said quietly. 'But I do miss him. I miss having someone to love. I lost both my husbands.'

'There are plenty of people still around for you to love,' Olivia chipped in.

Hattie felt another surge of guilt. How did Olivia feel, without a partner to love or love her? She'd never had a long-term partner since Oscar, only short-term flings that never seemed to develop into anything serious. How did that feel? Was she lonely?

Hattie followed Olivia's gaze to a point much further down the beach where Seth was cycling two elderly people along the promenade, but on a different route to his normal one past the beach hut. She didn't miss the flash of disappointment on Olivia's face, and she swore to herself she'd do something about it. There was still time. She would be a good mother too.

After Harvey left, promising to bring his twins to the beach to meet Hattie, a slim, petite woman in her late sixties – Valerie – arrived. She was a friend of Glenda's and came with a pair of tap shoes in a size five for Hattie to wear and a speaker that she linked up to her phone. After a quick introduction, she put on a Gene Kelly song and began tapping out a dance on the promenade just in front of the hut, indicating that Hattie should join her.

People sunbathing on towels on the beach rested their heads on their hands to watch. A small girl in a swimming costume, watched by her mother, stood nearby, giggling, attempting to copy Valerie's moves.

'Do you want to try?' Valerie asked Hattie, with a gentle, encouraging smile. She wore shorts, a sun top, a floppy sun hat and her tap shoes.

Some people might think her a little ridiculous, but Hattie immediately warmed to her. 'What the hell?' she said, putting on the shoes and trying the shuffle ball, ball change and step-heel.

A man walking his dog past the beach hut paused to give them a round of applause.

'You've already got the hang of it,' Valerie told Hattie, who felt herself smiling – really smiling – for the first time in a long while.

'Must be beginner's luck,' Hattie replied, her cheeks pink with the exertion.

They sat down on the deckchairs, and Valerie gave Hattie a flyer about a tap-dancing group she ran.

'There are all sorts there. Women in their thirties and others in their eighties. Some can do a high leg kick, others can just about manage a knee bend, but we all muddle in together, and the best thing is, we have a good chat after the lesson. You should come – I think you'd enjoy it.'

Hattie pulled a face that conveyed her doubt at attending an actual lesson. She thought of the stack of leaflets Olivia had presented to her over the months since Jesse died and suffered another pang of guilt at being so dismissive.

'I once felt like you do now,' said Valerie. 'When my husband died, I had to completely re-evaluate my life. We did everything together and sometimes we didn't do much at all, just watched TV or read the newspapers. When he wasn't there anymore, I tried carrying on what we did, but alone, and I quickly found that it wasn't much fun. I tried all sorts of activities and discovered that while I'd been watching TV with my husband, others were learning a new skill, making friends, keeping their minds alert and their bodies fit. Though I miss my husband, I'm enjoying the time I have left. I've found I've got a new lease of life.'

Hattie smiled and wrapped one hand around the other, resting them on her lap, finding it hard to believe.

'The way I think about it is that coming along to a group is like someone extending their hand to you,' Valerie said. 'Remember when you were a small child and you felt too frightened to step down off a wall or jump into the swimming pool – someone probably extended their hand to you. We're all from different backgrounds, have different life stories, yet we can all briefly hold hands, metaphorically speaking.'

Hattie glanced at Olivia, who was listening intently.

'Do come,' said Valerie. 'We'd love to see you there. You're a natural – I can tell.'

Hattie pushed on her sunglasses but knew that both Valerie and Olivia had seen the tremble in her bottom lip.

'I will,' she said thankfully. 'I will come. Thank you.'

'It was good of you to stop by,' Hattie said to Paul, later that afternoon. Olivia had gone to the shop to get something or other, and Hattie was keen to talk to the young journalist about her idea. Paul had arrived on a scooter. His face was pink with the heat, and he had a band of sweat across his body where he'd been carrying his messenger bag. He put it down and tried flapping his T-shirt to cool off.

'Have some water,' Hattie said, pouring him a glass and repositioning the sun umbrella so it offered them both shade.

Paul gulped down the water then got out his phone and notepad. Hattie waited patiently for him to test it out, wondering to herself what he'd do if he had to cover a breaking story. Would he be able to cope?

'So, Mrs Fryer,' he said eventually, 'the deckchair for hire is going well?'

'Yes, yes,' said Hattie. 'But this isn't really about that. I've had a brilliant idea and I want you to help me.'

Hattie showed him Beau's portrait and explained that they had to paint over it within the next few days, because of the council's guidelines on painting beach huts. She pointed further down the beach where someone else, who'd seen Beau's painting, had followed suit and decorated their hut, and explained that they too had been informed the painting had to go.

'I've heard that you can do some kind of petition or survey of people on the internet,' said Hattie. 'But I don't know how to do it. I thought you could help me with that. I think, here, on the beach, we should have a "beach hut gallery" every August, where owners are allowed to paint their beach huts however they like – as long as it's not rude or offensive – and they can leave the paintings there for a month. It would be a way to attract a new crowd to the beach and increase the tourist revenue. An exhibition. People can even make postcards out of the photographs of the huts and, that way, we can record the artwork too. What do you think? I think it's a brilliant way to encourage art and art appreciation, and it's free! People can see all the beach huts without having to pay anything, and it will cheer up the beachfront too. For those who aren't any good at art, perhaps they can offer their beach huts to local young people, like my granddaughter, to use as a canvas. It can all be shared on that social media thing. What do you think? If it needs to be run and organised by someone, I know the perfect person.'

Hattie's heart was racing. She hadn't felt so fired up about something in ages.

'You?' asked Paul.

'No,' Hattie replied. 'My granddaughter, Beau. She paints scenes for people who can't leave their homes much. Like the wall outside an old people's home, for example. Isn't that lovely? I want to give something back to her. I think it's time to give the young people a chance to shine, Paul, don't you? Will you help me? I might not be around for long.'

Paul blushed madly. He chewed his pen lid and nodded slightly.

'Great!' Hattie said. 'That's sorted then. Oh, do excuse me for a moment. Can I borrow this?'

She didn't wait for him to answer. She borrowed his scooter and started to ride along the promenade, a little shakily. She'd seen Seth in the distance and wanted to talk to him. She felt sure he could help Olivia shine too.

TWENTY-SIX

Beau had never shown anyone the scrapbook wrapped in a jumper and stuffed into a box under her bed. She knew it was laughable. But when she was twelve, it had brought her comfort to cut pictures out of magazines or brochures that came through the door of people she thought could be her dad. She'd never been able to throw the scrapbook away. Somehow knowing it was there, under her bed, made her feel that knowing him one day was a possibility. Even though Olivia had told her he didn't want to know her, had never wanted to be a father, she'd dreamed of him changing his mind. Coming back. Finding her. And now here he was, standing in front of her, clutching his phone in one hand, a small espresso cup in the other. He wore dark denim jeans and a green linen shirt and looked just like her; hair colour, eyes, the way his mouth curled up at the edges like a sleeping cat. That in itself blew her mind.

'Can you stop for a minute?' he asked, his tone slightly irritable.

He'd been pacing up and down the room behind Beau as she worked on the mural on the restaurant wall, talking into his

phone for the last half hour. She'd picked up that there was a
problem with money for the restaurant.

Beau turned to face him. He stood with his hands on his
hips and frowned as he scrutinised her work – an outline in
chalk, with codes of the colours she'd need for each section.

'How long is this going to take?' he asked, unsmiling. 'I think
you should scale it right down. Make it smaller. We don't have
much time.'

Beau felt the heat rise in her cheeks.

'It'll still be fantastic,' he said with a smile.

This was only the second time she'd met with Oscar, and
it wasn't going well. They'd talked on the phone a few times
and swapped friendly text messages, and as she'd told her
mother, he'd asked Beau to paint a mural on the restaurant
wall. Olivia had finally agreed to let her go on the condition
that she went with a friend, and so Wren had accompanied
her, which Oscar had made clear he thought was ridiculous.
When Beau had arrived at his flat that morning, a young
woman had answered the door wearing one of his shirts and
not much else and didn't seem to know who Beau was, which
had made her feel awkward and embarrassed in front of
Wren.

He'd given Beau the keys to the restaurant, and she'd gone
there to wait for him while Wren went shopping. When Oscar
finally turned up, he was clearly stressed, citing problems with
the restaurant investors. Beau desperately wanted them to get
on well, but in the back of her mind, she heard the sirens of
Olivia's warnings. She was determined to give Oscar a chance,
she was desperate for him to be someone she could like and
even love one day, but she wasn't going to be told what to do by
him – not when it came to her artwork.

'No, I don't think so,' she said, lifting her chin a little. 'I can't
make it smaller, and I can't rush it.'

Oscar let out a puff of amusement through his nostrils,

folded his arms across his chest and nodded. 'You're head-strong,' he said. 'You've inherited that from me.'

She shrugged. 'Maybe. Although Mum's pretty headstrong too.'

He let out a sudden bark of laughter, which made her jump.

'She never used to be! I always thought your mum was a people pleaser. She didn't like to upset people, and if she was annoyed about something, she'd keep it close to her chest, whereas I've always preferred it when people are more direct, get things out in the open. We were just different, that's all.'

Beau felt defensive and protective of Olivia. 'I don't think she likes confrontation. Nobody likes being shouted at.'

He glanced at her with a slightly guilty expression. 'No, of course not,' he said quickly. 'And I've learned over the years that I'm too confrontational. I think it was my training in the kitchen. You wouldn't believe what absolute bullies the head chefs could be. They would swear, shout and even throw things at you. You had to be tough to deal with that. I guess it rubbed off on me. Your mum couldn't cope with what I was like, I know that, but I've changed now. And you're a different kettle of fish to your mum too. I think you can stand up for yourself. You need to be strong if you're going to get anywhere in life.'

Again, Beau felt affronted on Olivia's behalf. He was belittling her by saying she couldn't cope with him and by saying that Beau could stand up for herself while Olivia couldn't. Beau bit her bottom lip. 'Mum's amazing,' she said. 'She brought me up on her own.'

Oscar raised his eyebrows and held his hands up in the air. 'I would have brought you up if she'd been honest,' he said. 'Was it strength or weakness that stopped her from telling me the truth? It's debatable.'

Beau was bright red now. 'I think she was scared of you. I think she was being strong.'

Oscar laughed and pointed to his chest. 'Am I scary? I

mean, really? I admit I drank way too much back then, and I ranted and raved and was rude, but I wasn't scary, Beau. I would never have deliberately hurt anyone. Christ, I'm not a horrible person – I was just going through a bad time. Anyway, you should get going with this if you won't make it smaller! I'm waiting for an important call from one of the investors and then I'll take you to lunch. Is your bodyguard coming with us?' He laughed again.

Beau shook her head. 'Wren's not meeting me until the end of the day. She's shopping and seeing a friend. What about your bodyguard – the one I met this morning? Is she coming with us?'

Oscar flashed her a grin. 'No,' he said, dragging out the vowel. 'She's nobody important.'

Again, Beau felt a little affronted, this time on behalf of the woman who'd been wearing his shirt at the door, and she flushed with sudden anger but then let it go. What could she say anyway?

At that moment his phone rang, and he walked quickly towards the back door and out into the yard.

She looked at her phone to see a message from Olivia, asking if she was okay. Quickly, Beau typed an answer.

All going well with Oscar and mural. Going for lunch soon!
See you later.

Lies. She was telling lies, but she wanted Olivia not to worry and to give herself and Oscar time to get to know each other. It wasn't going to be an immediate thing – the situation was new to them both. She'd begged Olivia to let her meet Oscar and get to know him, and she wanted to believe he was a different person to the man Olivia had described, so she was going to cut him some slack.

She picked up her chalk and started to draw, but it snapped in two and crumbled in her fingers.

'You can have one small glass,' Oscar said. 'I'll do the same. A small celebration for us.'

They were having lunch in a small French restaurant around the corner from Oscar's.

'I'm not sure,' said Beau. 'I don't really like wine...'

'Just one,' he said. 'It's sophisticated to have a small glass of wine at lunch. The French do it in style. Don't you ever have a drink with your mum?'

'Not really,' she said. 'Mum's always telling me not to drink.'

'She should get a life!' he said with a grin, before saying, 'No, that's very sensible of her, and I wish I'd listened to her more when I was younger,' in a voice that made 'sensible' sound incredibly dreary.

'I thought you didn't drink?' said Beau.

'I don't really. But I haven't signed up to total abstinence. I have the occasional drink, but it's under control now. What would you like to eat? I recommend the chicken.'

'I'm vegetarian,' said Beau.

Oscar put down his menu, deep frown lines on his forehead. 'Why?' he asked. 'You're missing out, young lady.'

'I don't want to eat animals. I've been vegetarian since I was ten.'

'But you'll eat animal produce like eggs, cheese and milk, and wear leather?'

Beau blushed and fell silent while he scanned the menu.

'Looks like there's only one vegetarian dish on there,' he said. 'So I guess that's what you'll have. Sorry, I should have checked with you. We could have gone to some sort of vegan place. Makes me realise how little I know you.'

Oscar seemed suddenly vulnerable and Beau gave a small

smile. 'It's fine,' she said. 'This will be lovely. Thank you. Really, I don't mind about the food. I just want to get to know you more. I feel like today has been a bit weird. You seem kind of stressed. Are you nervous about all this?'

Beau's heart was hammering in her chest. She was being direct, but she wanted to get the whole day back on track, to see more of the Oscar she'd met the first time.

The waiter brought over two small glasses of wine and placed them gently on the table. Oscar lifted his up and gestured for her to do the same. He gave her a warm smile and said, 'Cheers,' before clinking her glass. They both took a sip, and Beau tried hard not to show her dislike of the taste.

'I'm sorry, that's my fault. I know I can come across as a bit of an asshole at times,' he said. 'I do take some getting used to. I'm so stressed about this restaurant – it's taking its toll on me. I want to get to know you too. I think we're quite similar. Oh, hang on, sorry – my phone is ringing.'

Oscar pulled the phone from his pocket, rose from the table and went outside the restaurant to take the call.

Beau watched him through the window as he walked back and forth past the door, phone pressed to one ear, his hand over the other, his head bowed. He seemed to be outside for ages and, in that time, she wasn't sure what to do with herself.

Eventually, he came back inside, shaking his head.

'One of the investors has pulled out,' he said, slamming his phone on the table. The colour had drained from his face, and he finished his glass of wine in one gulp.

'It's all going tits up,' he continued with a wry grin. 'I need to find another investor – quickly. What about Hattie? She must have come into some money when Jesse died?'

'I don't know,' said Beau, frowning. 'I know he had properties, but I think they went to Alec, or...'

'Your mum maybe? Can you find out? Please? We need to act quickly, Beau.'

'I'll find out, but—' She stopped speaking, not knowing what to say.

'Thank you,' he said, turning to the waiter. 'Can I get another glass. And one for my daughter.'

Beau shook her head. 'No, I'm fine, thank you. Just water for me.'

'Daughter,' Oscar repeated. 'You're my daughter! I can't believe I've got a daughter! Isn't this just surreal? Right, let's get off to a better start.'

Beau wrapped her ankles around each other under the table and crossed her arms over her lap. He picked up his fork and tapped his glass a few times. The two nearest tables looked over.

'This is my amazing daughter!' he told them. 'I've only just found out I have a daughter. Isn't she fantastic? I think she's absolutely fantastic.' Oscar's eyes shone with tears.

Beau smiled then frowned, not knowing what to make of him. The diners raised a glass, and one lady clapped her hands together a few times. Beau's cheeks glowed red, and she stared at the menu, not seeing any of the words, which were dancing across the page.

'It's true,' he said quietly across the table. 'I really do. Hey, Beau, I think we're going to get on like a house on fire.'

Beau felt confused, part elated, part vulnerable, but in the pit of her stomach, she felt mostly wary. She wanted to know Oscar, wanted to know where she was from, her roots, who her mother had loved – and then despised. Then she had a thought that made her stomach turn in on itself: when was a house on fire ever a good thing? Surely, after the blaze, there would only be ashes left.

TWENTY-SEVEN

'Mum!' Olivia called for the third time, knocking on Hattie's front door, a growing sense of unease in her stomach. There was still no answer, so Olivia rifled through her bag to find the spare keys. With clammy hands, she let herself into Hattie's house, flicked on the lights and marched through each room, calling, 'Hello.'

She wasn't sure what she was expecting to find, but the house was empty. Olivia frowned, frantic scenarios playing out in her mind. Had Hattie fallen ill and been taken to hospital? Had she gone to the corner shop and tripped on the pavement in her ill-fitting sandals?

Moving to the telephone table, Olivia noticed a card in an envelope with Hattie's name on the front. She read the contents. It was from Francine and said that she wanted to put the past behind them and give their friendship another chance. She'd included her phone number too and drawn a little arrow pointing towards it, with 'ring me' written above. Olivia smiled.

She checked the hook where Hattie hung the keys and noticed that the beach-hut key was missing. Perhaps she was there?

Setting off towards the beach, Olivia was acutely aware that she didn't know what to do with herself while Beau was with Oscar. Her heart was in her mouth. Her stomach ached. She couldn't stand the fact that they were together and that she didn't know what was going on or how Beau was feeling. She'd checked her phone about one million times since Beau's last text message came through, saying everything was going well. She'd also called Wren, who'd told her the same story – that she'd called Beau and Beau had said she was going to lunch with Oscar in a French restaurant. She was going to meet her at 4 p.m. to catch the train home together.

Olivia sighed. That was another two hours away.

She longed to know what they were talking about and to see for herself that Beau really was okay. It wasn't that she thought Oscar was going to harm her – she would never have allowed any meeting to go ahead if that was the case – but more that she was worried he would disappoint Beau in some way. Being let down by someone you wanted to love and to love you back was a dreadful feeling. And the Oscar she knew was a complex person; reel you in, spit you out, build you up, cut you down. But just maybe he had changed.

'You can't control this,' Isla had told her. 'You have to let it play out and be there for Beau if it all comes crashing down in a heap.'

From the clifftop, Olivia could see down to the beach hut, where Hattie was sitting with Francine. The two women had their heads close together, obviously deep in conversation.

Olivia felt a rush of emotion. This was what she'd hoped for – for Hattie to be motivated enough to meet a friend, to have someone to talk to and share life with. She was delighted but felt something else too – the sensation that while Hattie and Beau were busy living their lives, she was wallowing in her quiet loneliness.

Hovering for a moment, she decided not to go down to the

beach – Hattie and Francine needed to catch up alone. And she decided not to text Beau again either. Beau wouldn't want her breathing down her neck as she took the first tentative steps towards getting to know Oscar.

'What about me?' she whispered.

An image of Seth came into her head, and she found herself scanning the promenade for his bike. She didn't see him, but she noticed Glenda, striding elegantly along the promenade like a lead ballerina, towards the beach hut, where Hattie was waving at her energetically.

Olivia walked along the beach, away from the hut, and her mind returned to Seth. She felt horribly guilty for asking him to leave the other night when he'd told her about Michael. She'd just been upset. Before that point, she'd loved the evening and enjoyed his company.

Brushing her lips with her fingertip, she remembered their kiss – she'd enjoyed that too. She wanted to see Seth again, but now that Oscar was on the scene, her head was crowded with thoughts of him and how to be around him.

Noticing a piece of driftwood on the sand, tangled in seaweed and among mermaid's purses and shells, she took a quick photo of it and sent it to Seth with a message. *I'll save this for you.* She picked it up and pushed it into her bag.

There was an immediate reply: an image of a storage room with the words: *I'll save this for* you.

Hours later, her fingernails bitten to the quick, Olivia sat bolt upright on the sofa when she heard Beau's footsteps outside the front door. She rushed to the hallway to greet her, asking questions before she'd even shut the door.

'How did it go?' she asked. 'Was it okay? What did you talk about? Did you get on alright?'

Beau's expression was inscrutable as she peeled off her bag and put her phone on the side.

'Yeah,' she said, her tone flat and her eyes not meeting Olivia's gaze. 'It was fine. We got on well. He's interesting. It was a bit stressful for him because an investor pulled out of the restaurant, so he started worrying about that. Understandably. But, you know, it was just bad timing. He's totally panicked about it and even asked if you or Granny had any money to invest. He said you'd get it all back, but I said I didn't know about all that. Anyway, yeah, it was... fine.'

Olivia felt heat rise to her cheeks. 'Oscar said what? He thinks Granny or I will give him *money*? I don't believe it! I literally cannot believe it.' She threw her hands up in the air and shook her head, exhaling so her cheeks puffed out. 'He's just incredible,' she said again. 'I knew it!'

'Oh, for God's sake, don't freak out,' Beau snapped. 'I knew you would. It was just a question, a comment. I was trying to explain about the day.'

'Well!' said Olivia. 'It's just a bit of a surprise, that's all. It's to be expected with him though.'

'Stop!' said Beau. 'I shouldn't have mentioned it! It was an off-the-cuff remark – he probably didn't even think it through.'

'I'm sorry he asked you and put you in that awful position,' said Olivia. 'I've been so worried about you today. Rightly so, it seems.'

Beau threw her bag down on the floor. 'God, Mum, I wish you'd stop worrying about me! You're so focused on me... And always so *sensible*... And... *you should get a life!*'

As soon as Beau said the words, she looked as if she regretted them, but she didn't apologise. She ran up the stairs, taking two at a time, and into her bedroom, slamming the door behind her.

Beau's words rang in Olivia's ears. *You should get a life!* A shiver, like cold water, trickled down her spine. It sounded like something Oscar would say.

A wave of anger washed over her. He had this way, even now, of reducing her, humiliating her.

She went upstairs and knocked on Beau's door before letting herself in. Beau was sitting on the floor, leaning against her bed. In her hands she held a scrapbook, open at a page of lists and drawings.

'What's that?' asked Olivia, sitting down next to her.

Beau shrugged, and Olivia peered over her shoulder. She saw in Beau's younger handwriting lists of things referring to an imaginary dad. Possible names. Possible jobs. There were illustrations too, of a man dressed in various outfits, some where he was talking to a girl.

Olivia swallowed hard, her cheeks flushing. Carefully, she put her arm around Beau's shoulders.

'I'm sorry, darling,' she said softly. 'I'm sorry I've not been honest with you in the past. I was trying to protect you, but I can see that in doing so, I've made things worse. How did today go really?'

Beau shrugged again. 'I want to make my own mind up,' she said, sniffing. 'I want to give it time. I want this to work out, the three of us – to get on together, a little family. A clean slate.' She looked up at Olivia, her face splotchy with tears.

Olivia held her tight and kissed the top of her head. 'I know you do. I'm sorry. I'll stop interfering and stop jumping to conclusions.'

From Beau's bed, her phone buzzed repeatedly. She lifted it up and checked the screen, before jumping to her feet. 'It's Oscar. He's on his way here.'

'What?' Olivia asked, her hand flying to her mouth. 'Why? I mean, why would he come here now... for money? Text him back and say now isn't a good—'

Olivia's sentence was interrupted by the sound of the doorbell ringing. They looked at one another.

'I'll tell him to go,' said Olivia. 'He can't just waltz in whenever he feels like it.'

'No,' said Beau firmly. 'I'd really like us to be together, the three of us, just to see what it's like to have a mum and a dad in the same room. Maybe then I can stop obsessing about it, imagining I've missed out on something amazing. Please, Mum – this is important to me.'

Olivia closed her eyes briefly and gave a slight nod, then took a deep breath and steeled herself for what was to come.

TWENTY-EIGHT

'This is so weird,' said Beau, biting her bottom lip and wrapping her arms around her waist. 'You two being here, *together.*' A wary smile played on her lips and she was blinking rapidly, which she did when she was nervous.

Olivia felt queasy. An image of Little Red Riding Hood popped into her thoughts, the sly wolf talking his way into her life.

Oscar was in the kitchen, taking things out of a carrier bag and placing them on the counter, as if he'd done it a thousand times before. 'You wait until you try my romesco and crispy potatoes,' he said. 'You'll never want me to leave.'

He laughed his loud, sudden laugh, making Olivia physically jump, opened a few drawers, selected a knife and a chopping board, and placed them down in position as if he was a surgeon preparing to operate.

She felt a combination of embarrassment at the state of her kitchen, indignation about him being there and numb with the shock of it all. She didn't really know what to do. This man she'd feared reappearing in her life for the last fifteen years, this man who'd made her so unhappy and who she'd told such a big lie to, was now in her home, acting as if this was all perfectly normal.

'Can I borrow this?' he asked, unhooking Olivia's denim apron from the peg on the back of the door and, when she nodded, pulling it over his head and tying the string at the back. 'This is new, very nice.'

Olivia pulled a face. What did Oscar know about what was new and what wasn't? 'It's about ten years old,' she told him.

'Of course. I'm sorry – it just feels a bit like we were never apart!' he said, with another laugh.

'I need a glass of wine,' she murmured.

She pulled the stopper out of a previously opened bottle, took a glass from the draining board and filled it with red wine, then felt suddenly aware of Oscar's gaze. 'Unless... is it too... difficult for you if I have wine?' she asked.

Oscar shook his head. 'No, you go ahead. I'll abstain.'

'You had a drink earlier, didn't you, Oscar?' said Beau. 'You said you sometimes do.'

Olivia felt her stomach crunch. She put down her glass. 'I thought you'd stopped?'

'I have,' said Oscar, turning his attention to chopping up red peppers. 'Ninety-nine per cent of the time. Occasionally I have one, like today. It was just one.'

'So can you stop at one?' Olivia said to Oscar's back.

'Obviously. Now where's your olive oil?' he asked crisply, clearly not liking the interrogation.

Olivia glanced at Beau, trying to communicate that the fact he'd had a drink in her company wasn't a great sign, but Beau simply shrugged.

Suddenly, Oscar stopped chopping and turned to face her.

'Honestly, Olivia,' he said. 'I can literally feel you worrying – it's like a forcefield around you. Don't. I'm not the man I was. I know I was a nightmare and have a lot of making up to do until you trust me again, but I'm fully repentant. I even meditate these days.'

Olivia didn't know what to think, so she busied herself with clearing a heap of laundry from the floor.

'I know I was a bit irritable today, Beau,' Oscar said. 'But it was the news about the investors – it completely threw me off. I can be prickly, I know that, but it's nothing personal.'

Ah, thought Olivia, the money. Was that why he'd invited himself in with a shopping bag of goodies – to soften her up and ask for investment? She opened her mouth to speak, to tell him that was totally out of the question, when he interjected.

'And I should never have asked about the possibility of investment from Jesse's inheritance,' he said. 'That was knee-jerk panic talking, and I can't believe I even said it! I've got someone in mind – a businessperson with a portfolio of restaurants. I've already contacted him. It'll work out.'

Beau threw Olivia an 'I told you so' look and then disappeared out of the room, saying she was going to get something from upstairs.

Oscar left the pan bubbling away and moved over to the wall behind the kitchen table, where there were numerous photographs of Beau in mismatched frames Olivia had found in charity shops. He studied them closely.

'Beau's great,' said Oscar. 'Absolutely great. You've done a fantastic job in bringing her up. It's... These photographs, they're... I've missed out on so much. I always wanted a daughter, you know?'

'She's my world,' Olivia replied. 'I did what I thought was right at the time, Oscar.'

'I know, I know,' he said. 'But I wish you'd told me the truth. My life would have been so different. Maybe you and I could have worked things out.'

Olivia was shaking her head. Hot tears stung the back of her eyes. 'No,' she said. 'It was over. That day, when you drove the car, that was too much.'

'That day in the car was dreadful,' he said, nodding, sitting down at the table in a defeated manner and pushing his shirt-sleeves up to his elbows. 'Let me explain. Before I came to meet you that day, I got an email totally out of the blue from my mother. She told me she didn't want to hear from me, that she'd moved on and remarried. She said my father was a bully and that all she had from our time together as a family were bad memories. She didn't even ask whether I was in a relationship, what I did for a career or how I'd been since she left. I'd wanted her to say sorry. After her email, I drank half a bottle of whisky and came to the restaurant. I shouldn't have done that, I know.'

Olivia didn't say anything, but she sat down at the table opposite him.

'I didn't care anymore,' he continued. 'I realised that I was a bully too, just like my dad. I knew how badly I'd treated you, and when I got in that car, I basically didn't care what happened. Until I saw that little boy – the sight of him kind of shocked me into seeing myself through someone else's eyes.'

'You ran away,' Olivia said quietly. 'You left me there.'

'I was ashamed, Liv. I was so ashamed. I *am* ashamed of how I was. I'm sorry.'

He reached over the kitchen table and gently took her fingertips in his before letting them go.

'I wish you'd told me the truth,' he went on, 'but I forgive you because what's the alternative? Holding a grudge for the rest of my life? Resenting you, who I loved so much and have thought about so many times since? I wish things had worked out differently between us, and I hope that you can forgive me. I would honestly love to be in yours and Beau's lives in some small way.'

Oscar looked into Olivia's eyes and held her gaze. She'd

been angry with him for so long, but he seemed genuinely repentant.

She opened her mouth to speak but couldn't find the words. She left her hand in his for a long moment before gently moving it away – just as Beau came back in the room.

'Shall I leave you alone?' she asked.

'No,' said Olivia. 'Of course not. Sit down with us.'

Olivia flushed. She'd used the word 'us' and it felt too intimate.

'So,' Oscar said, 'tell me about your life, Olivia. Is there a man hiding in the wardrobe upstairs?'

Oscar had changed his tone and was more upbeat in Beau's company.

'She doesn't have a man!' said Beau. 'Do you, Mum? She's been on a few dates though. What was that nutjob called who wouldn't leave you alone? Mark?'

'Yes, Mark,' said Olivia, rolling her eyes. 'We went on two dates and when I said it wasn't going anywhere, he would come into the shop I worked in, trying to win me over. My boss had to tell him to go and not come back. I've just not met anyone, and I've been busy with you, Beau, and with Granny since Jesse died. She's been very lonely.'

'She's not the only one,' muttered Beau. 'You're lonely too.'

'That's not good,' said Oscar. 'Not good at all.'

He briefly locked eyes with Olivia, but she quickly looked away.

'For goodness' sake, you two,' said Olivia. 'I am not!'

The meal Oscar prepared was amazing. Knockout good. Olivia ate so many crispy potatoes smothered in romesco that her stomach groaned. After dinner, Beau had shown Oscar her portfolio and photographs of all the murals she'd done, including the beach-hut painting of Hattie.

'This one is for a boy who has to stay inside on sunny days because of a rare skin disorder,' she said, pointing to an image of the garage door. 'And this one was a blank wall that the residents of an old people's home looked at, day in, day out. Now they can look at a pier, with twinkling lights and maybe imagine walking down it, feeling the fresh air on their faces.'

Olivia mentioned Seth and how he cycled older people around in a trishaw – part of a charity initiative.

'Doesn't he work?' said Oscar. 'Or is he just a volunteer?'

'He does work and there's nothing "just" about being a volunteer,' Olivia replied. 'He has a bike shop. He does the volunteer cycling in his spare time.'

'Perhaps we should call him Saint Seth,' said Oscar, winking at Beau and returning to the portfolio.

'Beau, I've had a thought,' he said. 'There's an exhibition in Winchester for amateur artists in a couple of weeks. You should exhibit your work. I'll have a word with the organiser if you'd like me to. The venue is opposite the restaurant. You could come too, Olivia, and maybe see the restaurant. I'll save you both the best table.'

Beau beamed. 'Great idea. Isn't it, Mum?'

Olivia nodded gingerly, but her mouth was set in a straight line.

'Don't look so worried,' said Oscar. 'As I said, I'd like to try to be a part of Beau's life. I can help, financially, and take the pressure off you – I can see your hands are full, having your mum to help and a teenager to support.'

'We're okay,' said Olivia. 'I've managed. I'm managing.'

But inside, Oscar's words struck a chord. She hadn't realised how much emotional and physical energy she'd put into Hattie and how much the last year had taken out of her.

'You could do with a hand,' he said, scanning the room. 'That's quite clear. Employ a cleaner if it's too much work. You need to spend some time on yourself. Be pampered.'

And just as soon as he'd offered his olive branch, she felt as if he'd snapped it in half and undermined her. What did a bit of peeling wallpaper matter if Beau was okay and Hattie was happier? Olivia was doing her best.

Beau was looking at her with a confused, penetrating stare.

Olivia opened her mouth to say something in her defence, but before she could get anything out, Oscar grinned and said, 'Don't take offence. I just want the three of us to get to know each other and to help in any way I can. It would be wonderful if we can have some sort of future together.'

Olivia remembered Elaine, the woman who'd said you had to deal with the past before you could move forward. Olivia wasn't convinced she was ready, but Beau's eyes were on her and she could almost feel her willing her to agree with Oscar.

She smiled and nodded.

'Great!' he said. 'Anyone for pudding?'

TWENTY-NINE

The TV weather map was awash with sunshine, but Olivia's mood was a dark cloud above her head.

'What's eating you?' Hattie asked her the following Saturday morning, when they were preparing for the next deckchair visitors. 'You seem very out of sorts. You've forgotten to bring the strawberry jam for a start.'

It was a stifling hot day. There was a heavy stillness to the air; people moved slowly along the beach, flopping onto towels with their hats over their heads. Wasps buzzed near fizzy-drink cans and melted pools of iced lollies on the pavement. The 'NO BBQ' signs were up, and a heat haze rose above the sea. Olivia looked inside the carrier bag she'd brought down to the beach – scones, cream, teabags, milk. No jam.

'Oh, damn it, I'll have to go to the shop. It's Oscar. He's being quite nice. He seems to be sorry for how he was and wants us to be closer. The three of us. He wishes I'd told him about Beau earlier and says it would have shocked him into changing.'

'You did what you thought was right at the time. Maybe he's had time to reflect and is better for it,' said Hattie, straightening her sun hat and draping a blouse over her shoulders. 'I mean, look at Francine. I feel like we're becoming firm friends all over again. We've been speaking almost daily!'

'I do want us to get along, and maybe we can spend some time together if he's hanging around in the UK, but it's so strange after I've spent all these years dreading him coming back!'

'Is he back for good?'

Olivia shrugged. 'I assume so. He hasn't mentioned going back to New Zealand, but I haven't asked him either.'

'If I were you, I'd keep him at arm's length and focus on other things and other *people* in your life, like Seth,' said Hattie, pulling up her sleeve to check her wristwatch. 'Oh look, Olivia, talk of the devil, here he comes. Would you believe the coincidence?'

Olivia straightened up, quickly tucked her hair behind her ears and pushed her hands into the pockets of her dungaree dress.

'Good morning,' said Seth, pulling up to the beach hut on his bike. 'Hattie, am I late? I couldn't remember if you said to come at eleven or twelve. Hi, Olivia. Thanks for suggesting this, but you could have texted me.'

Olivia frowned and looked at Hattie quizzically, but Hattie didn't acknowledge her. Instead, she brushed off Seth's question and gestured to two spare striped deckchairs, which were folded up and leaning against the hut.

'Why don't you take these chairs to the water's edge? It's so hot today. You can put your feet in the water like Jesse and I used to do.'

'But I need to get some jam,' said Olivia.

'Forget the jam.'

'But I need to be here when the visitors arrive. There's the English Channel swimmer, the two knitting sisters and—'

Hattie held up her hand to silence Olivia. 'I can cope. You two go and have a talk.'

Seth immediately carried the deckchairs down to the water, as if they were light as feathers, and set them up right next to the sea. He waved over to Olivia, and, speechless, she waved back. Frowning at Hattie, she kicked off her sandals and began walking towards Seth, who was waiting for her to sit down first, before he did.

'I spoke to your mum the other day,' Seth said. 'And I explained about my uncle and about Michael. She was very kind about it all and said it wasn't my burden to bear.'

Olivia nodded, wondering why Hattie hadn't talked to her about this. 'It's certainly not your burden,' she said. 'I'm sorry about the other evening. I was just a little shocked, you know, but I guess this town isn't very big. Thank you for the glasses – it means a lot to have them.'

Seth gave a little shrug and a small, apologetic smile.

'So what was it you wanted to talk to me about?' he asked. 'Your mum said you'd asked her to ask me. Seems a bit of a long-winded way to go about things. Is it about the space above the shop?'

Olivia cursed Hattie under her breath. 'No, no,' she said, her eyes darting from the sea to Seth to the sky to the people on the beach. She cleared her throat. 'I just wanted... I just wanted to... well... I...' She glanced nervously at Seth's expectant face, not knowing what to say. 'It's about the bike ride, it's about a bike.'

She exhaled and cringed but carried on regardless. 'I thought maybe I could come to the shop, and you could help me buy a new bike,' she said, not missing the disappointment on Seth's face.

'Of course. That's no problem at all. But did you need to see me here to talk about that? I thought, perhaps, you might want to talk about... what happened when we went out, and perhaps maybe that might happen again...?' He looked right into Olivia's eyes and gave a tentative smile.

Although she wanted to speak, although she wanted to say, *Yes, Seth, I'd like that to happen again; I really like you,* she couldn't say a single word.

He sat back in his seat, crossed his arms over his chest and looked out to sea. 'Don't worry,' he said. 'It's all cool. Let's leave things the way they are. We're friends, aren't we? Your mum said your ex is back on the scene. How's that going?'

Olivia opened her mouth, unsure how to answer. 'It's tricky. We've met a couple of times. We're going to an exhibition evening with him. I think Beau likes the idea of us putting the past behind us, but it's all very...'

'Complicated,' he said, standing up. 'I understand. You need to deal with that.'

The energy between them had changed, the tension released.

Seth reached into his bag for something and pulled out a frisbee. 'Want to do something uncomplicated?' he asked, smiling at her.

'Definitely,' she replied, relieved but wanting to say something to show she did like him. 'Seth, I... wanted to say— Oh, forget it, nothing. Sorry.'

'Let's just enjoy the moment – it's a beautiful day,' he said gently before running backwards a little way down the beach.

She gave him a grateful smile, and he crouched into a comical position before flinging the frisbee into the air towards her. Olivia held her breath as she watched it sail through the air – then lunged forward to catch it, almost tripping over. Clutching the frisbee in her hand, she grinned at Seth, who clapped and whooped in celebration. She pushed her feet into the sand and threw the frisbee back in his direction, and he launched himself onto the sand to catch it, just before it hit the ground.

'You're so good at this!' he called over after a few minutes of playing. 'It's so hot though – shall we play in the sea? Have you got your swimsuit?'

'Yes, there's one in the beach hut, but...'

Seth jogged over to her side. 'Come on – what else do you have to do?'

She looked up the beach at Hattie, who was talking to two women, the knitting sisters, who both had balls of wool on their laps and were handing Hattie needles. Seth was already stripping off his clothes to his swimming shorts, revealing his tanned, athletic figure. Olivia felt herself stealing a lengthy glance at his body.

'I'll be a minute,' she said, rushing to the beach hut and changing, before jogging back towards Seth.

Together they went into the water, through the shallows and out deeper until they were in to their waists. They began throwing the frisbee, and Seth invited others who were in the water to join in. He talked to them all, putting people at ease, praising their throws and catches in a humorous, kind way. Soon a large circle of people were playing, and during a few moments when one of the people playing swam out to collect the frisbee, which had gone astray, Olivia lay on her back and floated, staring up at the seagulls flying overhead, and realised she was feeling something she hadn't felt in a while: happy.

Seth's words rang out in her head: *Let's just enjoy the moment – it's a beautiful day.*

THIRTY

'I like this little garden, the house too,' said Oscar. 'But is it big enough for you both? Have you thought about moving somewhere more spacious?'

Oscar, Beau and Olivia were in the garden, a small square of grass with a plum tree in the middle, its branches laden with purple, juicy fruit, and a patio area with a bistro table and chairs. A small ivy-covered shed stood at the back of the garden, alongside a cluster of raspberry bushes. The garden was fenced, but you could see the tops of the neighbours' heads over it if they happened to be in their gardens.

'And maybe somewhere a bit more private?' Oscar added, plucking a plum from the tree and gesturing towards Donald's white head, just visible above the fence.

'Don't mind him,' said Olivia. 'He's always in his garden. You should see his climbing roses – they're divine. When I sit out here in the evening, I can smell their perfume in the air.'

'There's this tree that smells amazing in New Zealand,' said Oscar. 'Lemonwood. You'd love it.'

Olivia had been repotting some of the houseplants when Oscar called to ask if he could stop by to talk to Beau about the exhibition. She'd contemplated getting changed out of her gardening clothes and stopping what she was doing but decided instead to carry on outside. Beau and Oscar sat at the small bistro table, which wobbled every time one of them moved, until Oscar found a piece of wood to wedge under one leg.

Since they'd last met, Oscar and Olivia had texted each other a few times. Kisses were creeping into Oscar's texts, but Olivia kept hers neutral. He'd met with Beau once for coffee too, but it had been a short meeting, which Olivia thought was a good thing. Small steps.

'Sounds nice,' Olivia replied, pausing to smile at him. 'And it might be small, but it's been a great house for the two of us.' She didn't mention the obvious – that with only her salary to rely on, a larger house wasn't on the cards.

'Could have been the three of us,' Oscar said with a gentle laugh, biting into his plum.

Olivia tensed but then let it go. She'd been trying to look at the situation from Oscar's point of view and understand how he felt. 'Let's leave all that, shall we?' she said, returning to her pots.

'Yes,' said Oscar, 'I agree – let's leave it. So, Beau, how are you feeling about the exhibition?'

'Excited!' she said. 'I hope something comes of it. Maybe I'll get more commissions. I've got loads of ideas.'

'Why don't you tell me about them?' Oscar said. 'Show me more of your sketchbooks?'

While Beau talked, Olivia listened and carried on with the pots. She tried to relax into the situation; to imagine what it would be like if Oscar became a part of their lives in some way. If he carried on being like this, would it be so bad?

'What's this?' Oscar asked, picking up the driftwood boat Seth had made that she'd put on an outdoor shelf. He turned it around in his hands.

'Mum's admirer made it,' said Beau.

Oscar shot her a look. 'Admirer?'

Olivia shook her head. 'No. He's a friend. The volunteer I told you about. He makes things from driftwood and bits and pieces he picks up on the beach.'

Oscar tossed it down carelessly. 'Must have a lot of time on his hands,' he said with a laugh.

Annoyed, Olivia picked it up and balanced it carefully back on the shelf.

'No, it's good,' Oscar said. 'I like it. Hey, thinking of boats, I wanted to ask if you'd both like to come out on a boat trip with me, maybe the weekend after the exhibition? I learned to sail in New Zealand. We could go out for the day. I'll make a picnic, you and Beau can relax on deck, take photos, swim. We could have a carefree day together. No pressure.'

Beau nodded enthusiastically at Olivia. 'That sounds amazing, doesn't it, Mum?'

Olivia immediately worried about them spending a whole day together, but Glenda's 'fun sponge' accusation came into her thoughts, as well as Isla telling her to 'go with the flow'.

'It sounds... good,' she said, giving Oscar a small smile. 'Thank you.' She surprised herself by thinking that if perhaps Oscar did have a role to play in their future, it might not be so bad. Beau would be happy, wouldn't she?

'No problem,' he said. 'No problem at all.'

'I've got to make a call now,' said Olivia. 'Befriending call.'

'Sure. We'll finish off out here. Or shall I go?'

Olivia noticed Oscar's hand was trembling. A cynical, wary voice in her head wondered if he was aching for a drink but then decided it must be nerves. This whole thing must be difficult for him too.

'It's okay,' she said warmly, trying to put him at ease. 'Take your time.'

. . .

Edith was in a buoyant mood. She'd made friends with a new neighbour, Sheila, who played the piano and was going to teach Edith how to play too. In return, Edith was going to teach her how to crochet. Edith explained that she'd got talking to her when Sheila popped over with a package that had been delivered to the wrong address.

'We're going to keep our minds busy with each other,' said Edith. 'It's so nice to find someone who's interested in you and your interests and vice versa. Not very complicated, is it, but sometimes it seems almost impossible, like when you're six years old in the playground and everyone else is playing games together and you're sitting there on your own. It takes one person to come over and say hello, that's all. One person to extend the hand of friendship.'

'You're right,' Olivia said. 'It doesn't need to be complicated.'

She thought about Edith's words, and her mind drifted to playing frisbee on the beach with Seth. She knew she liked him, but with Oscar on the scene, she felt she needed to wait and see how things progressed with him and Beau. With the three of them.

While listening to Edith, she looked out the living-room window and watched Oscar leave, turning to give Beau a wave before he got into his car. She expected him to drive straight off, but he sat in the car for a while and then opened the driver's door, as if he was going to get out again. But after another moment he closed it, leaned his head into the headrest, then pulled away. Olivia frowned.

'Olivia, dear?' Edith asked. 'Are you still there?'

'Yes,' she said, turning away from the window. 'I'm sorry – I was distracted for a moment.'

THIRTY-ONE

The three generations of Fryer women were in Olivia's bedroom, in a cloud of spray hair chalk (Beau), body mist (Olivia) and powder puff (Hattie). It was a small room, with walls painted a dark shade of teal, exposed floorboards and a sash window jammed open with a cork drink coaster, and didn't often have guests.

The women stood in front of the huge gilt-framed mirror reclaimed from a clothing shop's dressing room that leaned against the wall because it was too huge and heavy to hang on the old-fashioned lath and plaster. The setting sun shone through the window and turned everything shiny a shade of pink or orange.

Though they were differing heights, the three women shared some similar features – an elegant neck, big eyes and the shape of their jawline – in varying degrees of definition.

Olivia stood in the sixty years between Beau and Hattie, sandwiched in the middle of youth and age. A wave of emotion swept over her. The last time they'd been together in her bedroom like this was on the eve of Jesse's funeral – their black dresses hanging in the wardrobe, nursing cups of hot tea, waiting, none of them wanting to sleep, to avoid the inevitable for as long as possible.

'You both look beautiful,' Olivia said. 'You *are* beautiful.'

Hattie did a little curtsey, pulling the edge of her dress, light blue with sequin trim, away from her very slim body. She looked ready for a ballroom dance, while Beau, dressed in a black bandeau minidress, looked ready to go clubbing.

'Do I look like one of those frilly toilet-roll covers?' asked Hattie. 'Glenda persuaded me to wear this, but she's more flamboyant than me.'

'No, Granny, you look like a film star,' said Beau. 'And, Mum, I haven't seen you dressed up so much in ages.'

Olivia blushed, vaguely aware that she hadn't made this much effort with her appearance in years. 'I'm not dressed up!'

She'd put on a slim-fitting dark grey dress and then taken it off, before putting it back on again. It did wonders for her curves. Her curls were piled on top of her head, and she wore red lipstick. Sitting on the edge of the bed, which was covered in an ancient, floral quilt, she pushed her heeled boots back under the bed and put on her flat thick-soled ones instead.

'It's a special night,' she said to Beau. 'Your first-ever exhibition!'

'World premiere!' said Hattie. 'I wish Jesse could be here to see you.'

Beau gave Hattie a hug before turning to Olivia. 'Are you dressed up because Oscar will be there?' she teased.

Olivia looked at Beau in the mirror and detected something in her demeanour, or was she just tense and nervous about the show?

'No,' said Olivia, sounding more definite than she felt. 'I'm not even a hundred per cent convinced he'll be there tonight, Beau – prepare for that. Tonight is about you and supporting you. I admit Oscar seems to have changed in some ways, but it's early days.'

'Besides,' said Hattie, 'it's Seth she likes.'

'Seth?' said Beau, looking worried. 'I think you should concentrate on one man at a time, Mum.'

'Don't be ridiculous,' Olivia replied, feeling flustered. 'You're both talking nonsense. I'm happy as I am, thank you. I have you two to take care of and that's enough.'

Beau opened her mouth as if she was about to tell Olivia something but seemed to change her mind.

'Ready?' Olivia asked, linking arms with Hattie and Beau. 'Let's go.'

Alec had offered to drive them to the venue, because Hattie had invited Francine and he seemed to be Francine's official driver.

'You ought to get a chauffeur's cap,' said Olivia as they squeezed into the back seat of the car, which smelled strongly of an interior valet cleaner. Olivia screwed up her nose, but she was touched that he'd gone to the bother.

'There's not one big enough for all Alec's brains,' said Francine. 'He went to Oxford University.'

'Here we go,' said Hattie under her breath, winking at Olivia.

'I was so proud of him,' said Francine.

'If you don't mind, I am here,' said Alec in his clipped voice. 'And that was thirty years ago. I have achieved things since then – I don't know why we have to keep harping back to ancient history.'

'That was where he met Amelie,' said Francine. 'The woman who broke his heart. She's married with three grown-up children now, without a thought for my darling Alec. If only I could give her a piece of my mind. That woman has a lot to answer for.'

'She has nothing to answer for,' said Alec. 'She didn't want to be with me. It's as simple as that.'

'Doesn't feel simple though, does it, darling?' said Francine quietly.

Hattie and Olivia exchanged glances. Alec sighed a deep sigh and switched on the radio. Classic FM.

The exhibition was held in a converted flour mill. It had been arranged by the local arts college and was a celebration of young people's talent. Several amateur artists from the local area each had a section where they exhibited their work.

The photographs of Beau's paintings were beautiful. Under each one she'd written a description of what the painting was of and who it was painted for. The painting of Hattie on the side of the beach hut was there, captured before it was painted over.

Olivia felt incredibly proud as people milled around Beau's stand, praising her work, but Beau seemed pensive. She was watching the door – waiting, Olivia knew, for Oscar to arrive.

'It's probably a work thing holding him up,' said Olivia, aware that she was making excuses for him but doing so to protect Beau. In truth, he was already over an hour late and so probably wasn't going to make an appearance.

'There he is!' said Beau, waving at Oscar, who was walking quickly towards them, taking off his jacket as he cut through the crowds.

Olivia felt a surge of relief. He reached Beau and Olivia and enthusiastically kissed them both, taking Olivia by surprise, as did his fragrance, which took her back decades. She waited for him to apologise for being late, but he didn't. She found herself feeling irritated about the way he could affect her mood so much.

When Beau moved away to talk to someone, he looked at her quizzically. 'Why are you angry with me?' he asked. 'You've got your cross face on.'

'I'm not and I haven't!' Olivia said, embarrassed. 'I just

thought you could have got here on time. I didn't even know you were definitely coming.'

Oscar smiled and narrowed his eyes. 'I'm pleased that you seem to want me in your life.'

Olivia fell silent.

'Have you changed your mind about me now?' he asked, taking her hand in his.

'What?' she asked, buying time, leaving her hand for a moment before pulling it away.

'Changed your mind about me. Do you want me in your life?' he asked, smiling tentatively at her. 'I'm not so bad, am I? You had me down as some sort of ogre, but you've got me all wrong.'

He rested a hand on her waist, and she didn't move away. She didn't know how to feel or what to say. There was something about Oscar – there always had been – and she found herself, yet again, wondering whether, if she'd done things differently, they could have had a long relationship. A good one.

Olivia swallowed, engulfed in a feeling of regret.

Oscar moved away from her to admire Beau's stand. Olivia watched him give Beau a hug and then introduce himself to a woman standing nearby.

'Are you alright?' asked Hattie, following Olivia's gaze. 'Is he worrying you?'

'I'm just doubting whether I've made the right decisions.'

'I think we all wonder that from time to time,' Hattie replied, taking Olivia's hand and squeezing it. 'I'm going to sit down for a minute, just over there. It's so hot in here.'

Linking arms with Hattie, Olivia walked her to a chair on the side of the room near the main entrance. After a while, Oscar, Beau, Alec and Francine were there too, asking if Hattie was okay.

'Stop fussing!' said Hattie. 'It's my shoes – they're too tight.'

'Put these on,' said Francine, slipping off her flat ballet pumps and giving them to Hattie. 'Let's swap.'

'Mum,' said Beau excitedly, 'that lady from the council, she's asked me to send her an idea for a mural on the sea wall at the back of the beach! Dad kind of persuaded her.'

Dad! It was the first time she'd referred to Oscar that way.

'That's incredible,' Olivia said. 'Nice job, Oscar.'

She raised her glass to him, and he toasted hers with his glass of water. They locked eyes.

'It was nothing,' he said. 'She mentioned a journalist had been in touch with her about a scheme you've come up with, Hattie, for a beach-hut exhibition each year. She's interested.'

'Is she?' Hattie said. 'Well, that's just brilliant.'

'You're a genius,' said Beau, giving Hattie a hug.

While everyone chatted, Olivia noticed two new arrivals making their way into the mill. The woman, who looked to be in her forties, was wearing a sundress and carrying a holdall, as if she'd been travelling, and the teenage boy was wearing a hoodie with the hood up, even in the heat of summer. They were clearly looking for someone, maybe one of the artists – but no, they'd gazed in their direction and were suddenly making a beeline for Oscar.

'Oscar?' the woman said as she tapped him on the shoulder.

'Dad?' the boy said.

Oscar spun round and froze. The smile on his face disappeared before hurriedly returning. Olivia's heart started to pound in her chest.

Oscar kissed the woman briefly on the cheek and pulled the teenage boy in for a hug.

'Um, who are you?' Beau asked, confused. 'Who's this?'

'I'm Oscar's wife, Lucy,' the woman replied. 'And this is our son, David. Who are you?'

Olivia's face burned. She rested her hand on Beau's shoulder.

'I'm Oscar's daughter,' Beau replied defensively. 'My name's Beau. This is my mum, Olivia.'

The woman's face paled and the boy's jaw dropped as he stared at Beau. Olivia felt bile rise in her throat.

Everyone turned to face Oscar, who stood still for a moment, open-mouthed.

'Oscar?' said Olivia.

'Oh...' Oscar started. 'I... It's...' Then he turned his back on them all and pushed through the groups of people, towards the exit. He didn't look back before he pulled the door open and let it slam shut behind him. Abandoning them.

And that's when Hattie appeared to faint.

THIRTY-TWO

'I'm a doctor,' said Lucy, dropping her bag, then kneeling and checking Hattie's pulse, instructing her to put her head between her knees and asking her son to get a glass of water. 'Make space, please – give her room,' she said. 'Does she have any known health problems?'

Olivia's heart was pounding. She couldn't compute what was happening. Oscar had a wife and son. She felt like a complete and utter fool. His wife was by her side, helping Hattie.

Blinking, trying to clear her head, she kneeled on the hard floor beside Hattie and passed her the glass of water David had brought over, gently rubbing her back and fanning her face with a paper programme. Seeing Hattie like this made Olivia feel helpless.

She turned to Lucy. 'She's on antidepressants, blood-pressure tablets and she's got psoriasis,' she said, then turned to Hattie. 'Can you tell us how you're feeling, Mum?'

'Like I'd rather you didn't tell the entire world about my medical problems,' she said. 'I'm fine. Stop fussing.'

'Blood-pressure medication can cause dizziness,' Lucy said. 'You might want to check in with your doctor.'

Beau, Alec and Francine moved in closer, creating a canopy of concern. The volume in the room seemed to increase a notch as more people piled into the venue: music, laughter, chatter.

'Perhaps it's just too hot in here,' Olivia said, her voice wobbling, staring at Lucy – the wife Oscar had forgotten to mention.

'I said I'm fine,' Hattie insisted after gulping down the water. 'It's because I've forgotten to eat and it's so bloody hot in here. Nothing more. I just need something to eat and to take off this ridiculous dress. It's too tight for me. I like stretch-waist trousers.'

With Olivia's help, Hattie stood up and thanked Lucy for her help.

'Do make an appointment with your doctor to get yourself checked out,' said Lucy. 'Pass that plate, David. Here – have something to eat.'

David passed Hattie the plate of canapés and Hattie reluctantly ate one.

'She needs a toasted teacake and a cup of tea,' said Francine, holding Hattie's hand. Then more quietly, she added, 'And less drama in her life, preferably.'

Olivia caught Beau's eye. She was standing quietly with one arm wrapped around her middle, fiddling with her necklace with her other hand. She was staring at David, who was finding one of Beau's photographs very interesting. Olivia tried desperately to think of a way to make it all better for Beau, but what could she say? Oscar hadn't been honest with them, and worse, he'd left them all in a moment of crisis; run away when things got tough. He was the worst kind of coward.

A horrible silence fell as they each struggled to process the last half hour.

'I'll take you home,' said Alec, clearly relieved to have something he could do. 'I'll bring the car around. Can you manage to walk to the door, Hattie?'

'Yes, thank you, Alec,' Hattie said. 'I'll be alright in just a minute.'

Olivia couldn't stop staring at Lucy. She was a bit younger than her, tall, slim and attractive, with blonde hair in a ponytail.

'Thank you for your help,' she said quietly.

'That's okay,' said Lucy, turning to Olivia. 'But I'm a little taken aback. It seems Oscar has a few things he needs to tell me. Now I need to sit down.'

She took a seat and leaned her elbows on her knees and rested her chin in her hands.

Olivia bit the inside of her cheek. She didn't want to defend Oscar but felt she should tell Lucy that he didn't know about Beau until very recently.

'Oscar didn't know about Beau until a few weeks ago,' she said, flicking her gaze to Beau, who wore a dazed expression. 'It's a long story, but he and I dated years ago. We broke up, I discovered I was pregnant and well, for various reasons, I... didn't tell him. He came back to the UK for this work thing and found out about Beau because he saw a photograph of us online and, well, they look similar, don't they?'

Lucy glanced at Beau and nodded. 'He told me about you,' she said. 'You were the one who got away.'

'I don't know about that,' Olivia replied. 'He wasn't in a very good place when we were together. I didn't know he'd got married. Or that he had a son.'

'He forgot to tell you about us?' Lucy threw her head back and laughed. 'That's why we came here. Things between us, well, they've not been great, and he wanted to take this opportunity in Winchester. We thought the break might help us, and we were supposed to talk after a month of him being here, but he seemed to fall off the radar. Now I can see why. Are you and he...?'

Lucy's hurt expression made Olivia feel guilty and ridiculous for having ever allowed herself to think, even if only fleetingly, that there might be something between Oscar and herself again.

'God, no!' she said, feeling herself turn the deepest of reds. 'Absolutely not. That all ended years ago.'

'But you might want to ask Oscar about the other woman he's seeing,' said Beau, piping up for the first time, her voice cutting through the ambient noise. 'There was someone staying at his flat. A woman who wasn't wearing much.'

Olivia cringed and felt furious with Oscar, wishing Beau hadn't chosen this moment to break that unsavoury news. She felt Lucy's pain like a punch.

Lucy's mouth twitched, and Olivia wondered if she was going to cry, but she squared her shoulders and sucked in her cheeks.

'Don't worry,' said Lucy. 'I will. Just before I ask him for a divorce.'

The mood on the drive home was subdued. For miles, nobody spoke. Alec put the radio on low, and a symphony of instruments did the talking instead. Poor Beau, who had earlier been incredibly excited by the prospect of the exhibition, was silently staring out the window at the passing cars. Her body was tense, her hands clasped together on her lap. Olivia seethed with anger towards Oscar.

'He's such a coward,' she said quietly. 'I can never forgive him for letting Beau down like this. Compare him with Jesse, who was so heroic, and you wonder why someone like Oscar gets to go round causing so much harm, while someone with a heart of gold like Jesse – and my dad – were killed. Where's the justice?'

Beau put her headphones on and closed her eyes. From

beside her, Hattie sighed, reached over for Olivia's hand and gave it a squeeze.

'I think we should talk less of cowards and heroes,' she said. 'Oscar has his own issues, perhaps all the way back from childhood. It must be awful being him, running away all the time. Imagine how he feels right now?'

Olivia shook her head slowly. She didn't want to think about how he was feeling any longer. Rather than continually forgiving him, she thought Oscar needed to take responsibility for his mistakes, be answerable for his wrongdoings.

'It's easy to say all that sympathetic, philosophical stuff when you're not directly affected though, isn't it?' said Francine. 'Sometimes you have to put yourself first.'

Alec lowered the volume on the radio and cleared his throat. 'I've recently learned that it helps to know that you can take responsibility for your own feelings. It certainly helps me. You can't help what happens, but you can control how you react to it. So, Olivia, rather than let Oscar's actions dictate how you feel, you can take back control by being unaffected by him. Don't let him steal any more of your life.'

Olivia rested her head back on the seat. She had an awful, sinking realisation that, even from thousands of miles away, Oscar had been affecting her life for years. But why? Was it that she'd tried to 'fix' him and failed, just as she'd done with Hattie when her dad died?

She squeezed her eyes closed and opened them again, blinking in the flash of headlights. She caught Alec's eye in the rear-view mirror, and he gave her a brief, kind smile. It felt like someone reaching out to her in the dark, someone who understood. A brother maybe.

It was agreed that Hattie would stay at Olivia's house overnight in case she felt unwell again. When Alec pulled up outside,

Olivia asked if he and Francine would like to come in, out of politeness more than anything.

'Yes,' they said in unison.

Olivia was surprised – she'd expected them to say no, that they too would want to put an end to this awful evening, but obviously it had unsettled them all.

They traipsed into the house and crammed into the living room. Hattie changed into a pair of Olivia's pyjamas then sat by Francine on the small sofa, Francine talking intently to her.

Alec perched on the edge of an armchair, pulling books from the shelves, flicking through, and placing them back again. Beau disappeared to her room to change, and Olivia quickly shoved dirty dishes into the sink and put the kettle on. Her head ached from the two glasses of Prosecco she'd knocked back at the exhibition, so she drank a big glass of water. Making a platter of buttered toast to accompany the tea, her head split into a hundred different thoughts.

She jumped when someone knocked on the front door.

'I'll get it,' she called, walking through the hallway, expecting it to be Donald, complaining about where Alec had parked.

She opened the door and instead found Oscar, swaying slightly, like a reed on a riverbank.

She scowled at him. 'You're not welcome and you're drunk,' she said, but he pushed past her and stumbled into the hallway.

Beau, in her tracksuit, her make-up wiped off, appeared at the top of the stairs and sat down on the top step, arms hugging her knees.

'Please tell me you haven't driven here, Oscar,' Olivia said.

'God, you're obsessed! No, I didn't drive,' he said. 'Taxi. Can I talk to you both, please? Please, Olivia?'

She gestured towards the living room, and he staggered in, exclaiming, 'Jesus!' when he saw everyone in there. 'Can I talk to you in private?' he asked.

She shook her head. 'You can say everything you need to say here.'

Oscar pushed his hand through his hair and sighed a deep sigh. There was a moment of silence and then he burst into tears. Great big, sobbing, messy tears.

Immediately, Olivia was transported to the time they were together, when he would behave badly, then feel sorry for himself and cry. Like a child.

There was a collective intake of breath. Alec passed Oscar a box of tissues so he could blow his nose – which he did, noisily.

'Look,' he said, sniffing, 'I know tonight was a bit of a surprise, and yes, I'm married and I have a son. We were having a rough time, so they stayed in New Zealand while I came over here to work on the restaurant. I was going to get round to telling you about them, but I was enjoying getting to know Beau and being with you, Olivia. I thought perhaps... you and me... that we had unfinished business.'

Olivia shook her head in dismay. 'But what about Lucy? You can't just abandon people like that. You, of all people, know what that feels like. We promised each other we'd be honest!'

Oscar looked at her with red eyes and nodded.

Beau came into the room, blinking in confusion. Olivia sighed. She didn't want her to see Oscar like this – in a messy heap of tears – but she steeled herself. Perhaps Beau should see every side of him and then she'd better understand.

'It's been so great to meet you, Beau,' he said tearily. 'I've enjoyed every minute.'

Beau gave the slightest nod. 'I'm tired,' she said. 'I think I'm going to go to bed, leave you guys to it. Is that okay, Mum?'

'Of course,' Olivia said.

Oscar looked crestfallen. He sat down on the edge of the sofa with his head in his hands.

Olivia felt anger rising in her. 'We do not have unfinished business, Oscar. It was finished years ago,' she said firmly. 'I've let you back into my life, into *our* lives, and it was a mistake. You've proved yourself to be what I always knew you to be. You've proved to me that I was right about you all along. I can't trust you; I can't rely on you. I want you to leave and get out of my life, just as I did all those years ago. Now!'

'Oh, get off your high horse for a minute, will you?' said Oscar.

'Just get out of my house!' shouted Olivia. 'Now!'

'Come on – you heard what she said!' said Alec, punching numbers into his phone. 'I'll get you a taxi. You need to sleep it off.'

'What the hell do you know?' Oscar said meanly.

'I know enough,' said Alec. 'I think you should go.'

'I remember your dad saying that exact same thing to me!' Oscar laughed, standing up and swaying.

The taxi arrived in minutes, and Alec led Oscar out of the house. Olivia, her whole body shaking, watched through a gap in the curtains as Alec paid the driver and gave him instructions.

'Thanks,' Olivia said, when he came back inside. 'I'm literally shaking with anger. But that's the end of it. No more Oscar. I'm sorry to have dragged you all through this.'

Beau had come back downstairs, and everyone looked pale and shocked and glum. Olivia swallowed. She felt overwhelmed and responsible.

'I should have handled this all differently,' she said. 'I'm sorry, Beau. This hasn't worked out at all well. I know you wanted it to be different. I should have put my foot down from the off, but he managed to worm his way back in. For God's sake, I actually started to think he'd changed. What an idiot!'

So used to holding herself together, suppressing her emotions and putting everyone else first, Olivia allowed herself to cry. Beau gave her a bundle of tissues, and Hattie wrapped her arms around her.

'You're the best mum there is,' said Beau. 'I could see that Oscar is a difficult person. When I went to do the mural at the restaurant, he was irritable and snappy. He got cross too, but then he was all nice again, and I thought he maybe liked you, and you might like him one day, so I thought I shouldn't say anything in case you had a future together. The thing is, I worry about you, Mum – I worry about you being lonely. You're always doing stuff for me, or for Granny, even the old people you befriend on the phone, but what about you? What will make you happy? What do you want to do?'

Olivia blinked at the question. Her mind went to the cycle ride she'd been on with Seth, to her sketchbook of designs. She'd like to do both of those things more.

She cupped Beau's face in her hands. 'I'm not lonely,' she said. 'Well, sometimes I am. I guess I would like to have a relationship with someone. I feel like I've had my heart sealed away for rather a long time, like I've been in a strange kind of limbo, living with a mixture of anger at Oscar and guilt at lying to him. Yes, I've felt – *do* feel – lonely at times.'

Saying it out loud was a relief.

'You're not the only one who sometimes feels lonely,' said Alec. 'It's very quiet at home on my own! Like a morgue!'

He laughed a little bit, and Francine patted his knee.

'You should come over here,' said Olivia. 'Or we could meet up at the beach hut.'

'I'd like that,' Alec replied.

'I know everything there is to know about living in a silent house,' Hattie said. 'With Jesse gone, the bungalow is horribly quiet. I still haven't got used to it, even now.'

'I've got an idea about that, Hattie,' said Francine.

THIRTY-THREE

Francine moved into the spare room of Hattie's home a week later. They'd decided between them that it made sense for the old friends to be together, to put past hurts aside and keep each other company. They'd trial it for a few weeks, to see if it would work out.

'You travel light for the Sultan of Brunei!' Hattie said when Francine arrived with two huge travel trunks, four unmarked cardboard boxes, two suitcases, a crate full of kitchen equipment and a long-haired black-and-white cat.

'Stop it!' said Francine with a laugh like an old-fashioned school bell.

When Olivia visited a few days after Francine's arrival, Francine was at the stove, cooking a stew with dumplings, while Hattie sat on the sofa, slipper-clad feet up on the footstool, reading a magazine.

Olivia put her head into the kitchen to say hello to Francine and noticed that the calendar boxes had gone from being completely empty a couple of months ago to being crammed full of words written in Hattie's squiggly old handwriting: names of people to meet at the beach, times, activities. And by the side of the calendar, Francine had hung a meal planner, which boasted robust breakfasts, lunches and dinners.

'Your social life is busier than mine,' Olivia said, taking a seat in the living room.

Hattie lowered her magazine and put her feet down. 'It's exhausting,' she said with a little puff of laughter. 'But it's been rather nice, meeting up at the beach with Francine, Glenda and the girls. The days are quite busy, especially now Francine expects us to have three square meals a day.'

Olivia's eyes moved to the wall behind Hattie where she had up a number of framed photographs of herself with Jesse. Francine had removed a few, to make room for some of herself and Alec.

Following Olivia's gaze, Hattie raised her eyebrows and smiled a pointed smile.

'I see she's making herself at home,' Olivia said quietly.

'She's going to redecorate the spare room,' said Hattie. 'She's chosen ever such a bold colour. I'm just going with it.'

'And is she good company?'

'Marvellous company. She never stops talking. In fact, I think I'll have to go to the beach hut to get some peace and quiet. Seriously though, we play cards, we do the crossword, watch a TV programme or two. We've been for some long walks. We haven't talked a great deal about the past – all that was a long time ago. She does aqua aerobics, but I've got line-dancing with Glenda, so I don't want to overdo it.'

Olivia found herself beaming.

'Yes, you should smile,' said Hattie. 'You achieved what you wanted to achieve, didn't you?'

'We've raised a lot of money for the befriending charity,' Olivia said. 'Almost two thousand pounds.'

'And you wanted me to find a friend. Well, I've got a friend in residence! And quite a few others too. We've arranged to meet up at the beach some Saturday mornings. Glenda wants us all to do that cold-water swimming, but I'm still not keen on getting in the sea, after Jesse.' Hattie twisted the corner of a cushion in her fingers, as if pinching the pain.

'How are you feeling about him now?' Olivia said softly.

Hattie's eyes immediately filled with tears. She pulled a tissue from her cardigan and blew her nose. In the background, Olivia heard the sounds of bowls and cutlery being pulled from the cupboards and drawers.

'I don't cry all the time, but I do still miss him so very much. When someone dies, when your dad died and then Jesse, it's just so completely shocking. I can't describe the feeling, but knowing you'll not see them again is so painful. I wake up in a panic, knowing I've lost the person I love. But I'm learning that being with other people helps take my mind elsewhere – I'm learning to enjoy life again. I know you understand what I mean, what with losing your dad at such a young age. You poor, sweet thing. I couldn't bear how sad you were.'

'I felt the same about you,' said Olivia.

They smiled sadly at each other.

'But you were just a child,' said Hattie. 'It shouldn't have been that way. I'm sorry if I wasn't very strong for you.'

'Nothing to be sorry about – I understand,' said Olivia, the heat rising in her body. It was the first time Hattie had acknowledged how much Olivia had taken onto her little shoulders.

Hattie smiled gratefully and raised her eyebrows as Francine started to sing along to the radio in the kitchen.

'There's one other really nice thing, you know, about having Francine here, in that Alec visits a lot, and he's like Jesse in many ways,' she said. 'He's a connection to Jesse, I suppose. He'll sit and talk to me about his dad, which is very nice, because other people have a habit of not mentioning him, because they're frightened I'll get upset. Apparently, before he died, Jesse told Alec that his favourite place to be in the world was sitting in his deckchair on the beach, next to me, having a cup of hot coffee on a cold morning. That's why I got this done. Jacob said it didn't really hurt and he was right.'

Olivia frowned as Hattie twisted her body, pulled down the neckline of her knitted jumper and bared her shoulder, where there was a small tattoo of two striped deckchairs next to each other.

Olivia's hand shot to her mouth. 'Oh my God!' she cried, cracking up laughing. 'I can't believe you did that! You've always hated tattoos!'

'People can change, and I'm not getting any younger, am I?' Hattie said. 'I need to do as much as I can, while I can, one of them being part of this new initiative with Beau.'

Hattie grabbed her phone from the coffee table and located the *Echo* website. 'It came up today,' she said. 'Paul, that young journalist, has been very supportive of it all.'

Olivia scanned the news story, which reported that the local council liked the idea of the beach-hut gallery and were prepared to trial the idea the following August with a small selection of beach huts. They'd done a survey of beach-hut owners and had an overwhelmingly positive response – people thought it was a wonderful idea.

She grinned. 'That's such a marvellous idea,' she said. 'I wish I'd thought of it.'

'Beau wants to paint Jesse next time, from this photo,' Hattie said, smiling.

She pulled a photograph from the pages of her diary and showed it to Olivia. It was of Jesse, sun hat on, money belt slung around his hips, red waistcoat over a short-sleeved shirt, socks and sandals, a huge grin on his lips, squinting in the sunshine.

Olivia and Hattie smiled at one another.

'And how about you, my dear daughter?' Hattie asked, pushing the photo back into the pages of her diary. 'You were very brave the other evening to admit how you've been feeling. I've been thinking about that job in Dublin. Do you think you could still go there? Do you want to? Perhaps a fresh start is what you need. I know you changed your plans because of me. I've never really thanked you for that.'

Olivia screwed up her nose. 'I think when I accepted the Dublin offer, I was running from my fears of Oscar returning. But this is my home. You, Beau, my house, the beach. I need to find a new job, but I'd also like to hire out the deckchairs in the summer season, like you and Jesse did. Always seemed like a lovely way to spend the summer months, and we have hundreds of them in storage. I've been thinking too about my fabric designs, about printing them on a bigger scale. I need to invest in some equipment, and I thought I'd use the inheritance money Jesse left for me. Do you think he'd be happy with that?'

Hattie nodded. 'That's a lovely idea, and yes, he would. And dare I ask, has Oscar been in contact?'

Olivia sighed. 'He's asked me to meet him for a walk on the beach. I'm not sure there's anything more to say. He says he's going back to New Zealand.'

'Just sit down and tell him how you feel,' said Hattie. 'Life is one big conversation, isn't it?'

They both looked towards the door, where Francine was coming through, carrying a tray with a steaming bowl of stew and dumplings, a half pint of Guinness, cutlery and a napkin.

'This will put hairs on your chest, my friend,' she said.

'They'll go well with your tattoo,' said Olivia.

'I'm not sure that's such a good look,' said Hattie, accepting the tray and winking at Olivia. 'Thank you, Francine. Gosh, I'm going to have to wear bigger clothes! I'll have to wear Jesse's.'

Francine left the room to collect another bowl of food from the kitchen.

'Truth is, I already do,' she whispered to Olivia, pulling up her trouser leg to reveal that she was wearing a pair of Jesse's socks, too big for her feet, but pulled up high to her knees.

'Doolally, aren't I?' she said, looking for a moment as vulnerable as a child.

Olivia rose from the armchair and moved across the room to sit next to Hattie.

'I love you,' she said, wrapping her arms around her mother and leaning her head on her shoulder.

Hattie wrapped her arms around Olivia and held her tightly. 'I love you too,' she replied.

The sea was rough; grey and white. The sky was the same colour, the sun straining to get through any cracks in the clouds. A warm September wind blew Olivia's hair into her eyes as she opened the beach hut and boiled the kettle, ready for Oscar's arrival. She set up the two deckchairs, spacing them far apart, wondering what he was going to say and then wondering why she was giving him her time. She felt impatient for the meeting to be over, to go and get on with the next part of her life. Oscar had already taken up far too much of it.

'Tea?' she asked when he arrived, gesturing for him to take a seat.

She handed him a mug of hot tea, and he sipped it, staring out to sea.

'So,' Olivia said, choosing to sit on the step of the beach hut, rather than on the deckchair, 'here we are.'

Oscar looked in her direction and gave her a sad smile. 'I've never known where I belong,' he started.

Olivia internally rolled her eyes but didn't say a word.

'I've always been looking for something. Searching. And when I've found something good, I've destroyed it. When things have got difficult, I've run away. I'm not very brave. I've had therapy and thought I was making progress, but I just keep returning to this place where I want to run and hide. Climb a tree. Stick my head in the sand. My whole life I thought I could prove myself by being successful, being someone worthy, but it's not really what's important, is it?'

Olivia fished around for something to say but couldn't find anything, so she just took a sip of her tea. She felt weary. A part of her wanted to tell Oscar that she was bored of listening to his self-pity, but another, bigger part of her felt sorry for him. She'd spent so long fearing his return, fearing a reprisal over Beau, worrying about his fragility, but now she knew she'd done the right thing. The alternative would have been this: trying to find a way to fix a problem she couldn't fix and that wasn't hers *to* fix.

'Like I said, I'm going back to New Zealand,' he continued. 'I'm going to try to work out things with Lucy, although she's requested a divorce. I asked Beau if she'd like to come – there are some amazing art colleges over there.'

'You've done what?' Olivia asked, almost dropping her mug.

'She said no. She's such a good artist, but she's more interested in this beach-hut summer exhibition thing. Bit small town, really.'

Olivia sighed. He just couldn't help himself.

'I think the summer exhibition will be absolutely brilliant,' she said. 'I'm glad she's happy here. This is her home.'

'She's welcome to come and see me,' said Oscar. 'Whenever she wants. I know you said you wanted me out of your life, but Beau is still my daughter. I want to keep in touch with her, be a part of *her* life.'

'I'll leave that up to her,' said Olivia. 'She can make up her own mind. Oscar, can I ask you a question?'

He nodded.

'When your mum left you and your brother, how did you feel?'

'Frightened, furious, like I wasn't good enough. Helpless. Hopeless.'

'And what got you through?' she asked.

'The hope that she might come back,' he said without missing a beat.

'So, when you realised that she wasn't coming back, how did you feel?'

'The same again – furious, like I wasn't good enough. Unlovable. Grief-stricken.'

'Are you able to consider that her leaving wasn't about you?' Olivia asked. 'That it was about her – an adult who had her own unrelated set of problems, that you probably know nothing of, that you can't control and you couldn't have fixed?'

'Yes, yes,' said Oscar, 'but the damage is done. She damaged me.'

'Damage can be repaired, and blame is a waste of time,' said Olivia. 'Grief and loss ease. Maybe you've given her enough of your time now. Maybe you've licked those old wounds for long enough. Why not give yourself permission to be the person you'd like to be?'

It was as if she was talking to herself, but in terms of the anguish she'd felt over Oscar. She wasn't sure if he was really listening, but she felt sure she was making perfect sense.

He put down his tea and stood up, preparing to leave. 'Beau might look like me,' he said, 'but she's got your head and your heart. If only—'

He said something else, quietly, but it was lost in the wind, and Olivia decided she didn't really care what it was.

She watched him walk away along the promenade, past the little beach shop with inflatables and buckets, and postcards curling at the edges, straight away reaching for his phone, not once looking back in her direction.

Sighing and raising her eyebrows, she felt light-headed with relief. Oscar returning, and leaving, had given her a renewed sense of perspective.

She started to pack up the deckchairs into the beach hut and froze when she felt the strange sensation that someone was standing next to her. Quickly, she glanced over her shoulder, but there was nobody there. On the breeze, she imagined she heard the sound of an old man singing, or was it the seagulls cawing?

She looked up and watched a gull soar confidently and courageously across the sky. Her own words ran through her thoughts on repeat: *Why not give yourself permission to be the person you'd like to be?*

THIRTY-FOUR

Seth's home was on the edge of the New Forest, a short drive from Milton-on-Sea. Olivia drove towards his address, carefully crossing the cattle grid which separated the New Forest from the busy main A roads, preventing the wild pony population from wandering into danger.

She slowed and wound down her windows, waiting while a pony walked along the road in front of her and another sidled past, pausing to chew on a bush. In the distance, past the heath-land, she saw glimpses of other ponies, sheltering from the midday sunshine in dense woodland. Further still, she could see the outline of Seth's converted barn – he'd shown her photos on his phone when they'd gone on the bike ride. A flutter of excite-ment grew in her stomach.

When the ponies had moved out of the way, she drove towards the barn, parking up on the roadside verge and walking the last few metres.

The property was part stone, part wood, and surrounded by a wild garden boasting trees and an extensive allotment, where Seth was digging. He'd stripped to the waist while he worked, and Olivia couldn't help noticing how deeply tanned his shoulders were.

'I hope you're wearing high-factor sunscreen,' she said, making him jump.

He turned round to face her. Resting his hand on his spade handle, he beamed at her, before bursting into a lovely peal of laughter.

'You made me jump!' he said, quickly laying down his spade, pulling on his T-shirt and walking towards her. 'Come in, please, come in. Welcome. I'm so glad you're here.'

She followed him into the cool barn, where he offered her a glass of water and some blueberries, freshly picked. She took a few and, with her heart thumping in her chest, opened her mouth to say what she'd come to say.

'Seth?'

He opened his eyes wide and nodded.

'When you asked me on the beach that time how I felt about what happened on our bike ride, I said nothing. What I meant to say was that I liked it very much and that I'd like to go on another one with you, at some point, if you would also like to.'

Seth paused for a moment before punching the air above his head with both fists and whooping so loudly, Olivia burst out laughing.

'How about right now?'

'Now?' she said. 'I don't have a bike with me and—'

'Come with me,' he said. 'I've got something for you.'

She followed him outside to a small stone workshop at the back of his garden. Blinking in the sudden darkness inside, she waited for her eyes to adjust and watched Seth pull a sheet off a bicycle.

'I found this lovely vintage bike at an auction and decided to restore it for you,' he said. 'You mentioned you had a bike a long time ago that you loved. You said it was light blue, so I thought you'd like this one. Why don't you try it? We can cycle to the beach from here – I know some quiet country lanes we can go down. Come on – let's do it.'

Olivia's eyes were fixed on the bike. It was the most beautiful opaque pale blue – the colour of sea glass. Seth wheeled it out into the light and adjusted the seat to her height, before adding a wicker basket onto the front.

'It's beautiful,' she said. 'I love it. Thank you.'

'My pleasure,' he replied. 'Let me grab a few things and we'll go.'

Minutes later, they were cycling along a quiet country lane, where the trees growing on both sides of the lane leaned towards each other, forming a green, leafy arch. He probably normally cycled like the wind, thought Olivia, but Seth pedalled slowly beside her, asking after Hattie and Beau, listening and responding with genuine interest.

'There's quite a steep part here,' he said when they came to the summit of a gentle slope. 'You can either go down with your brakes on the whole way, or just freewheel and enjoy the ride.'

Olivia peered down the steep hill and suffered a moment of fear, of self-doubt. She pushed her fingers down on the brakes, but when Seth set off, yelling and laughing, his feet away from his pedals, she released her fingers and let her pedals spin.

Gathering speed, the hedges at the edges of the lane blurring, she opened her mouth and screamed. She felt like a seagull soaring across the sky, cawing at the top of her lungs.

At the bottom of the hill, she didn't stop, just carried on cycling behind Seth through the countryside, until they reached the edges of the town and came down to the beach.

Along the promenade they travelled, beach huts on their right-hand side, the beach and sea to their left. Over the sea, the sun was setting, pouring its golden yolk onto the water.

Reaching Hattie's beach hut, windswept and grinning, Olivia got off her bike, leaned it carefully up against the beach

wall, near the enamel 'Deckchairs for Hire' sign, and unlocked
the beach hut. Seth carried Hattie and Jesse's striped deckchairs
outside and set them up next to each other, facing the sunset.
The smell of fish and chips wafted into their noses from a shop
at the top of the cliff. Out of his bag, Seth pulled a bottle of
wine, opened it and poured Olivia a very full glass.

'Are you hungry?' he asked.

She nodded.

'You wait here, enjoy that wine, and I'll get us some fish and
chips. Nothing like eating them out of the paper, next to the sea,
is there? Salt in the air and on your chips too. I remember you
saying that.'

While Seth dashed to the fish-and-chip shop, Olivia sipped
her wine and watched the sun sink further into the sea, turning
the sky a vibrant shade of orange.

'Grub's up!' Seth said, appearing with two packs of newspa-
per-wrapped fish and chips. He handed her one and sat down
in the deckchair, telling her a story about enjoying 'batter bits'
and vinegar on bread as a child.

As they ate and drank and talked, the wind died down and
the air became still and quiet. Night fell, and as the multicoloured lights twinkled on the pier, Seth and Olivia pulled
their deckchairs a little closer, linking fingers in the darkness.

A LETTER FROM AMY

Thank you so much for choosing to read *The Lonely Hearts Beach Club*. I really hope you enjoyed it, and if you did and want to keep up to date with my latest releases, just sign up at the following link. Your email address will never be shared and you can unsubscribe at any time.

www.bookouture.com/amy-miller

I'm sure many of us have fond memories of seaside holidays; sandy beaches, deckchairs, windbreaks and melting ice creams. The idea for this book came from my own memories and experiences of the seaside. As a young child, I enjoyed holidays on the English coast with my grandparents and my mum. I remember my grandparents snoozing together on deckchairs in the sun, and my mum once hiring out deckchairs for us – I gave mine to my teddy bear and sat on the sand next to him!

Also, when I first got to know my parents-in-law, I loved meeting them at their beach hut in Bournemouth, where they would sit together, happily soaking up the sun. There's something about the joyful, iconic image of two people sitting side by side in deckchairs at the beach – the sort of image you see in old photographs and on vintage postcards – that I love.

The sight of two deckchairs together evokes happy, nostalgic memories: thoughts of conversation, laughter, companionship and sunshine. However, I'm at the stage in life when many friends are losing their parents, or who are supporting a grieving parent, suddenly alone after their life partner has died. It made me think about the impact of loss on those fond memories, those seaside snapshots – that there would be one empty deckchair.

Making a nod to the 'sandwich generation', so called for being at an age where you're supporting both children and parents, I thought about how people my age want to help their bewildered, grieving parent but sometimes feel at a loss to know what to do. That's when I came up with the concept of hiring out that empty deckchair to find a friend. I wanted to highlight the importance and significance of making simple connections with people and how conversations, however brief, can help a person feel less alone.

It draws on 'befriending' – a wonderful initiative supported by various charities, where people are encouraged to 'befriend' an isolated person to help improve their mental health and wellbeing. In my story, Olivia is a volunteer phone 'befriender', but I must make it clear that the conversations she has are entirely invented and are probably not true to life! Also invented is the story location – it's loosely based on where I live, but the town name and locations are fictional.

A note about the character Seth, who rides elderly people around on a trishaw. He was inspired by an amazing non-profit global initiative, Cycling Without Age (cyclingwithoutage.com), that I've seen operating in my own area, where volunteers cycle elderly people around on trishaws. I've seen the smiles of those older people, enjoying the views of the beaches and the sea from the trishaw – and I take my hat off to those volunteers.

facebook.com/AmyMillerBooks
twitter.com/AmyBratley1

ACKNOWLEDGEMENTS

I would like to thank the amazing team at Bookouture, including Commissioning Editor Lucy Frederick and Digital Publicity Director Kim Nash, as well as my agent Veronique Baxter at David Higham Associates. I'm very grateful to my friends for sharing stories with me about supporting a parent through a bereavement and about being in the 'sandwich generation', family who introduced me to the simple joys of seaside life, and to people who have confided in me about their feelings of isolation, particularly during the pandemic.

After coming up with my 'deckchair for hire' idea, for Olivia to find Hattie a new friend, I did some research online and discovered that there are schemes dotted around towns in the UK such as 'Happy to Chat' benches and 'Buddy Bench' initiatives, where people can sit down and have a chat with another person. In a world when everyone is busy rushing around and often on their phones, I think this is a wonderful idea to help people reach out to one another. I've also been told about schemes in cafés that have a specific table where visitors can meet new people – another great idea to combat isolation.

In researching the different themes in my book, I found newspaper articles and websites helpful. Inspiring the events in my opening scene, I found newspaper articles about a 'human chain' rescue at Durdle Door, Dorset, useful, as well as an article on globalrescue.com about how to tell if swimmers are in trouble in the sea. I regularly swim in the sea myself and have been told by swim coaches that people often go very quiet and still when in difficulty or at risk of drowning, contrary to what we might think.

I read about isolation and researched the effects of bereavement on charity websites including childbereavementuk.org, sueryder.org, and befriending initiatives run by charities such as ageuk.org.uk, though my own story is entirely fictional. I found theguardian.com, theconversation.com and collegeofpsychic studies.co.uk useful when researching and thinking about the psychic world, which I very briefly touch upon.

In terms of beach life, I enjoyed spending time at my local beaches watching the fabric of deckchairs catch in the breeze, searching online for vintage photography and watching the Postal Museum's curator's tour of *Wish You Were Here: 151 Years of the British Postcard* on YouTube.

Finally, thanks to my family and friends for their words of encouragement, patience, and support along the way.

Printed in Great Britain
by Amazon

26442230R00169